P. C. Doherty was born in Middlesbrough and educated at Woodcote Hall. He studied History at Liverpool and Oxford Universities and obtained a doctorate at Oxford for his thesis on Edward II and Queen Isabella. He is now the Headmaster of a school in North-East London, and lives with his wife and family near Epping Forest.

P. C. Doherty's previous Hugh Corbett medieval mysteries are also available from Headline.

SATAN IN ST MARY'S
'Wholly excellent, this is one of those books you hate to put down' *Prima*

CROWN IN DARKNESS
'Brings the harsh medieval landscape of Scotland to vivid life' *Publishers Weekly*

SPY IN CHANCERY
'A powerful compound of history and intrigue' *Redbridge Guardian*

THE ANGEL OF DEATH
'Medieval London comes vividly to life . . . Doherty's depictions of medieval characters and manners of thought, from the highest to the lowest in the land, ringing true' *Publishers Weekly*

THE PRINCE OF DARKNESS
'P. C. Doherty sustains the suspense throughout his action-packed narrative and the complex plot has many ingenious twists and turns' *Million*

MURDER WEARS A COWL
'Historically informative, excellently plotted and, as ever. superbly entertaining' *Cads*

Also by P. C. Doherty from Headline

Hugh Corbett medieval mysteries
Murder Wears a Cowl
The Prince of Darkness
The Angel of Death
Spy in Chancery
Crown in Darkness
Satan in St Mary's

The Assassin in the Greenwood

P. C. Doherty

HEADLINE

First published in 1993
by HEADLINE BOOK PUBLISHING

First published in paperback in 1994
by HEADLINE BOOK PUBLISHING

10 9 8 7 6 5 4 3 2

ISBN 0 7472 4245 3

Printed and bound in Great Britain by
Cox & Wyman Ltd, Reading, Berkshire

Hodder and Stoughton
A division of Hodder Headline PLC
338 Euston Road
London NW1 3BH

To my son Michael – the best drawer of pigs!

Prologue

In his cold, cramped cell in the monastery outside Worcester, Florence the chronicler lifted his milky, dim eyes and stared out at the darkness beyond his cell window. How should he describe these times? Should he recount all that he had heard? Was it true for instance that Satan himself, the prince of darkness, had risen from the depths of hell with his horde of black-garbed legions to tempt and terrorise the human soul with visions from the pit? He had been told that an evil sea of demons, rumbling and boiling over the face of the earth, amused themselves disguised as snakes, fierce animals, monsters with crooked limbs, mangy beasts and crawling things. At midnight, so Florence had heard, the heavens rumbled with thunder and lightning flashed above a restless sea of heads, hands outstretched, eyes glassy with despair.

Another monk, a member of his community, claimed to have seen a chariot speed through the sky pulled by stallions with fiery eyes and fetid breath; inside a grinning skeleton wearing a crown of brambles.

It was a time of killing. Great Edward was in Scotland hunting down the rebel leader Wallace while in France, the silver-haired Capetian, Philip le Bel, plotted in his secret chambers beneath the Louvre Palace. He was gathering his armies, thronging the roads of Normandy with lines of men

1

moving snakelike, cavalry, men-at-arms, archers and spearmen, pouring north to throng on France's northern borders where they waited for the order to cross into and destroy the Kingdom of Flanders.

Florence had heard such mutterings in the refectory as Father Abbot entertained royal messengers, dusty and dark-eyed, who rode from the coast. These couriers kept the King's generals in London informed of French ships in the Narrow Seas for had not Edward prophesied that when the French fleet sailed, Philip would deliver his hammer blows against Flanders and perhaps against England's southern coast?

In which direction would Philip's armies march first? The pope in Avignon crouched behind his throne and waited. Edward of England tossed restlessly in his soldier's bed as his mind worried at the problem. The merchants in London also waited; if Philip conquered Flanders then England's trade, the shiploads of wool sent to the looms and weavers of Ghent and Bruges, would stop summarily and fortunes would be lost. All of Europe held its breath. Chroniclers like Florence could only dip their quills and pen the direst warnings and prophecies of what might come to pass.

In the dark streets and alleyways of Paris, which ran together in a spider's web on the far side of the Grand Pont, more practical men laid their schemes and drew up plans to discover Philip's true intentions. Sir Hugh Corbett, Edward I of England's most senior clerk in the chancery, master of the King's secrets and Keeper of the Secret Seal, had flooded the French city with his agents: merchants ostensibly looking for new markets; monks and friars supposedly visiting their mother houses; scholars hoping to dispute in the schools; pilgrims apparently on their way to worship the severed head of St Denis; even courtesans who hired chambers and entertained clients, the clerks and officials of Philip's secret chancery. Their task was dangerous for William of Nogaret, Corbett's rival at the French court, together with Philip's master spy, Amaury de Craon, waged a silent but bloody war against Corbett's legions of spies. Two English clerks had already disappeared, their disfigured corpses later washed up on the muddy banks of the Seine. Another three of Corbett's 'pilgrims' were now rotting cadavers on the great scaffold at Montfaucon. A comely courtesan, young Alisia, with silken skin and a tangle of corn-gold hair, had been brutally beaten to death in her chamber at The Silver Moon where so many of the French King's chancery clerks were accustomed to sup and drink.

So the bloody chess game was played: pawn against pawn, knight against knight. Knowledge was the prize at stake. When would Philip give the orders to march? Where would his troops attack in Flanders? If Philip kept the advantage of surprise then all would be well, but if Edward of England got to know then so would his Flemish allies who would mass their forces against Philip's advance.

Publicly, however, Edward and Philip were the best of friends – the closest of allies even. Edward had married Philip's silver-haired sister Margaret whilst his own son, the Prince of Wales, was to be betrothed to Isabella, Philip's one and only daughter. The French sent Edward a pair of costly silken gloves with jewels crusted around the cuff. Edward responded with a Book of Hours, each page a glorious tapestry of colour. Philip called Edward 'his dear coz'. Edward replied, sending tender greetings to 'his dear brother in Christ'. Yet in the alleyways and musty taverns, each King waged a silent war.

In The Fleur de Lys tavern which stood on the corner of Rue des Capucines, Ranulf-atte-Newgate, Corbett's manservant and ostensibly Edward's unofficial envoy to the French court, sat in the corner of the taproom with Bardolph Rushgate. A young man of indeterminate parentage and mysterious past, Bardolph, despite his boyish features and golden love-locks, was a perpetual English student, financed by the English Exchequer to visit this university or that. He was instructed not to take any degree or study the mysteries of the Quadrivium but to collect information on behalf of his masters at home. Now he leaned back against the wall, eyes closed, pretending to be much the worse for drink. Ranulf, too, acted as if in his cups, his red hair tousled, eyes half-closed, mouth slack. He had even rubbed some chalk into his white face to make himself look more pallid. To all outward appearances they were two Englishmen who found the strong wines of Paris too rich to stomach.

'Do you think the wench can cope?' Bardolph muttered.

'I hope so.'

'How many are there now?'

Ranulf looked through the fug of the noisy tavern and studied the group of relic-sellers. They seemed more interested in staring back than in selling any of the trinkets from their trays which now lay stacked on the floor beside them.

'How many?' Bardolph repeated.

'Six,' Ranulf replied.

His stomach churned as his hand went beneath the table, seeking reassurance from the thin, stabbing Welsh dagger stuck into his belt and the dirk at the top of his long riding boots. Once again Ranulf felt his leather sack containing a small crossbow and a sheath of bolts.

Above them, in one of the narrow closets which the landlord grandly described as 'a chamber', Clothilde, a buxom wench with skin as dark and smooth as a grape, was earning her silver. She bounced across the battered old four-poster bed, her legs and arms wrapped round Henri de Savigny, a cipher clerk from Philip's chancery. Ranulf had been playing him for days. The French clerk, as lecherous as any dog on heat, couldn't believe his luck at

4

finally being favoured by such a high-class courtesan when at first she had refused him. No fool, however, Henri knew the price she asked: a copy of the cipher Philip had sent to his generals on the borders of France.

At first the clerk had refused. He even protested that he would go to Nogaret and reveal all. Bardolph Rushgate had countered that. Wouldn't the very confession be a partial admission of guilt? De Savigny had licked his thick red lips, peered once more at Clothilde's luscious bosom and reluctantly agreed in exchange for a bag of coins and Clothilde's favours free of charge. And what was the point in refusal? Henri had seen the ciphers, which had meant little to him, so how would any English Goddamn understand them? Now he was lost in his own spiral of pleasure, hands running up and down Clothilde's smooth back. He revelled in the way she thrust back her head and her jet black hair swung like some halo of passion around her, whispering and pleading that he do more.

Clothilde looked over de Savigny's shoulder at the small roll of parchment he had tossed on the table. She didn't care a whit. Ranulf-atte-Newgate had been an attractive prospect, and even more so with the bag of coins he had offered her. Enough silver for Clothilde to leave Paris, go back to Provence and buy a small farm or even a tavern. Men were so stupid! They'd sell so much for a single night with her. Clothilde continued her pretended gasps and whispers of ecstasy. She saw the door open and momentarily froze. Ranulf-atte-Newgate slipped like a shadow into the room. He tiptoed across, took the parchment, winked at Clothilde and left, gently closing the door behind him.

'May we have that, Monsieur?'

Ranulf whirled round. Two of the relic-sellers stood at the top of the stairs. One lounged against the wall chewing on a piece of straw, the other leaned against the rail of the stairs. Ranulf cursed. Somebody had betrayed them. He heard Clothilde giggling in the room behind him. Ranulf smiled and nodded his head.

'Your sister?' he mocked. 'She sends her best regards!'

The straw-chewer shifted and, as he did so, Ranulf smashed his fist into the other relic-seller. Straw-chewer did not have time even to lift his dagger as Ranulf, light as a cat, struck out with his own, slicing a deep gash into the side of his neck. He thundered downstairs, crashing into the taproom.

'Run, Bardolph, run!' he yelled.

The perpetual student needed no second bidding. Both he and Ranulf fled from the tavern before the other relic-sellers recovered their wits. Their leader shoved two of his companions towards the stairs.

'See what's happened!' he rasped.

The two men kicked their tinker trays aside, brought out the arbalests they had concealed on hooks beneath their cloaks and raced across the taproom and up the stairs. One of their companions was unconscious, the other dying, blood bubbling from the wound at his neck. They ignored him. One sent his boot crashing against the chamber door which flew back on its leather hinges. Clothilde and de Savigny looked up in astonishment but neither the clerk nor the courtesan had time even to protest. Nogaret's men pointed their crossbows and sent a bolt deep into each lover's neck.

In the darkening streets below, the rest of Nogaret's men were pursuing Ranulf and Bardolph. The two English agents ran like the wind, slipping and scrabbling on the dirty cobbles.

'Who told them?' Bardolph hissed.

'Clothilde!' gasped Ranulf. 'Who else? She did not say who she was meeting or de Savigny would never have been allowed to enter the tavern alive. She must have told them merely that tonight we would act. She sold her favours to both camps.'

Bardolph stopped at a corner, leaned against the wall and gasped for breath.

'The lying bitch!' he breathed. 'I'll kill her!'

'No need,' Ranulf answered, pushing him on. 'She and de Savigny will already be dead – as will we be soon if you don't run!'

The two Englishmen fled deeper into the warren of alleyways. Ranulf had prepared for such an eventuality. As long as they reached the riverside they would be safe. He had the precious roll of manuscript. Others in 'Master Long Face's' service, as Ranulf secretly called Corbett, would provide safe passage to Boulogne and a ship to England.

At first they could hear the cries of their pursuers but gradually these faded. The streets were black, the cobbled alleyways running off them shrouded in darkness. The good citizens of Paris slept. No one was about except withered, hideous beggars whining fruitlessly for alms. Ranulf and Bardolph thought they were safe. They left a street of dark, high-gabled houses and were half-way across the open square when they heard a shout.

'There they are! In the King's name, stop!'

Ranulf and Bardolph fled. A crossbow bolt whirled past their heads. They had nearly reached the mouth of an alleyway when Bardolph suddenly groaned, flung his hands forward and crashed to the cobbles. Ranulf stopped and ran back.

'Don't leave me!' pleaded Bardolph. Ranulf let his hand run down the man's back and felt the cruel barb embedded at the base of his spine. 'The wound is grievous.' Ranulf looked despairingly across the square at the dark shapes hurrying towards him.

'Then don't leave me alive!' Bardolph wept. 'Please, Ranulf, do it! Do it now!'

He shook his sweat-soaked face and peered closer.

'Please!' Bardolph insisted. 'They'll keep me alive for weeks!'

Ranulf heard the slap of leather on the cobbles.

'Look!' he hissed. 'Look over there! We are safe!'

Bardolph painfully turned his head and Ranulf swiftly slit his throat, breathed a prayer and hurried into the shadows.

The forest had always stood there, the trees providing a canopy to shield the earth from the sky. Beneath this veil of greenness which stretched as far as the eye could see, the forest had witnessed murder as long as it had seen man himself. First the small dark people who burnt their victims in hanging cages to atone their angry war gods or placate the great Earth Mother whose name should never be mentioned. They were replaced by more warlike men who hung their victims from oak or elm in sacrifices to Thor and one-eyed Woden. These, too, had gone to dust, supplanted by men who, though worshipping the white Christ, built temples to their own captains of power.

The trees had seen it all: the gnarled oak, the elm with its branches stooped with age. The forest was a dangerous place, a living thing, and through its green-dappled shadows slunk masked men who knew the secret paths and where to avoid the treacherous morass. Only a fool would wander from the beaten track which wound through Sherwood Forest, either north to Barnsleydale or south to Newark and the great road down to London.

The tax-collectors thought of the legends about the forest as they slowly moved the King's money in ironbound chests, chained and padlocked in covered wagons, to the Exchequer at Westminster. The two tax-collectors were following a secret route, going by little used pathways and tracks so not even the local sheriff, Sir Eustace Vechey, had knowledge of their whereabouts. The convoy was protected by a small column of dusty archers and a few outriders who anxiously scanned the trees on either side for signs of ambush. It was a hot day. The sun was now high in the sky like a disc of molten gold and the soldiers sweated and cursed under their chain-mail cotes and tight-fitting iron helms. If they could only reach Newark and the safety and the coolness of the castle!

The principal tax-collector, Matthew Willoughby, spurred his horse forward, his assistant John Spencer galloping close behind. The two men rode ahead of the column, searching the horizon for an end to this treacherous forest. All they could glimpse was a sea of green and the white dusty track.

'At least it's empty,' Willoughby grated.

Spencer looked back at the convoy. 'Do you think we are safe?'

'We have to be. The King needs this money. It's to be at the Exchequer within a week and at Dover by the end of the month.'

They stood stroking their sweat-covered horses, not waiting for the wagons to catch them up. Spencer rose high in the stirrups.

'We will pause . . .'

The rest of the sentence was lost. A long feather-tipped arrow sped out from the trees, caught him full in his soft throat and sent him retching on his own blood out of the saddle.

Willoughby looked round in horror. Three of the escort were already down and two of the cart drivers were now a bloody mess still sitting in their seats, heads flung back, barbed arrows sticking out of chests or stomachs. There was a second volley of arrows. Some of the horsemen panicked whilst archers fell like skittles before they could even string their bows.

'Stop!' a voice rang out from the darkness of the trees. 'Master Tax-collector,' it continued, 'tell your men to drop their weapons. Take the lead yourself.'

One of the horsemen, braver or more stupid than the rest, drew his sword and urged his horse forward. Two arrows took him full in the chest and sent him crashing to the dust. One archer had an arrow from his quiver. He was running for cover behind one of the carts. He never reached it. An arrow, steel-pointed and a yard long, caught him full in the cheek, going in one side of his face and out the other. The man tossed and turned, giving strangled cries, sending up white puffs of dust from the forest trackway.

'Enough!' Willoughby shouted despairingly. 'Your weapons – place them on the ground.'

He let go of the sweat-soaked hilt of his sword as a group of men, armed and hooded, dressed in Lincoln green, faces covered in black leather masks, stepped out of the trees. They moved soundlessly, like wraiths or those will-o'-the-wisps which hang above the marshes, so silent and terrible that Willoughby thought they were demons from the wild pack of Herne the Huntsman. But these were no ghosts. They were men of war, carrying sword, dagger, buckler, and each with a long bow and a quiver of arrows, either slung over their shoulders or strapped to their sides. More of them appeared at the edge of the forest. Willoughby scanned the line of trees. Forty or fifty assailants he counted anxiously to himself. God knew how many more lurked in the darkness. He chewed his lip nervously. He had how many? He looked back along the trackway; at least seven dead, only thirteen surviving. The man with the arrow through his face was still screaming. One of the outlaws moved across, grasped him by the hair and quickly slit the exposed throat.

'Oh, Christ's sweet mother!' murmured Willoughby. 'No more deaths!' he shouted.

An outlaw stepped forward. One of Willoughby's men suddenly plucked a dagger from his sleeve. Willoughby saw dark figures in the forest's gloaming and, before he

could shout, bow strings thrummed and the unfortunate
soldier slumped to the ground, choking on his death blood.
The outlaw leader stepped closer.

'Get down, Master Tax-collector.' The voice was
muffled. 'Do not be so foolish as to attempt anything. The
lives of what remains of your men are in your hands.'

Willoughby wiped the sweat from his face.

'Do as he says!' he shouted. 'No more foolishness!'

Willoughby stared at the outlaw leader but could glean
nothing about him. He was tall and had a strong northern
accent but cowl and mask completely concealed his face.

'You will follow us!' the outlaw shouted. 'Anyone who
disobeys will be executed.'

The whole convoy was turned round and forced to
retrace their tracks for a while before the horses were
unhitched, their chests taken from the wagons and the long
line of outlaws, their prisoners and the gold, disappeared
into the green darkness.

Willoughby had never been in a forest so dense. The
trees closed in, blocking out the sun. All the clerk could do
was trudge helplessly, following his captors along a
trackway known only to them which ran between the trees.
Only once did they stop to slake their thirst at a small
brook, then the march continued. One of the carters, who
had bravely stumbled on despite an arrowhead in his thigh,
eventually collapsed. The outlaw leader whispered quietly
to him. The carter smiled. The outlaw went behind him.
Willoughby saw the glint of a knife. He heard a hissing
sound and the carter writhed as his life blood spurted.

The day drew on. Darkness fell but the march
continued. Now and again they crossed an open glade.
Looking up, Willoughby glimpsed the star-studded sky and
a hunter's moon. The undergrowth came to life with the
sounds of small animals. Now and again an owl softly
swooped to its prey which shattered the silence with a
terrible scream.

At last, as Willoughby thought he could plod no further, the line of trees broke and they entered a broad moonlit glade. Pitch torches had been lit and fastened to poles dug into the earth. Willoughby looked around. At one end of the clearing rose a huge escarpment of rock, the caves at the base probably serving as living quarters. Near these a huge fire was being lit, logs being thrown on by other outlaws who greeted their fellows with cheers and the prisoners with derisive calls.

'Guests for our banquet!' one shouted.

He came up, face covered in dirt, and peered at Willoughby.

'Rich venison!' he muttered. 'The King's own deer. Look.' He pointed to where a fat buck was being gutted and cleaned by a nearby stream in preparation for roasting. The outlaw leader approached.

'The banquet is for you, Master Tax-collector!'

'I will not eat with you,' he replied.

Immediately arrows were notched to bows.

'You have no choice,' the outlaw leader challenged.

'What is your name?' Willoughby asked.

'Oh come, sir, you know my name and my title. I am Robin Hood, Robin of the Greenwood, the Great Wolfshead, the Master Archer.'

'You are a murdering knave!' retorted Willoughby. 'And a liar to boot. You took the King's pardon. When you are caught, you will hang!'

The outlaw leader stepped closer and grasped Willoughby by the wrist. The tax-collector flinched at the hate-filled eyes behind the mask.

'This is my palace,' the wolfshead continued. 'This is my cathedral. I am King of the Greenwood and you, Master Tax-collector, are my servant. You need to be taught the due respect owing to me. Take his hand!'

Immediately three outlaws sprang forward and, before the tax-collector could resist, thrust his open hand against a tree trunk, splaying out his fingers. The outlaw leader, humming a tune, drew his dagger and neatly sliced off the top of the tax-collector's fingers. Willoughby, screaming in agony, collapsed on to the grass. Blood pumped out from the stumps, covering his robes with small pools of glistening red.

The outlaw leader strode away and returned, bearing a small bowl filled with black tar. Willoughby's hand was grasped again as the man styling himself Robin Hood coated the stumps with hot tar.

Willoughby could bear no more. He closed his eyes and screamed himself into a dead faint. When he recovered the pain had receded to a savage ache. The tax-collector, holding his damaged hand against his chest, stared round the glade. The chests taken from the carts had now been emptied and were being thrown on to the roaring fire. The horses had disappeared. Willoughby glimpsed the weapons of his escort piled beneath a tree whilst their former owners sat in a long line near the fire, pale and frightened in the glare of the torchlight. All fight had gone out of them; they looked terrified by the cold-blooded ruthlessness they had witnessed.

The outlaw leader came and squatted before Willoughby. He thrust a piece of roasted venison into his good hand and placed a goblet of thick red wine beside him. Willoughby looked away. The meat roasting over the fire gave off mouth-watering smells and the tax-collector, despite his pain, realised he hadn't eaten since the previous evening.

'I am sorry,' murmured Robin Hood, the mask still over his face, 'but I had no choice. Look around you, Tax-collector. These are savage men, wolvesheads. If they had their way they would kill you all. They hate you, despise your royal master, and see the money from those chests as rightfully theirs. Now come, sit with us by the fire – and keep a civil tongue in your head.'

He pulled the unresisting tax-collector to his feet and

pushed him across the clearing, giving him a place before the fire. Willoughby watched as the outlaws began to carve huge chunks of glistening meat; braving the flames of the fire, each outlaw hacked off a chunk and forced it into his mouth, chewing vigorously until the juice ran down his chin. Willoughby, despite his discomfort, nibbled at his meat and took the occasional sip from his wine cup. Did they intend to kill him? he wondered. Would any of them survive? Beside him the outlaw leader remained silent.

Most of the talking was being done by a huge giant of a man whom the others called Little John. He apparently was the leader's lieutenant and had been absent from the attack on the convoy. He, too, wore a mask across his face, as did the woman on his right. She was dressed in a smock of Lincoln green; the hem hung high above her riding boots whilst the bodice was drawn tightly across her breast. She displayed no shame in the presence of so many men, noted the clerk. Around them outlaws talked and chattered; a few sang songs. The tax-collector's eyes grew heavy, the pain in his hand worsened. He gulped some wine to dull the pain. At last his eyes grew heavy-lidded with sleep and, despite the mocking calls of the outlaws, he folded his arms and stretched out on the grass, no longer caring what might happen.

He awoke the next morning, cold and damp, his mutilated hand throbbing with pain. The fire was no more than a smouldering mass of ashes. Willoughby looked around but the glade was empty. He picked himself up and walked across to the caves. He glimpsed rough, makeshift beds made out of ferns and branches. He looked around again, moaning as the pain in his hand flared back to life.

'Jesu miserere!' he whimpered. 'Nothing.'

Oh, there were scraps of food on the ground, and above him in the trees birds chattered angrily at being bereft of their spoils. Willoughby felt sick from pain and the coarse wine. For a while he knelt, sobbing for breath and retching at the bitter taste at the back of his throat. He heard a twig snap and looked up.

'Who is there?' he called.

No answer. Willoughby glimpsed a flash of colour amongst the trees but his eyes were blurred with tears after his violent retching. He squatted on the ground, head thumping and his body aching, his clothes all soiled. There was no sign of the outlaws. No indication, apart from the scraps of food and the smouldering ash, of their wild banquet the night before.

Willoughby sat cradling himself for a while. Again, out of the corner of his eye, he glimpsed a flash of colour but his mind felt battered and his body drained. He dared not concentrate. A ring of pain encircled his hand. He felt feverish and almost wished he had died quickly the previous day. A huge magpie, bold and daring, swooped from the trees and started pecking with its cruel yellow beak at a piece of fat-caked meat. Willoughby got to his feet and walked to the line of trees. He looked up. Once again, he caught the flash of colour and stared fixedly.

'Oh no!' he sobbed. 'Oh, Christ, have mercy!'

He fell to his knees and stared round. Other snatches of colour caught his gaze.

'Oh, you bastards!' he murmured, and then crumpled to the ground like a child, whimpering and crying. From the overhanging branches of the trees around the glade, every member of his retinue, stripped of clothes and boots, hung lifeless by the neck.

Chapter 1

'Murder, Sir Peter, that's why the King has sent me north!'

Sir Hugh Corbett, Keeper of the King's Secret Seal, stared across the table at Sir Peter Branwood, under-sheriff of Nottingham, now acting-sheriff after the mysterious murder of Sir Eustace Vechey. Corbett propped his elbows on the table and ticked off the points on his fingers.

'The outlaw Robin Hood has reneged on his pardon. He has re-formed his coven of outlaws and wolvesheads and taken refuge in Sherwood Forest. From there he has attacked merchants, pilgrims, and finally royal tax-collectors. He has pillaged and plundered. Now he has murdered the King's officer in these parts! That, Sir Peter, is why I am here!'

The smooth-faced Branwood never flinched. He leaned his head on his hand and scratched his close-cropped dark hair.

'And you, Sir Hugh,' he said slowly, 'must realise that I would gain great personal satisfaction from capturing this malefactor. He has murdered my friend Sir Eustace, injured and killed retainers and officials from this castle. He hampers our administration. He has even attacked and pillaged my manor outside Newark on Trent, burning my barns and slaughtering my cattle.' Branwood licked his lips. 'He has brought my name into mockery and continues to harass and revile my office as well as the Crown.' He got

17

up and went to look through one of the arrow-slit windows. 'Just look out there, Sir Hugh.'

Corbett rose to join him.

'You see the castle and town walls – and what else?'

'Forest,' replied Corbett.

'Yes,' sighed Branwood. 'Forest! Are you a hunting man, Corbett?' He did not wait for a reply. 'Go in there as I have with mounted men, and within a bowshot of leaving the path you will be in a darkness so dense not even the brightest sun above can diminish it. Chase a deer and you'll find your skills hard pressed. Hunt an outlaw and you finish up hunting death itself.' Branwood walked away from the window. 'In Sherwood, Master Clerk, it is very easy for the hunter to become the hunted.' He rubbed his hands on his dark green gown and re-hitched the sword belt round his slim waist. 'The soldiers you take with you,' he continued, 'cannot be trusted. Some may well be in the pay of Robin Hood.'

He caught the disbelieving expression on Corbett's face.

'Oh, yes, there are sympathisers even here. How else did Robin Hood gain access to murder Eustace Vechey? This God-forsaken town and castle are built on a crag with as many secret tunnels and passageways as you'd find in a rabbit warren. Some of the tunnels reach the forest itself.' Branwood paused. 'Now let us say you do trust the soldiers,' he continued. 'Once in that forest, their mood changes. They are superstitious and fear the place. They still believe the small dark people live there who might cast spells and carry them off to Elfin Land. Three days ago . . .' He turned and pointed to his burly serjeant-at-arms, seated at the table. 'You tell him, Naylor.'

The serjeant-at-arms stirred; his black leather jerkin studded with steel points creaked as he moved his arms. His craggy face and balding head reminded Corbett of a piece of stone brought to life only by sharp, restless eyes.

'As Sir Peter says, we went into the forest.' The soldier

glared coldly at Corbett. 'Within a quarter of an hour, the time it would take a man to snatch a meal, two of my soldiers were missing. Neither horses nor riders have been seen since. The following day Robin Hood himself entered Nottingham and impudently pinned a rhyming ballad on one of the postern gates of the castle about how Sir Eustace Vechey was well named – being useless as a sheriff as well as a man!'

Naylor's eyes moved from Corbett to the clerk's two servants, Ranulf-atte-Newgate and Maltote the messenger, who sat quietly at the end of the table.

'And how,' he sneered, 'does His Grace the King think a clerk and two manservants will resolve all this?'

'I don't know,' Corbett replied slowly. 'God knows, the King's mind is taken up with the French threat against Flanders but he cannot have his tax-collectors and soldiers hanged like barnyard rats and his sheriff mysteriously murdered.' Corbett spoke to Branwood. 'When did these attacks begin?'

'About six months ago.'

'And the robbery and murder of the tax-collectors?'

'Three weeks ago. A peasant found Willoughby wandering witless in the forest and brought him in.'

Corbett nodded and looked away. He had seen Willoughby in London. He would never forget that meeting. The once proud exchequer clerk was reduced to a shambling wreck. Dirty, dishevelled and ill-clad, Willoughby simply stared at his mutilated hand and recounted time and again how his companions had died. The King's anger had boiled over at the sight and Corbett had been forced to witness Edward in one of his black rages. He kicked furniture over, pounded on walls till his fists were bloodied, scattered papers from his table and dragged hangings from their hooks. Even the royal greyhounds had the sense to cower and hide. Corbett had effaced himself until the royal rage abated.

'Am I the King?' Edward roared. 'To be made a mockery of in my own kingdom? You will go north, Corbett, you understand? You will go to bloody Nottingham and see Robin Hood hang!'

So Corbett had come to Nottingham. He bore the King's message of angry disapproval to the sheriff Sir Eustace Vechey but, on his arrival at the castle, discovered Vechey had been poisoned in his own chamber.

'Tell me again,' Corbett said, breaking free from his reverie, 'how Sir Eustace died.'

'Sir Eustace,' Branwood began slowly, 'was in the blackest pit of depression. On Wednesday evening he dined here in the hall. He hardly spoke. He ate sparingly though he drank well. At last he got to his feet, said he was retiring early and, followed by Lecroix his manservant, took a goblet of wine up to his chamber. Vechey slept in a great four-poster bed, Lecroix on a pallet in a corner of the same chamber.'

'Was there any food in the room?'

Branwood made a face. 'A little. A plate of sweetmeats, and of course the cup of wine. However, when Vechey's corpse was discovered, Physician Maigret tasted both the sweetmeats and what was left of the wine. Both were found to be harmless.'

'Did anyone visit him in the night?'

'No. Vechey locked his chamber door, leaving the key in the lock. Two soldiers stood guard outside, Vechey's personal retainers. No one came near that chamber.'

'You talked of secret passageways?'

'Oh, they may exist under the castle but Sir Eustace's chamber is on the floor above. Not even a rat could squeeze in there.'

'And the windows?'

'As here, mere arrow slits.'

'So,' mused Corbett, 'a man is poisoned in a locked chamber. No one entered, no one could force their way through a window and there are no secret passageways. And you say he only ate and drank what you did?'

Branwood snorted. 'Even better. He made myself, Lecroix, and Physician Maigret taste everything before he did. You see, Sir Eustace had nightmares about Robin Hood. He believed the outlaw wanted him dead, if not by an arrow or dagger then by poison.'

Corbett shook his head and went back to the table.

'So this man leaves the table in good health. He takes a goblet of wine upstairs, perhaps eats a sweetmeat, yet neither of these was tainted?'

'Yes,' Branwood said softly. 'Go to the chamber yourself, Master Clerk. Naturally Sir Eustace's corpse has been removed, but on my orders and those of Physician Maigret, nothing else. The wine and sweetmeats – everything is still there.'

'I would like to question the servant Lecroix.'

'He will be found for you but is surely not responsible,' Branwood explained. 'Lecroix is simple-minded and deeply loved his master.'

Ranulf-atte-Newgate spoke up clearly, tired of the way Naylor was glaring at him. 'But you said, Sir Peter, that Lecroix slept in the same chamber. Surely Sir Eustace Vechey's death throes would have woken him?'

Branwood shrugged. 'Vechey had drunk deep, as had Lecroix. The fellow sleeps like a log. And according to Physician Maigret, certain noxious potions can kill quietly and swiftly.'

Corbett rubbed his face and walked over to the window, drawn there by a clamour from the castle bailey below. He stared down at the small crowd of retainers who had gathered round a makeshift execution platform on which a red-masked headsman was standing. Corbett stood transfixed as a man was hustled up the steps, hands bound behind his back. His head was thrust down on the block, the axe rose, glinting in the sunlight, and fell with a loud

21

thud. Corbett flinched and looked away as hot blood spurted in a curving arc.

'Master, what is it?'

Ranulf and Maltote left the table and peered over Corbett's shoulder.

'See,' Ranulf whispered to Maltote, 'the eyes still flutter and the lips are moving.'

The round-faced Maltote, who could not stand the sight of blood, his or anyone else's, briskly walked away, praying not to faint. Corbett looked at the sheriff.

'A bloody business, Sir Peter?'

'No, a lesson,' Branwood replied, toying with a ring on his slim brown hand.

Corbett flinched as the axe fell again. He caught the glint of amusement in Branwood's eyes.

'What is happening?' Corbett jerked his head towards the window.

'You are a visitor to Nottingham, Sir Hugh. There's an outbreak of plague in the city.'

Corbett shivered and turned away. Thank God, he thought, he hadn't brought Maeve and baby Eleanor here.

'A house in Castle Street,' Branwood explained, 'was taken by the plague and a group of night watchmen, in accordance with city regulations, had the place shut up, marking the door and windows with crosses.'

Corbett breathed a prayer; if the plague visited any house, all the occupants suffered.

'Anyway,' continued Branwood, 'a man, his wife, a girl, a boy, and two servants were declared dead. The corpses were to be removed to the lime pits outside the city gates. Now usually everyone stays away in these cases but this time an inquisitive relative, braver than the rest, came to pay his last respects. He hid in the shadows and, when one of the corpses was dragged out, saw the head roll to one side. The throat had been cut.' Branwood nodded at the window. 'The night watchmen were murderers. They'd killed the entire family and plundered the house. Now they pay the price, to the King and to God.'

Corbett walked back to the table, trying to close his mind to the repetitive thuds followed by murmurs from the small crowd of spectators.

'I need to inspect Sir Eustace's corpse,' he demanded.

'It's been moved.' Branwood shrugged. 'Because of the heat. To a death house in a garden near the postern gate.'

'No time like the present,' Corbett replied briskly. 'Sir Peter, you'll show us the way?' The under-sheriff led them out, Naylor, Ranulf and Maltote following. Corbett looked carefully around. For a royal castle Nottingham was painfully neglected. The paint on the walls was mouldy and flaking; the paving stones underfoot uneven, damp and cracked. Branwood led them through a dirty kitchen. The walls were spattered with traces of meals long past whilst bloated flies buzzed lazily over pools of blood as a sweating cook and his grimy-faced scullions hacked at a chunk of beef. Corbett glimpsed a tub of dirty water covered in scum. He swallowed and quietly vowed he would be careful what he ate here. They crossed an empty yard, passed down more passageways and into a small garden. Perhaps under previous sheriffs it had been a bower, but now the chipped statue in the centre was almost hidden by a wild tangle of brambles and weeds.

'Better care should be taken,' Ranulf murmured.

'We are King's officers not gardeners!' Branwood snapped. 'And, thanks to Robin Hood, poor Vechey could hardly take care of himself.'

They fought their way through the high grass and gorse to a small stone building with a flat roof whose cracked door hung askew on leather hinges. Branwood pulled it back and waved Corbett in. The stench was so pungent he pinched his nostrils.

'Today is Friday,' he muttered to himself. 'Vechey died late on Wednesday evening.'

23

He stared round, took a thick tallow candle left just inside the door, struck a tinder and moved deeper into the darkness. Ranulf and Maltote wisely stayed outside. The dead sheriff's body had been laid on the floor, a dirty linen sheet flung over it.

'I am sorry,' Branwood called in through the half-open door, 'but we knew you were coming, Master Corbett, and Physician Maigret told us not to dress the corpse until you had inspected it.'

Corbett pulled back the fetid sheet and tried not to think or reflect. If he did so he would gag or retch. Vechey had been middle-aged, balding, a slightly podgy man though the stomach was even more swollen with the trapped gases. The eyes were still half-open. Corbett tried not to look at them but examined the lips which had turned a purple hue, particularly the open sores at each side of the mouth. In his earlier days the clerk had performed military service in Wales and knew enough physic to conclude that such blotches were the result of poor diet, too much meat and very little fruit. He carefully scrutinised the dead man's fingers and nails but noticed nothing untoward except that the skin of Vechey's hand felt like wet wool. Corbett sighed, pulled back the sheet, blew out the candle and walked back into the garden.

'Does Sir Eustace have any family?'

'He has a son in the King's army in Scotland and a daughter married to some Cornish knight; he was a widower. His remains will probably be interred in one of the city churches until Sir Eustace's son declares his intentions.'

'You can take him away,' Corbett murmured. 'God knows that body has suffered enough!'

Naylor rejoined them, marching purposefully through the long grass. He seemed more friendly and grinned at Corbett.

The Assassin in the Greenwood

'They are all ready. I've summoned them to the hall,' he announced.

Ranulf, sitting on a stone wall sunning himself, squinted up at this serjeant-at-arms against whom he had taken an instant dislike. 'Who is ready?' he asked.

Before he received an answer, three others came through the garden: a friar, small, balding and brown as a berry, his face glistening, eyes almost lost in rolls of fat. Beside him was a young clerk, with thick hair cut painfully short. He was dressed in a fustian knee-length sleeveless jupon. Underneath his jerkin was of padded silk with slashed sleeves, and on his dark head sat a small tasselled skull cap. A clerk, Corbett thought, but a fop. Nevertheless, he liked the fellow with his boyish face and laughing eyes. Beside him stood a severe figure with steel-grey hair and a long white face, his chin deeply cleft. He was dressed in a blue quilted gown, fringed at the neck and cuff with dyed black lambswool, which almost hid his spindly legs. Branwood waved them over.

'Sir Hugh Corbett, may I introduce three members of my household. Friar Thomas, my clerk Roteboeuf, and Physician Maigret.'

Hands were clasped and shaken, Corbett introducing Ranulf and Maltote. He glared as Ranulf winked fleetingly at his fellow. Corbett knew his manservant was already poking fun at the young clerk's name which, translated from the Norman French, meant 'Roast Beef'. The quick-witted young man caught the exchange of grins.

'My name,' he laughed loudly, 'indicates my origins but not the quality of meals received here in the castle.'

The murmur of laughter, shared by all except Maigret and the sombre-faced Naylor, was halted by Branwood putting up his hands and loudly declaring, 'Sirs, we have problems enough but, I assure you, either the cook changes his ways or he goes!'

25

'Who knows?' Roteboeuf quipped. 'Sir Eustace, God rest him, may have been poisoned by his own cook.'

'He would not have died so quickly,' Maigret snapped, his eyes flickering with annoyance as he scratched the tip of his nose. 'Sir Eustace was murdered. And you, Sir Peter, had a narrow escape.'

Corbett glimpsed the annoyance on Branwood's saturnine face.

'What does the physician mean, Sir Peter?'

'The night Sir Eustace died, we had been dining at table in the hall. I left after Sir Eustace. Later I returned for a half-finished cup of wine. I drank it but the taste was acrid so I threw it away. After I retired I began to retch and vomit. I spent the night in the latrines. My bowels had turned to water.' Sir Peter cleared his throat. 'The next morning I felt weak. I thought it was something I had eaten until Sir Eustace's corpse was found when I consulted Physician Maigret.'

'He had been poisoned,' the doctor declared triumphantly, as if daring anyone to contradict him.

'With what?' Corbett asked.

'I don't know, but if Sir Peter had finished that cup of wine he would surely have died. I told him to fast for twenty-four hours and drink as much water from the castle well as possible.'

Corbett stared round the group. 'You did say someone was waiting for us?'

'Ah, yes, the two guards and Lecroix are in the small hall.'

'The same two who guarded Sir Eustace's chamber?'

'Of course.'

'Then we had better not keep them waiting. And I would like everyone,' Corbett continued, 'to be present at the interrogation.'

They went back into the castle and into the small hall. Corbett noticed this too shared the general air of decay which hung over the whole castle. A dirty, flagstoned room, its narrow windows were protected by wooden shutters or a few glazed with horn. Along the hammer-beam roof Corbett glimpsed huge cobwebs and on the dirty white-washed walls hung dusty shields bearing the faded escutcheons of former sheriffs. The fireplace was battered and the grate still full of last winter's ash. There were no carpets or rugs on the floor which was instead thickly covered with lime. There were two wall seats covered in cushions but these were ragged and faded. There was very little in the way of furniture except two grease-covered trestle tables on the dais as well as a number of makeshift benches and stools. On one bench, pushed against the wall, sat three lack-lustre figures. They stood up as Corbett entered. The two guards looked morose and greasy-haired, while Lecroix, skull-faced under a mop of tousled black hair, was rather obese with an unkempt moustache and beard to hide his hare lip.

'Let us make ourselves comfortable,' Branwood suggested.

Benches and stools were moved into a horseshoe pattern, everyone self-consciously taking their seats as Sir Peter once again introduced Corbett.

'Sir Peter,' he began briskly, trying to dispel the tension, 'tell me once again what happened on the night Sir Eustace died.'

'We all gathered here. The food was rancid as usual. The cook said it was roast pork but it was wet, soggy and tasted of salt.'

This drew a snigger from his companions.

'Some of us drank ale, others wine.' Sir Peter stroked his chin, trying to remember. 'There was a dish of vegetables and some marchpane.'

'And nothing happened at the meal?' asked Corbett.

'Those who were hungry ate, then as usual we sat about talking.'

'Sir Eustace included?'

'Yes.'

'For how long?'

Corbett studied the faces of the rest of Branwood's household; from their expressions he deduced the sheriff was telling the truth.

'Oh, about an hour and a half, then we went to bed.'

'And what happened next?'

'I was up early the next morning. As I have explained, I had been unwell all night,' Branwood continued. 'I attended mass and came down here to break my fast. I expected Sir Eustace to be here. When he wasn't, I went up to his chamber and asked the two guards if he had risen.'

They shook their heads as if anticipating Corbett's question.

'We never hears anything,' one of them replied in a thick country accent. 'We hears nothing so Sir Peter bangs on the door.'

'And then what?'

Lecroix pulled himself out of his reverie.

'I woke up,' he muttered. 'You see, sir, I am a heavy sleeper.'

'More like a heavy drinker!' snapped Maigret.

'I had drunk deeply,' Lecroix cried, 'but I was tired!'

Corbett watched him carefully. He noticed the man's flickering eyes, the drool of saliva down his tangled beard. This man is not full in his wits, he thought, the mind of a child in the body of a man.

'Master Lecroix,' he said softly, 'no one is accusing you. Just tell me what happened.'

'I was asleep on the trestle bed on the other side of the chamber. I always sleep there. Sir Peter's loud knocking woke me up and made my head even more sore. I went across to Sir Eustace's bed to pull back the heavy drapes. He was just lying there.' Lecroix's lower lip began to tremble and his eyes filled with tears.

'Continue,' Corbett said quietly.

'I knew there was something wrong. My master's body was twisted, his face turned to one side and his mouth open. His eyes were staring. They reminded me of a dog I had seen crushed by a cart.' Lecroix put his head in his hands. 'Sir Peter was still knocking and my head was hurting so I went and unlocked the door.'

'And you went in, Sir Peter?' Corbett asked.

'We all did,' the sheriff explained. 'I sent one of the guards here down to the hall. Naylor, Roteboeuf, and of course Physician Maigret joined me.'

'When I went in,' Maigret explained, 'Lecroix was kneeling by the bed weeping.' He patted the servant on the shoulder. 'He was devoted to his master. One of the bed curtains had been pulled aside and it was as Lecroix has described; Sir Eustace lay sprawled as if he had suffered some dreadful seizure. By the appearance of his skin, his eyes and mouth, I immediately concluded he was poisoned.'

Corbett got to his feet and shook his head in disbelief.

'Sirs, let me repeat the obvious. Sir Eustace drank and ate only what you did at supper?'

'Yes,' Sir Peter replied. 'And, remember, Master Clerk, he insisted on Lecroix, Maigret and I testing everything for him.'

'Did he eat or drink anything else?'

'No,' replied Maigret. 'When he left the hall I went up with him to his chamber. Lecroix bore his wine cup for him. Sir Eustace was lost in his own thoughts. He was almost beside himself with fear about your visit, Sir Hugh. He believed the King would hold him personally responsible for the robbery and murder of the tax-collectors. Anyway, I wished him good night, took the wine cup from Lecroix and put it in his hands. Even then Vechey asked me to taste it, so I did.'

29

Corbett came back and stood over the manservant.

'Lecroix!' he whispered.

The servant looked up, his face made even uglier with fear.

'Inside his bed chamber,' Corbett continued, 'your master drank the wine. Anything else?'

'Just the sweetmeats,' Lecroix murmured. 'He always kept a small tray there, but I ate some as well.'

'Did he drink any water?'

'No.' Maigret spoke up defensively. 'There's only a bowl of washing water. Both I and Roteboeuf here tested this and examined the napkin on which he dried himself. There was nothing untoward. You can see for yourself, Sir Hugh, they are still there, as are the sweetmeats and what is left of the wine. I insisted that the room be sealed so nothing could be tampered with.'

'Maigret speaks the truth,' Roteboeuf added. 'I ate some of the sweetmeats. I even examined the water in the bowl.'

Corbett stared at the mildewed wall and momentarily closed his eyes. Something was wrong here, he thought. How could a man be poisoned in a locked room and yet no one trace the source of the poison which killed him? He sighed heavily.

'Look.' He held up his hands. 'Sir Eustace died of poisoning. How it was administered and who administered it are a mystery. However, surely he would have suffered spasms, cried out in pain and woken Lecroix?'

'Not necessarily,' Maigret answered quickly. 'God knows what killed Sir Eustace Vechey but there are poisons, Sir Hugh – white arsenic, henbane, foxglove – which can kill as quickly as an arrow to the heart. Remember, Sir Eustace was not a fit man. He was overweight and his heart was growing weak. He may have taken only a few seconds to die.'

Ranulf, leaning against the wall, now unfolded his arms and stepped forward.

'Is it possible,' he asked, 'that Lecroix or anyone else could have changed the wine or water?'

'No,' Maigret explained. 'I saw to that. In Sir Eustace's chamber the windows are mere arrow slits. I examined them carefully. Nothing had been thrown out, and even if it had, how could it have been replaced? There was no more water or a jug of wine in the room.'

'So,' Corbett concluded, 'we have Sir Eustace who dines and wines but only what you eat and drink and even then it is first tasted by others. He goes up to his room with half a cup of wine which was apparently untainted. The same applies to a tray of sweetmeats he kept there and the water with which he washed his hands.' He glanced at Lecroix. 'Your master did wash before he retired?'

The man nodded.

'So, Sir Eustace retired to his bed, locked in a chamber with the key on the inside?' He stared at Branwood who was watching him carefully.

'Yes,' Branwood replied. 'Lecroix opened the door. I heard the key turn.'

'And you, sirs,' Corbett pointed to the soldiers, 'never left your post and no one visited Sir Eustace that night?'

Both men shook their heads.

'On the same evening,' Corbett continued, 'you, Sir Peter, returned to the hall for a cup of wine you had left. Now, if our good physician is to be believed, that too had been poisoned. A mere sip of it turned your bowels to water.' Corbett looked at the friar who had been sitting on a stool, hands on his knees, half-dozing. 'Father, I beg your pardon, where were you when Sir Eustace's corpse was discovered?'

'I had gone back to the chapel to clear up after saying mass. Sir Peter sent a servant for me. I went up and did the only thing I could. I anointed the body and blessed it.'

'You have seen many corpses, Father?'

The friar's merry eyes met Corbett's.

'Aye, Sir Hugh, more than you have. I served as King's chaplain with the armies on the Scottish march.'

'And when you saw the corpse and anointed it, would you say that Sir Eustace had been dead for hours or had died shortly before Sir Peter knocked on the door?'

The friar narrowed his eyes.

'The corpse was growing stiff,' he replied haltingly. 'Still supple though there was a tightness to the limbs. Sir Eustace retired an hour before midnight. I anointed his poor remains somewhere between eight and nine in the morning.' He stared up at Corbett. 'To give you an honest answer, Sir Hugh, I believe Sir Eustace may well have been dead by midnight.' The friar laughed sourly. 'The witching hour when more souls go to God than at any other time.'

Corbett scratched his brow, genuinely perplexed as well as tired and weary after his journey. He rubbed his eyes. Nothing, he thought to himself, there is nothing here, not even a loose thread.

'So,' he breathed, 'we do not know how Sir Eustace died or who killed him?'

'Oh, yes we do,' Sir Peter spoke up. 'The wolfshead Robin Hood!'

'How could he?' Corbett retorted. 'Enter a castle at the dead of night and administer a deadly potion to a man already on his guard against him? Why do you say that?'

Sir Peter dug into his wallet and tossed a greasy piece of parchment across.

'Because that's what Robin Hood claimed he did.'

Chapter 2

Corbett stared in disbelief at the scrawled writing on the parchment:

> Sir Eustace Vechey, self-styled Sheriff of Nottingham, executed by order of Robin Hood. Peter Branwood, self-styled Under-Sheriff, executed by order of Robin Hood.

Corbett mouthed the words slowly and stared at Branwood. 'So you too were supposed to die. But why didn't you show me this immediately?'

'I told you that Robin Hood was responsible! Vechey is dead and so should I be. There's no doubt this wolfshead has sympathisers in the castle. I thought,' he coughed self-consciously, 'I thought I should watch you. See what conclusions you drew.' He shrugged. 'Now you have it.'

Corbett stared at the parchment again. 'By the cross!' he swore. 'This outlaw does take on styles and titles! He finishes his letter: "Given at our castle in the Greenwood".' Corbett tossed the parchment back at Branwood. 'I want to see that bastard hang from the castle walls! Where was this proclamation left?'

'It wasn't. It was despatched by arrow into the outer bailey.'

Corbett looked at a huge cobweb in the corner of one of the roof beams.

'The letter proves one thing,' he declared. 'It says "by order of", so the poisoner must be in the castle. I don't accept that some criminal has the God-given power to go through stone walls.' Corbett paused. 'You did say there are secret passages here?'

'In the cellars below, yes, a veritable warren. The castle and town are built on a huge crag. The caves and tunnels were used by people long before the Romans came.'

'But why?' Ranulf stepped forward, ignoring the surprised looks from Sir Peter's household. 'Why should an outlaw murder one of the King's sheriffs and attempt the assassination of another? He must have known it would only bring royal fury down upon his head.'

Corbett nodded. Ranulf was correct: the outlaw and his band could roam the greenwood, plundering at their will. Other outlaws did the same in forests up and down the kingdom. So why attract attention to himself?

'Sir Peter, my manservant's question is significant.'

The under-sheriff shrugged and spread his hands.

'First, Sir Eustace issued a proclamation saying this Robin of Locksley or Robin Hood should be killed on sight. He also called him a coward, a caitiff and a traitor. The outlaw replied by demanding Sir Eustace do public penance for his remarks or suffer the consequences. Sir Eustace refused and . . .' His voice trailed off.

'But why poison?' Corbett insisted. 'Why not in public as Sir Eustace was travelling through the town?'

'Master Clerk, you have served as a soldier?'

'Yes, I have.'

'You have seen men lose their courage? Well, so did Sir Eustace. He refused to venture out of the castle. He became obsessed with the idea that there was a traitor here in the castle, perhaps in his very household. Vechey changed. He was nervous, agitated, neglecting himself and drinking far too much.'

Corbett stared round. Too many ears here, he thought.

He leant over and whispered in Sir Peter's ear. The sheriff looked at the guards and Lecroix.

'You may go.'

The soldiers hastened from the hall but Lecroix was sluggish. Dragging at his straggling moustache, he shuffled to the door then abruptly turned round.

'My master was tidy,' he declared as if refuting Ranulf's and Branwood's assertion.

'What do you mean?' Corbett asked.

'Nothing,' Lecroix replied. 'He was just tidy, especially in his own chamber.' And he shuffled out.

Corbett waited until the door closed then turned to Roteboeuf.

'You are the clerk of the castle as well as Vechey's secretarius?'

The young man cheerfully nodded.

'Did he say anything to you? Anything at all?'

'No. Sir Eustace kept to himself, glowering and throwing dark looks at everyone.'

'I tried to speak to him,' Father Thomas put in. 'But he told me to look after my own business and he would look after his.'

'And you, Sir Peter, why should Robin Hood try and kill you?' Corbett caught the glint of hatred in the man's eyes. 'Sir Peter?'

The sheriff splayed out his fingers and studied them carefully.

'Eight years ago I was travelling north through Barnsleydale. I was and still am hoping to marry the Lady Margaret Percy. I had bought her a piece of silk, costly and very precious. Robin Hood and his outlaws stopped me, took my gifts, stripped me naked, tied me to my horse and left me to public ridicule.'

You hate well, Corbett thought, noting a muscle flicker high in Branwood's cheek. The under-sheriff swallowed hard.

'When Sir Eustace issued his proclamation, I openly defied Robin Hood, calling him a coward, a skulking caitiff, the illegitimate son of a yeoman farmer. I challenged him to a duel *à outrance* on the High Pavement of Nottingham.' He pulled a face. 'You know the outlaw's reply.'

'You are sure,' Corbett asked, abruptly changing the conversation, 'that the outlaw himself never comes into Nottingham?'

'Why do you ask?'

'Because I think he might be captured by stealth, rather than by force. His Grace the King is most insistent that he is taken. Once this threat is removed, Edward intends to take the field against the Scottish rebel William Wallace.' Corbett looked at Ranulf, the strange words on the parchment his manservant had brought from Paris running through his brain. He blinked. 'Yes, as I was saying, the King needs the roads north free for supplies and men. Robin Hood is to be killed.'

'How?' Branwood sneered. 'By you and two servants?'

'No,' Corbett replied, stung to the quick. 'You have heard of Sir Guy of Gisborne?'

'Yes, he holds the lands near Stifford on the Lancashire border. He was once sheriff here during Robin Hood's early depredations.'

'Well,' Corbett replied, 'Guy has offered his services to the King and they have been accepted. No man knows the forest better than Gisborne. He is now at Southwell with a dozen trained foresters and sixty archers.' Corbett was pleased to see the hauteur drain from Branwood's face. 'Tell me,' he continued quickly, 'what do you know of the outlaw?'

Branwood seemed discomfited by the reference to Gisborne and Corbett cursed his own ineptitude; it might appear that the King had no confidence in Branwood while Gisborne's presence was supposed to be secret.

'Robin of Locksley,' Branwood began slowly, gathering his thoughts, 'was born a yeoman farmer. He inherited the small manor of Locksley with some fields and pasture rights. As a young man he fought in the King's armies in Wales where he became skilled in the use of the long bow.'

Corbett nodded. He had seen the strength and power of this weapon, increasingly used by English archers instead of the crossbow. The height of a man in length and, fashioned out of polished yew, a skilled bowman could use it to loose four arrows each a yard long, capable of piercing chain mail, in the space of a minute.

'Robin of Locksley was born for war,' Branwood explained. 'He took part in the troubles in the old King's reign but then came back to Locksley where he was drawn into a fight with royal verderers who, some say, murdered his father. Robin killed three of these and fled to Sherwood for sanctuary.'

Corbett listened carefully; what Branwood was telling him agreed with the information he'd gathered before he left Westminster.

'Robin was a skilled bowman,' Branwood continued, 'a good soldier who knew the forest paths like the back of his hand. He was joined in the forest by Lady Mary of Lydsford together with a Franciscan nicknamed Friar Tuck.'

Corbett looked at Friar Thomas who grinned back at him.

'Not all friars are men of God,' he quipped. 'Old Tuck was a rogue who had his cell at Copmanhurst near Fountaindale. When the King issued pardons to Robin Hood, Tuck was sent to fast on bread and water in one of our houses in Cornwall where he later died.'

'What else?' Corbett asked.

'Others joined Robin,' Roteboeuf spoke up. 'A huge giant of a man, bigger than Naylor, called John Little, nicknamed "Little John", an ex-soldier and a savage man. Robin's other principal lieutenant was Will Scathelock or Scarlett.'

'You see,' Branwood intervened, 'Robin of Locksley was quite unique. He imposed discipline on his own coven and was careful not to hurt the peasants or those who might betray him. He plundered churchmen or lords, and those he could not terrorise into silence, he bribed.' Branwood shrugged. 'You know the rest of the story. Six years ago His Grace the King came north. He issued pardons to Robin and his men, even,' he added bitterly, 'giving the wolfshead a place in his household chamber. Robin took his men to serve in the Scottish war.'

Corbett held up hand 'I saw him,' he murmured. 'A tall, swarthy-featured man, his hair black as a raven. He always wore Lincoln green under the royal tabard. He was a captain in the company of royal archers. Harsh-faced,' Corbett mused. 'He reminded me of a hunting peregrine. Enough,' he concluded. 'Sir Peter, what do you propose now?'

'Tomorrow morning,' the under-sheriff replied, 'I intend to take a company into Sherwood Forest. I suggest, Sir Hugh, that you come with us.'

'Is that safe?' Corbett asked.

'No, Master Clerk, it isn't. But what can I do? Stay shut up in the castle like some widow in mourning? I am the King's officer in these parts. I cannot allow Robin Hood to ride roughshod over the King's authority here.'

'Shouldn't we wait for Gisborne?'

'Gisborne can do what he wants!' Branwood snapped. 'Now, you wished to see Vechey's chamber?'

Corbett nodded and Branwood, dismissing the rest apart from Naylor, led them up a spiral stone staircase to the second floor. The dead sheriff's room was still sealed and locked. Branwood removed the wax, opened the door and waved Corbett in.

The bed chamber was as tawdry as the rest of the castle. A great battered four-poster shrouded in thick serge curtains dominated the room. A long, iron-barred chest stood at the foot of the bed. There was a table, some stools, two other chests, and in a corner a stout oaken lavarium bearing a large pewter bowl. At the other side of the room was a trestle bed with a straw mattress and some woollen blankets.

'Lecroix slept there?' Corbett asked.

Branwood nodded. Corbett kicked aside the dirty rushes and stood in the centre of the room. It was a stark, almost monastic cell. The walls were plastered with lime and the only windows were three arrow slits in the far wall. Branwood lit a cheap oil lamp and handed it to Corbett, who went across to the bed and pulled back the curtains. The bed was dirty and stale, the bolster, sheets and blankets faded and grimed with dirt. Branwood was correct. Sir Eustace's neglect of himself was more than apparent. Corbett scrutinised the sheets, bolsters and blankets but smelt nothing except stale sweat and body odour. He then examined the goblet still containing a little wine but this, too, seemed harmless as did the few sweetmeats on a pewter plate in the middle of the table. The flies had been busy over them. Corbett summoned up his courage, closed his eyes and popped one into his mouth, chewing it carefully until its cloying sweetness became too much. He went over to one of the arrow-slit windows and spat it out, wiping his mouth on the back of his hand.

'Ranulf! Maltote!' he ordered. 'Examine the rushes!'

Whilst they did this Corbett tested the water, now stale and laced with dirt.

'Master,' Ranulf called out, 'there's nothing amongst the rushes.'

Corbett stared bleakly at Branwood.

'You are right, Sir Peter. There's nothing here, so how was Vechey poisoned?'

'I am no physician. Maigret said the potion must have been powerful. Henbane, arsenic or foxglove.'

Corbett picked up the napkin from the lavarium, it bore finger marks and Corbett caught the odour of sugar and sweetmeats. He remembered the sores round Vechey's mouth.

'What happens, Ranulf, if you have scabs and wipe your mouth with a napkin?'

'The napkin often grazes them and the bleeding starts again.'

'Well, that napkin was definitely used by Vechey. There are blood specks on it.' Corbett waved his hands in exasperation. 'There's nothing here,' he murmured. 'God knows how Vechey was murdered.'

'Come,' Sir Peter called, almost jovially. 'Sir Hugh, you must be tired. Let me at least show you around the rest of the castle then perhaps you can rest.'

Corbett was about to refuse but realised such information would be necessary and they all followed Branwood as he led them up the three floors of the keep and on to the battlements. Sir Peter stood by the crenellations with Corbett half-listening as he described the rest of the castle. The clerk relished the cool breezes and enjoyed the beginning of a glorious sunset. Then something in Sir Peter's words caught his attention. Corbett followed the direction of Branwood's outstretched hand and stared north, beyond the crowded houses and streets of Nottingham, where the green sea of forest stretched as far as the eye could see.

'You see the problem, Sir Hugh? How can you hunt a man in such a vastness? Horsemen are useless, foot soldiers are terrified. There could be an army hidden there and you would not realise until you stumbled into a trap.'

'Does the outlaw use horses?'.

Sir Peter smiled maliciously. 'Now that's the outlaw's weakness. A poor horseman, he much preferred to go on foot. Of course, amongst the trees a mounted soldier is useless.'

He then led Corbett and his party down through the three floors of the great keep, along dusty passageways, under arches where the stone was fretted in a dogtooth pattern, and out into the dusty baileys. In the inner bailey the makeshift execution platform was now being washed down. Beside it, the decapitated corpses of the criminals were being shoved into arrow chests, the tops nailed down before burial in one of the town cemeteries. A grey-haired woman keened beside one of these whilst the hard-bitten soldiers took the decapitated heads and fixed them on poles, as if they were pumpkins, to display along the castle walls.

Half-naked children played in the dust, impervious to the horrors around them. Farriers were busy, the fires of the smithies blowing hot and fierce, and the sound of hammer on anvil was deafening. Chickens scrabbled for corn, competing with the lean, dirty pigs. A group of castle women washed clothes in vats of greasy water whilst a small girl, armed with a wand, tried to impose order amongst a flock of geese alarmed by the snarling of one of the mastiffs. In the outer bailey soldiers were training in a half-hearted fashion until Naylor appeared when they set to vigorously against the quintains and stuffed figures fastened on poles.

The castle was a military stronghold circled by walls, the great keep its hub whilst the garrison and their families slept in rooms and outhouses built against the walls. It was well served: Corbett saw the fowl coops, the small rabbit warren, its burrows already covered with nets as the warrener hunted for fresh meat and a large dovecot standing on the outskirts of a small orchard. Although the garrison seemed busy and purposeful, Corbett sensed that the castle was under siege, as if the garrison dare not venture beyond the gates.

'How many soldiers do you have here?'

Branwood stopped and stared up at the red-gold sky.

'A full muster. One knight, five serjeants-at-arms led by Naylor, twenty mounted halberdiers, thirty foot and about the same number of archers.'

Corbett looked up at the castle wall where Sir Peter's pennant, three golden castles on a sarcenet background, snapped defiantly in the evening breeze.

'Do you think it is wise to enter the forest tomorrow?'

'As I have said,' Branwood snapped, 'I have no choice. I have to display defiance to the outlaw. But, come, I will show you the cellars.'

He led them back into the keep, through an iron-studded door and into dark, cavernous cellars, well above a man's height, which stretched under the floor of the keep. The cellars had small alcoves or recesses; two mangy cats hunted in their darkness as Sir Peter led them by hogsheads of wine, iron-hooped barrels of beer, sacks of grain and other supplies.

'You said there were secret entrances?' Corbett asked.

Sir Peter, who had taken a sconce torch from the wall, beckoned them over to an alcove, moved a sack of grain and showed them a trap door.

'As I have explained, the castle is built on a stone crag riddled with passageways and tunnels. This is one entrance but there could be others we do not know about.'

'Don't these make the castle vulnerable?'

'No. If a siege began these trap doors would be sealed.'

He led them back up the steps and ordered Naylor to show them their own chamber, saying he had other pressing duties to attend to.

Corbett ignored the polite snub. Naylor took them to their own room on the second floor of the keep, the same passageway as Sir Eustace's. The chamber was long, low and black-beamed but fairly clean. The hard stone floor was swept and laid with fresh rushes, some still green and supple. The sheets and blankets on the trestle beds were clean. There were chests and coffers, some with their locks unbroken, a table, one box chair, a bench and a number of stools. The walls had been freshly limewashed though rather hastily: the workmen covering the flies that had died there and barely disguising the scrawled picture of a lion drawn by some long gone artist. There were pegs for their clothes and a large black crucifix bearing the twisted, tortured figure of the dead Christ.

Once Naylor was gone, a servant brought up a wooden tray bearing a jug of cold ale and some cups. All three drank thirstily and then began to unpack the saddlebags. Corbett saw Maltote pick up his sword belt to throw on the bed.

'No, Maltote!' he ordered.

The messenger dropped it as if it was hot and Ranulf grinned at him.

'I have told you before,' he whispered. 'Old Master Long Face hates you to touch weapons.'

'I heard that, Ranulf,' Corbett shouted over his shoulder. 'Maltote, you are one of the best horsemen I have ever met but you know my orders. Never, in my presence, touch a sword or dagger. You are more dangerous than a drunken serjeant waving his sword around a packed tavern.' Corbett stared at him suspiciously. 'You are carrying no dagger?'

The round-faced messenger stared owlishly back, his childlike eyes full of apprehension.

'No, Master.'

'Good!' Corbett murmured. 'Then finish unpacking. Go down to the castle buttery. Steal or beg something to eat and drink and then ride to Southwell. I showed you the way as we entered Nottingham. Go to the crossroads and take the Newark road south. You'll find Sir Guy of Gisborne lodged at the sign of The Serpent. Tell him that we have arrived in Nottingham and that tomorrow we enter the forest. However, he is not to move until he has spoken with me. Bring him back with you, not to the castle but ask him to lodge at the tavern at the foot of the crag. What was it called?'

'The Trip to Jerusalem,' Ranulf added. He was sharp-eyed for any ale house they passed, to slake his thirst, draw the unsuspecting into a game of dice or sell his 'miraculous' medicines to those stupid enough to buy them.

'Bring him there,' Corbett ordered.

Maltote nodded, washed his hands and face at the lavarium and scurried out.

'You are too harsh on him, Master.' Ranulf grinned. 'He has great ambitions to become a swordsman.'

'Not whilst I am alive,' Corbett muttered. 'Ranulf, he's lethal. Did you see him at the Lady Maeve's supper before we left Bread Street? He was gutting a piece of meat and nearly took his fingers off.' Corbett turned back to his packing. 'And who is this Master Long Face?'

'No one,' Ranulf guiltily replied. 'Just someone we both know.'

Corbett grinned to himself, laid the last of his clothes in one of the chests and hung his two robes on a peg. He tried not to think of his wife Maeve who had so neatly folded everything, chattering like a magpie as she tried to hide her unease at her husband's departure. A picture of her flashed into Corbett's mind: ivory white skin, those deep blue eyes, that beautiful face framed by long golden hair.

'I should be with her,' he muttered. 'Going with her, baby Eleanor and Uncle Morgan to our manor at Leighton.'

Corbett opened his saddlebags and took out his small writing tray, neatly laying out parchment, ink horn, knife and quill. He looked up. Ranulf was moodily staring through one of the arrow-slit windows.

'Come on!' Corbett urged, sitting down in the chair. 'Let us unravel the mysteries here, eh?'

Ranulf made no move so Corbett shrugged, picked up a quill and dipped it into the blue-green ink.

'Primo,' he announced, 'the King's business in London.'

He unrolled the greasy piece of parchment his servant had brought back from Paris. Corbett smoothed it gently. Bardolph had paid for this with his life and Corbett guiltily remembered visiting the dead man's wife in Grubbe Street near Cripplegate. The King had promised her an allowance but the woman had just screamed, cursing him, until Corbett had retreated from the house.

'What did Bardolph die for?' he declared loudly. 'What does this cipher mean? *"Les trois rois vont au tour des deux fous avec deux chevaliers".*'

'The three kings,' Corbett translated, 'go to the tower of the two fools with the two chevaliers.'

Corbett closed his eyes and tried to picture the crude map of northern France his clerks had drawn up at Westminster. Philip now had his armies massed there, tens of thousands of foot soldiers, squadron after squadron of heavily mailed knights, carts full of provisions. Once the harvest was in his army would cross into Flanders. But where? Did this cipher hold the secret?

'Where will the blow fall?' Corbett murmured to himself. 'Will the French army roll like a wave or will it form into an arrowhead and strike along one road against a certain city?' Edward's Flemish allies had sent importunate pleas for such information. If they only knew Philip's route of march, his battle plan, they would counter it; but their army was small, too thinly spread to provide against all eventualities.

Corbett remembered the King at Westminster, white-faced with rage.

'We are like a cat watching a thousand rat-holes. Where will that bastard in France aim his blow?'

Corbett had replied by urging his myriad of agents in Paris to worm the secret out. Now they had the information but it made no sense.

'What does it mean?' the King had shouted. 'By God's tooth, what does it mean?'

Corbett had quietly explained that the cipher was new, concocted by one of Philip's principal clerks. It would be known only to the King, his inner group of counsellors and his generals on the French border.

'Why can't you break it, Corbett?' the King had begged.

'Because it's like nothing we have ever seen before.'

The King had raged and mimicked him.

'Your Grace,' Corbett quietly insisted, quoting a famous maxim from logic, 'any problem must always contain the seeds of its own solution.'

'Oh, God be thanked!' Edward had snarled and gone on to stare at Corbett with his half-mad, blood-shot eyes. 'And what happens if you unlock the cipher, Clerk? Philip now knows we have it. The bastard might change it!'

Corbett disagreed. 'You know Philip cannot do that. The military preparations are made – any change in plan would cause terrible chaos. He has time on his side and could invade any time during July.'

'In which case,' the King snarled, 'you have only days!'

Corbett closed his eyes. Just before he'd left Westminster his conclusion about Philip was proved correct: the French had taken other precautions about the cipher with deadly consequences for himself. Corbett sighed, opened his eyes and stared down at the cipher. The briefer such messages were, the more difficult to unravel.

'"The three kings go to the tower of the two fools with the two chevaliers." What does it mean, Ranulf?'

His manservant still gazed gloomily through the window.

'Do you miss London?' Corbett asked. 'Or are you still smarting over the Lady Mary Neville?'

Ranulf heard his master but stared bleakly at the sunset, trying to control the rage seething within him. He had loved the Lady Mary Neville with every fibre of his being: her dark, lustrous hair, those lips he had crushed against his own when she had invited him into her bed, wrapping her cool white body round his. Then she had discarded him as she would a piece of needlework. She had fluttered her eyelashes and said she really must return north in the company of Ralph Dacre whom she described as a distant kinsman. Ranulf knew different: Dacre was a court fop with his curled, prinked hair, tight hose, buckled shoes and a blue quilted jerkin which hung just above his elaborate codpiece. So Lady Mary had tripped out of his life, leaving him to seethe with discontent. Ranulf glared over his shoulder at Corbett. Affairs of the heart were his personal business.

'It's not just the Lady Mary!' he snapped.

'You mean the clerkship?'

'Yes, Master. Thanks to you, I am skilled in French, Spanish and the use of protocol, but the King still refuses to elevate me to the position of clerk.'

'He is playing with you,' Corbett replied. 'He wishes to test you.'

Ranulf sneered. 'Thank you, Master, but I suspect the clerkship will slip as easily through my fingers as the Lady Mary Neville did.'

Corbett went across, grasped his manservant's shoulders and swung him round.

'Is this the famous Ranulf-atte-Newgate, the lady's man, the roaring boy! I need you, Ranulf, yet you lean against the wall like some lovelorn maid!'

Ranulf's green, cat-like eyes blazed with anger.

'It's true!' Corbett snarled. He went across to the crucifix and put his hand over the figure of Christ whilst lifting the other to take an oath. 'I, Sir Hugh Corbett, Keeper of the King's Seal, do solemnly swear that if you assist me in these matters, if you break this damnable cipher, you, Ranulf-atte-Newgate, will attend the service in St Stephen's Chapel, Westminster where you will be accepted as a clerk and receive your fee and robes.'

Ranulf knew an opening when he saw one. He grinned.

'So, Master, why are you wasting time? There was no need for the oath.'

'Oh, yes there was!' Corbett retorted. He sat down at the table again. 'But let's leave the cipher for the time being and concentrate on matters in hand.' He picked up a fresh piece of parchment and began writing.

'Item – Robin of Locksley, Robin Greenwood, Robin Hood was, is, an outlaw. He's a skilled bowman, a good war-leader, he has been pardoned once and has returned to the forest to continue his depredations. According to Willoughby, there was a woman present and a huge giant of a man. So this Lady Mary of Lydsford and his erstwhile companion John Little must have rejoined him.'

Ranulf sat down opposite him.

'This Robin,' he interjected, 'has returned with a vengeance. He not only plunders but kills and maims. The attack on the tax-collectors was particularly murderous. He has a hand in the murder of Eustace Vechey and has tried to kill Branwood.'

'But why?' Corbett mused. 'Why the deaths? Why the personal vindictiveness?'

'Perhaps Robin expected higher things after his pardon?'

'Item – the people in the castle,' Corbett continued. 'What do you think of them, Ranulf?'

'Branwood has a hatred for Robin. Naylor is a surly bastard. Friar Thomas . . .' Ranulf shrugged. 'You know these priests. However, it's Roteboeuf who puzzles me. Have you noticed, Master, the two forefingers of his right hand are severely calloused and he wears a leather wrist guard on his left?'

'In other words, a professional bowman?'

'And Lecroix?' Corbett asked.

'A half-wit, dedicated to his master.'

'And Vechey's death?'

'God knows, Master, how he was poisoned. But I agree, there's a traitor in the castle. Branwood might know, perhaps Naylor, Father Thomas, or even our good friend Roteboeuf.'

Corbett stretched for another quill and, as he did so, heard shouting from the parapet walk. At the same time he felt a hiss of air before a steel arrowhead hit the far wall. Corbett just sat astonished, the shouting outside increased and other arrows whirred into the room. Ranulf grabbed his master and hurled him to the floor. Outside in the corridor they heard the sound of running feet. Ranulf looked up towards the window. He heard something thud dully against the wall outside and saw splashes of blood on the window sill. There was a sound of men running along the galleries and Naylor yelling outside the door: 'Sir Hugh Corbett, for God's sake, the castle is under attack!'

Chapter 3

Corbett and Ranulf opened the door and ran into the corridor beyond. Both men hurriedly wrapped their sword belts round them and followed Naylor as he clattered down the stairs. In the inner bailey all was confusion. Soldiers ran up the steps to the parapet walks. Screaming women grabbed protesting children. Dogs barked in the far courtyard near the stables while another thrashed on the ground, an arrow in its back. Branwood came hurrying out, dressed in half-armour, his sword drawn.

'The bastard!' he shouted, white-faced. 'That bastard outlaw has the impudence to attack us here! Sir Hugh, for God's sake, stay inside!'

And before Corbett or Ranulf could protest, he almost pushed them back into the keep. They stood in the hot darkness watching the shadows lengthen as Branwood, Naylor and other officers of the garrison tried to impose order. The baileys were cleared of people, the howling dog put out of its misery. Two soldiers entered, carrying a third between them, an arrow embedded in his shoulder. An hour passed before Branwood re-appeared, his face grimy and soaked with sweat. In his hand he carried a dirty sheet.

'The attack's over,' he muttered and grinned mirthlessly. 'One soldier wounded, a dog killed. The biggest blow was to our pride. And this.' He led them into the hall, placed the sheet on the ground and undid it carefully. Corbett gagged and Ranulf quietly swore. A severed head lay there. The side of its face was severely bruised, the eyes rolled back in the sockets, the hair blood-soaked. It was difficult even to estimate how old the victim was or what he'd looked like in life. Around the severed neck hung loose tendrils of skin and muscle.

'For sweet Christ's sake!' Corbett breathed. 'Sir Peter, I have seen enough. Who is it?'

'Hobwell. He was my squire.' Branwood pushed the blood-soaked bundle away with his foot. He went across to a small table and slopped wine into three goblets whilst bawling for Naylor to come and take the head away.

'Where to?' the serjeant asked.

'For God's sake, man!' Branwood roared. 'Who gives a damn? Bury it!'

Once Naylor left, Branwood served the wine. They sat on a bench at the table on the dais.

'Who was Hobwell?' Corbett asked. 'Your squire, I know, but why this?'

'A week ago,' Branwood began, 'Hobwell pretended to be a wolfshead, fleeing to the forest for safety. He was to join the outlaw band.' The under-sheriff shrugged. 'The rest you can guess at. Hobwell was betrayed and Robin Hood has sent his answer.'

A serjeant ran into the hall. 'Sir Peter,' he shouted breathlessly, 'news from the town. Five or six outlaws, hooded and masked, attacked from a cart. Under bales of straw they had a small trebuchet.'

'A catapult!' Sir Peter whispered.

The soldier shrugged helplessly. 'The cart's still there but the outlaws have fled.'

The soldier left. Sir Peter sat with his face in his hands.

'So,' Corbett exclaimed, 'Hobwell was betrayed, the outlaws decapitated him and pitched his head back into the castle, along with a volley of arrows, two of which nearly struck us.'

Sir Peter lifted his face. 'Welcome to Nottingham and Robin Hood's greetings to the King's Commissioners!' He stared round the hall. 'Look,' he whispered despairingly. 'Look how dark it is becoming.'

Corbett followed his glance and noticed the dying rays of the sun piercing the arrow slits high in the wall.

'I hate this place,' Branwood continued. 'It's accursed and haunted. It never brought luck to anyone. A hundred years ago, the present King's grandfather hanged twenty-eight Welsh boys, hostages because of a rebellion in Wales. They were left to dangle from the walls and people say their ghosts still walk here, bringing ill luck. Guy of Gisborne will confirm that. Sir Eustace suffered because of it and now it's my turn.'

Branwood's sombre words were interrupted by Naylor bursting into the hall.

'For God's sake, come!'

'What is it, man?'

He leaned against the wall, panting for breath.

'In the cellars – Lecroix has hanged himself!'

They followed Naylor down the stairs and into the darkened cellar.

'I came down to broach a beer cask,' Naylor explained, pointing to the candle placed in a recess.

The flickering flame made Lecroix's body appear even more ghastly as it hung from the rafters, twirling in a macabre jig. Corbett and Ranulf stared, horrified by the poor servant's grotesque appearance; eyes popping, tongue caught between his teeth, his neck and head twisted awry and his breeches urine-stained.

'Get Physician Maigret and Friar Thomas!' Branwood ordered.

'Oh, for God's sake!' Ranulf snarled. 'Master, hold the body.'

Corbett closed his eyes and gripped the corpse round the waist whilst Ranulf sawed through the rope with his sword. They laid the cadaver gently on the damp earth floor just as Brother Thomas and Maigret arrived. The physician took one look at the body and turned away, hand over his mouth.

'Dead as a nail!' he exclaimed.

'How long?' Corbett asked.

Maigret knelt, put the back of his hand against the dead man's cheek and neck. 'Oh, about an hour.'

'So he must have died during the attack?' Corbett asked.

'I would think so,' Maigret snapped, wrinkling his nose disdainfully.

Corbett crouched on one side of the corpse, Friar Thomas on the other. The cleric whispered words of contrition in the dead man's ear and sketched a blessing in the air as Corbett carefully examined the corpse. He satisfied himself that the hands and ankles were free from any rope marks then undid the dead man's belt. He lowered his head and sniffed at Lecroix's mouth, trying to ignore the streaks of saliva drying on the dead man's beard. Corbett pinched his nose and looked up at Branwood.

'He was drunk when he killed himself. His breath stinks of stale wine!'

Naylor, who had been busy lighting the sconce torches, trudged deeper down into the cellar.

'There's been a wine cask broached.'

Corbett stared into the darkness. He saw a wooden box lying lop-sided, beside it a pewter cup.

'He was a toper,' Maigret commented.

Corbett nodded and stared up at the piece of rope still wrapped round the rafters and once again at the box and fallen cup.

'Did any of you see him this evening?' he asked.

'I did,' Friar Thomas replied, his fat face now drained of

any trace of humour. 'Just before the attack I met him on the stairs. He was deeply in his cups.'

Corbett once more examined the corpse, paying particular attention to the fingers, noticing how callused those of the left hand were.

'He was left-handed?' he asked.

'Yes, yes,' Branwood murmured. 'Sir Eustace was always cursing Lecroix because he served from the wrong side.'

Corbett got to his feet, wiping his hands on his robe.

'God knows why,' he announced, 'but perhaps the attack tipped the balance of his mind. I suggest Lecroix came down here to hide. He broached the cask of wine and, in his cups, decided to take his own life. He stood on that box, slipped the rope over the beam and the noose round his neck, kicked the box away and his life went out like a candle flame.'

Corbett stared down. Something was wrong but he couldn't place it. He closed his eyes. He had seen enough for one day. He was exhausted after the hot, dusty journey up the ancient Roman highway, Branwood's revelations, Vechey's death, the grisly attacks on the castle, and now this.

'Sir Peter,' Corbett declared, 'you are right, this castle is accursed.'

'Well, tomorrow,' Branwood retorted, 'we will carry the curse back to the forest. I am going to take this outlaw alive and string him up like a rat in the market place. Naylor, remove the body!'

'Where?'

'In the death house next to his master. Friar Thomas, keep a still tongue in your head. No one will miss poor Lecroix, and who cares if he was a suicide? He and his master can be buried together.'

The sheriff led them out of the cellar back into the hall where scullions were laying the high table for the evening meal. Just inside the door of the hall, servants were waiting with bowls of water and napkins. Everyone washed carefully and took their places at the high table. Friar Thomas said the benediction and Sir Peter ordered the evening meal to be served. Both Corbett and Ranulf felt queasy after what they had seen in the cellar as well as their visits to the kitchens earlier in the day but the food proved to be quite delicious: a young piglet, its flesh soft and sweetened, served in a lemon sauce, whilst Sir Peter was generous in filling everyone's wine cup with chilled wine of Alsace. He grinned at his guests.

'I cannot guarantee the food and drink are not poisoned but an armed guard now stands in the kitchen. I have sworn that if anyone else dies, the cook and his scullions will hang.'

'Physician Maigret,' Corbett insisted, 'my apologies for asking you this again, but you do know what poison killed Vechey?'

The physician's eyes snapped up. 'No, but I suggest a concoction ground from a dried noxious plant – henbane or belladonna.'

Corbett sipped from his cup. 'And you cannot guess how it was administered?'

'I have told you once,' the physician retorted, 'we have scrutinised everything Vechey ate or drank at table or in his chamber. Why do you ask now?'

'I was thinking of Lecroix. Could he have been the culprit? Could there have been a private feud between him and his master, and then, overcome by remorse, Lecroix took his own life?'

'I'd thought of that myself,' Maigret trumpeted.

'But why?' Friar Thomas intervened. 'Lecroix was a simple man. He could hardly fill a goblet, never mind buy some deadly potion and then administer it in a way no one can discover.'

Corbett sipped at his wine. Lecroix, he thought, might be the murderer but there was something in that cellar, something he had seen which was out of place, and whilst the conversation turned back to the outlaws' recent attack on the castle, Corbett brooded on what he might have missed.

More courses were served: fish in a tangy sauce, roast beef in an onion stew, small loaves of wheaten bread. Corbett ate quietly, half-listening to Sir Peter's plan for the following morning. His eyes grew heavy. Images of Maeve flickered through his mind then Uncle Morgan bawling out some Welsh song, Edward screaming at him from the throne at Westminster about that damnable cipher, three kings visiting the two fools' tower with the two chevaliers . . . A grinning Ranulf nudged him awake.

'Master!'

Corbett smiled and picked up his wine cup. His stomach felt heavy, one of those rare occasions when he had eaten far too much and drunk too fast. Corbett loosened the belt around his waist to make himself more comfortable – then sprang to his feet.

'Of course!' he whispered to his startled companions. 'Of course!'

'What's the matter, man?' Branwood shouted.

Corbett looked at him. 'Sir Peter, my apologies but I have just realised that Lecroix was murdered.'

'What do you mean?' Branwood snapped.

'Nothing,' Corbett replied sourly. 'Except the way a man puts on his belt. Where is Lecroix's corpse now?'

'Where it was left, under a sheet in the cellar. You know soldiers, Sir Hugh, they are superstitious and refused to remove the corpse of a suicide except in daylight hours.'

'Then we had better go down,' Corbett insisted.

At Branwood's order, soldiers appeared with torches and led them down to the cellar. Corbett crouched in a pool of light and pulled back the sheets covering the corpse.

'Lecroix was left-handed?' he asked.

'Is this necessary?' Roteboeuf asked languidly. 'God's tooth, man! Having to look at Lecroix when he was alive was enough to put you off your dinner!'

Corbett ignored the sniggers. 'The corpse has not been disturbed?'

'Of course not.'

'Well,' Corbett said, 'look at the belt.'

'Oh, for God's sake!' snapped Branwood.

Corbett tapped Lecroix's belt.

'You notice how the tongue at the loose end of the belt lies to the left?'

'So?'

'Lecroix was left-handed. I found that out when we examined the corpse earlier. This belt should be on the other way round, looped through the clasp, with the tongue of the belt hanging to his right.'

'He was so bloody drunk,' Naylor muttered, 'it was a wonder he could put it on at all.'

Corbett shrugged. 'I thought of that, until I remembered something else. See how this belt is fastened?' He undid the belt carefully and held it up. 'Now all the holes on this belt except for one are undamaged, for the simple reason that they were never used. A belt is a very personal article. We fasten it the same way every day – unless, of course, we become fatter.' Corbett moved his finger to a hole further up the belt, well away from the one Lecroix had used. 'See how this hole has been torn, slightly gouged? We can tell, from the specks of creamy leather underneath, that this was very recent.' He put down the belt and got to his feet. 'So I ask you first, why did Lecroix put his belt on the wrong way? Secondly, we have seen the hole he always used – so why is this one, much further up the belt, so recently damaged?'

Everyone stared back, Sir Peter open-mouthed, Naylor blinking as if he could not follow Corbett's reasoning. Friar

Thomas looked expectant whilst Corbett caught a glint of understanding in Roteboeuf's eyes.

'My opinion,' Corbett concluded, 'is that this belt, on one occasion, was taken off Lecroix and used to bind something which strained against the belt, forcing the gouge marks around the second hole. I'll go further. This belt was strapped around Lecroix after he died. Or should I say was murdered?' Corbett knelt once more at the side of the corpse and pushed back the sleeves of the dead man's threadbare gown. 'Let us, for the sake of argument, maintain that Lecroix was murdered. Someone either took him down here or found him in a drunken stupor. Remember, Lecroix was not the most intelligent of God's creatures, God bless him, and even without wine often lapsed into a very deep sleep. With so much wine down him, I doubt very much whether he would remember his own name. So,' Corbett concluded, 'the murderer, once Lecroix was deep in his cups, took off the poor fellow's belt and bound it round him in such a way as to secure his arms.' Corbett took the belt and then carefully looped it round the corpse, threading the belt through the buckle and fastening it so Lecroix's arms were tightly pinned to his body.

Ranulf heard the murmur of agreement and grinned to himself. At last Old Master Long Face had shown them he was no fool for the belt fitted exactly at the point where the hole was recently gouged.

'Do you follow my meaning?' Corbett stared round. In the pool of torchlight they all nodded, their faces tense and watchful.

'See,' he repeated, 'the belt is now linked around the arms. Lecroix, in his drunken stupor, cannot move his hands. Our murderer then takes the drunken Lecroix, forces him to stand on that box, slips his neck through the waiting noose and knocks the box away, leaving him to kick and slowly choke to death. Now when I was here first, I thought of this possibility and so carefully examined the wrists.' Corbett undid the belt and pushed the sleeves of the gown even further back, pointing to the angry welts high on each arm just under the elbow.

'He was murdered!' Branwood declared.

'Oh, yes,' Corbett continued. 'A dreadful death, gentlemen. Lecroix may have taken minutes to die. Once he was dead, the murderer slipped out of the shadows, took off the belt and quickly wrapped it round the corpse's waist. As the assassin was right-handed, the belt was fastened differently from the way Lecroix would have tied it. And who would notice it? Who would discover the hole in the belt or the weals round the arm? Or, if they did, put all these items together?' Corbett got to his feet and shook his head. 'I only realised this when I undid my own belt in the hall.'

'But why?' Roteboeuf leaned forward.

Corbett noticed the clerk's face was pallid and covered in a sheen of sweat.

'Why should anyone murder poor Lecroix?'

'For two reasons,' Ranulf intervened, winking at his master. 'Isn't it obvious, sirs? First, if Lecroix committed suicide it's only natural to draw the conclusion that he did so out of remorse for killing his master. Such a death would also hide the real truth.'

'Which is?' Branwood snapped.

'I know what Ranulf is going to say,' Corbett intervened. 'Lecroix brooded over his master's death. Perhaps he saw or remembered something amiss in that chamber and the murderer realised this. But what was it, eh?' Corbett stared round. 'Did the man say anything to anyone here?'

'He spoke to me,' Roteboeuf called from the shadows where he stood. 'He kept saying his master was a tidy man.'

'What did he mean?'

'I don't know. He just kept mumbling about how tidy his master was.'

'But he was not!' Ranulf almost shouted. 'I mean, this

castle needs cleaning, painting . . .' His voice trailed off at the angry murmurs his words provoked.

'What Ranulf is saying,' Corbett tactfully added, 'is that the wolfshead's depredations unhinged Sir Eustace's mind. What is more important,' he continued briskly, 'is that Lecroix was murdered because he saw something which may have unmasked his master's assassin. And, on that, sirs, I bid you good night.'

Corbett left the cellar, Ranulf following behind him. Not until the door closed behind them, did Corbett allow himself a smile. He undid his belt and threw it on the bed.

'Well, well,' he grinned. 'So we have set the cat amongst the pigeons! Vechey's murder we had to accept but we have won one victory. The assassin now knows we are not so stupid as he thought.' He sat down on the bed and stared at Ranulf. 'I'll tell you this, Ranulf-atte-Newgate, faithful servant and would-be clerk: if we discover the murderer of Lecroix or Vechey, we will trap Robin Hood.'

Corbett went to the chest at the bottom of the bed. He took out a small iron-bound coffer no more than a foot long and secured by three locks which he undid with one of the keys which swung from his belt.

'Master?'

'Yes, Ranulf.'

'I accept what you say but look at it another way – we are here alone in a castle surrounded by murderers. What's the use of knowledge if it leads to our own deaths?'

Corbett rummaged in the small coffer, took out a roll of parchment and tossed it to Ranulf.

'True, true,' he murmured. 'But isn't that always the case, Ranulf? Now let me add to your woes. Robin Hood may not be the only person seeking our deaths.'

'You mean the murderer in the castle as well?'

'No, there could be someone else.'

The colour drained from Ranulf's face and he slumped down on the bed.

'Oh, sweet Mary, help us!' He looked down at the parchment Corbett had thrown at him. 'Is it something to do with this business?'

'No, worse.' Corbett drew in his breath. 'Before we left Westminster, after our audience with the King, do you remember he followed us down to the courtyard and took me aside?'

'Yes,' Ranulf replied. 'You and the King went into the small rose garden. You were there some time. I wondered what was wrong. His Grace not only ignored me but left his bosom friend the Earl of Surrey kicking his heels.'

'It was over the cipher,' Corbett blurted out, shame-faced. 'And I should have told you before.'

'What? Does the King know the truth about the tower of the fools and the three kings taking their two chevaliers?' Ranulf jibed.

'No, the cipher is a mystery to him as it is to me.' Corbett licked his lips. 'The French King and his two murderous advisers, our old friends Sir Amaury de Craon, may God damn him, and Nogaret, realise we have the cipher. They know that we know that time is on their side. Soon Philip's armies will cross into Flanders. We know,' Corbett continued caustically, 'that the French will do anything to stop us solving their cipher. Now you are a gambling man, Ranulf. To put it bluntly, the French have decided to protect their wager. They have an assassin, a skilled killer, a murderer whom we know only by the name given to one of Satan's devils – Achitophel.' Corbett now stared directly at his servant. 'Well, Amaury de Craon and others of his ilk believe their cipher will be entrusted to me. One of our spies in the Louvre Palace sent our noble Edward the rather chilling news that Achitophel has been sent to England to kill me. And, if necessary, those who work with me.'

Ranulf's jaw dropped. He stared in stupefaction at his master. He wasn't frightened of danger. Ranulf had been born fighting and raised in the fetid alleys and runnels of Southwark. But if anything happened to Sir Hugh Corbett, who would care for Ranulf? Who would bother if he never became a clerk or received further preferment in royal service?

'Who could it be?' he stuttered.

'Anyone. A strolling player, some priest, a beggar on a corner. Even worse, Achitophel always remains in the shadows. We know he is responsible for the deaths of at least a dozen of our agents in France and the Low Countries. Sometimes he – though it could as well be a woman – strikes himself; at other times he hires someone else to carry out the task. Achitophel may be in this castle now or he may have spent good silver to buy the services of someone here. They will have one task and one task only: to kill me.'

Ranulf leaned back on the bed and groaned.

'Achitophel,' he murmured, 'an assassin in the castle, outlaws in the forest, the King screaming about a cipher no one understands!' Ranulf raised his voice. 'The three kings go to the two fools' tower with the two chevaliers.' He closed his eyes. 'Hell's teeth, Master!'

'But let's leave that,' Corbett replied briskly, getting to his feet. He took out his writing implements, smoothed out a piece of parchment on the table and pulled the candle closer. 'Improve your reading, Ranulf. Tell me again what the clerk at Westminster wrote about Robin Hood.'

Ranulf sat up and unrolled the parchment Corbett had given him, studying it carefully with lips silently moving. Ranulf was proud of his ability to read and never lost an opportunity to demonstrate his skill to his master.

'Sir Peter Branwood has already told us most of it,' Ranulf began. 'The outlaw was born Robin of Locksley. At the age of sixteen or seventeen he fought with Simon de Montfort against the King.'

'Stop!'

Corbett raised his face from the parchment and stared at the sliver of night sky through the arrow slit window. He felt uncomfortable. At Westminster the King had glossed over this. Was there something Edward hadn't told him? Simon de Montfort, Earl of Leicester, had forty years ago led a most serious rebellion against the King. De Montfort, who had owned lands around Nottingham, had only been defeated after a bloody battle at Evesham. Was Robin Hood nurturing old grievances?

'How old does that make Robin now?' Corbett abruptly asked.

Ranulf screwed up his eyes in concentration. 'Evesham took place in 1265 so the outlaw must be in his mid-fifties, about fifty-five or fifty-six.'

'Mm!' Corbett mused. 'Old, but there again, the King and his generals are much older and quite capable of leading the most taxing campaigns in the wild glens of Scotland.'

Ranulf shook his head. 'What I can't understand, Master, is that according to what this clerk has written, Robin Hood was an outlaw who preyed only upon the rich. He was well known for his generosity, especially to the poor who openly supported and protected him. True, he did fight pitched battles in the forest but never once did he engage in wanton killing or secret assassinations such as the murder of the tax-collectors and poor Vechey. So why now?'

'Perhaps his mind has turned?'

Ranulf wearily threw the parchment back on the bed.

'Master, I am tired. This day has been long enough.'

He began to undress and Corbett, feeling his eyelids grow heavy, did likewise. He blew out the candles and lay for a while staring into the darkness. Images pressed in on him. The cipher, Maeve's face as she said farewell, the old King shouting in his fury, Lecroix swinging by his neck from that beam and Vechey's corpse lying cold and forgotten in the death house. Outside a dog howled at the summer moon and bats flitted against the castle walls. From a nearby stand of trees an owl hooted mournfully. Corbett shivered, rolled over and fell asleep wondering what tomorrow would bring.

Just outside the castle, Achitophel the assassin sat drinking in The Trip to Jerusalem. The murderer steeped in the blood of Philip's opponents carefully sipped his wine and stared round the crowded tavern full of soldiers and servants from the castle. Achitophel kept in the shadows. He stared through the open window at the dark mass of the castle and carefully plotted Corbett's death.

Chapter 4

The next morning Corbett and Ranulf breakfasted on ale and a loaf of bread fresh from the castle bakery then went down into the courtyard. The sky was overcast with thick black clouds massing, threatening rain. Branwood joined them, dressed in a chain-mail jacket with its coif pulled over his head. He cradled a visored helmet in his arms.

'I hope it doesn't rain,' he moaned. 'If it does we will have to turn back.'

'Is this wise?' Corbett asked.

'Again, yes. We have no choice.'

A soldier came running down the keep steps carrying a small banner displaying Branwood's coat of arms.

'Even if the townspeople see that we can enter the forest and return, it will be a victory.'

Branwood turned and shouted orders. The courtyard became a milling hive of activity as grooms edged horses out, men mounted and serjeants-at-arms ensured all equipment was ready. Wives holding children came to bid farewell. Corbett reckoned that their force was about thirty mounted men and the same number of archers. At last, Sir Peter shouted the order to move.

Naylor blew a shrill blast on a horn, the gates swung open and they left the castle, taking the winding route down under the gatehouse, through Brewhouse Yard into

Castle Street then up Friary Lane which led to the market place. Sir Peter rode in front, Corbett and Ranulf behind whilst Naylor went up and down the column to maintain good order. As they passed the townspeople some looked surly but most shouted good wishes and Corbett gathered that Branwood was, despite his office, fairly popular in the town.

They entered the market place, past the houses and stalls of the Guild of Poulterers now preparing for a day's busy trade: feathers floated in a soft breeze and women and children plucked carcasses. These were handed over to the apprentices to be slit and gutted before being washed in huge vats of scalding water and hung over the stalls for sale; beggars and dogs fought for the giblets tossed into dirty puddles.

Two children screamed with delight as they tried to ride a pig. A dog bit one of the children and was immediately chased, howling and yelling, into Branwood's column of archers where it received further punishment before escaping up an alleyway. A group of wild men, garbed in rags, their faces painted brown and green, performed a strange dance around the skull of a goat impaled on a rod. They ignored Branwood's order to clear the way and only retreated when Naylor advanced on them with drawn sword. The column crossed the cobbled market place into the streets leading down to St Peter's Gate where the crowds became more dense and the air stank with the odour of stale sweat as citizens moved from stall to stall, bartering noisily with the tinkers, apprentices and journeymen.

For a while the column had to pull aside as a herd of cattle, lowing with fright, were driven up towards the slaughter houses. These were followed by a cleric who had been caught with a whore and was being led through the streets for public humiliation. Both the man and his paramour had been stripped just short of decency, tied back to back, and were now being paraded through the city by two grinning beadles. The soldiers joined in the laughter then turned to watch as a madman jumped on a haberdasher's stall. The fellow wore a pair of dirty, makeshift boots and a ragged gown and carried a large ash pole. His eyes, wild as an animal's, scrutinised the soldiers as he loudly declared that he was the Angel Gabriel sent by God to warn them of impending judgement. The soldiers did not believe him and the 'angel's' important message was drowned in cat-calls and jeers. Naylor, an iron helmet on his head, the broad nose-guard almost obscuring his face, screamed for silence and, going ahead with drawn sword, began to force a way through the crowd.

At last they reached the city gates and the column debouched on to the white, dusty track which wound between the broad fields beyond the city wall. Ahead of them lay the fringe of Sherwood Forest, its dark greenness almost touching the lowering black clouds. Corbett glanced across at Ranulf and noticed how hollow-eyed his servant looked, his face pale with anxiety.

'You slept well, Ranulf?'

The manservant turned and spat.

'A little trouble. I hate forests,' he muttered. 'The darkness, the noises. Give me Southwark's alleyways any day.'

Corbett tried to reassure him but even as they entered the forest, began to share Ranulf's feelings. Sir Peter stopped in a small glade, sending forward scouts on either side of the trackway to search out any possible ambush. Then the whole column was ordered forward, swallowed up by the green darkness. They became acutely aware of the eerie silence. The sky disappeared. Corbett became conscious of every sound from the horses and men on the track and the darkness from the surrounding trees. The sweat broke out on the nape of his neck and he began to scrutinise the forest on either side, his imagination further agitated by the lack of bird song, the sound of bracken snapping and strange scuffling noises from the undergrowth. Corbett urged his horse forward.

'How deeply do we ride, Sir Peter?'

'Perhaps an hour, two hours. Then we'll swing round and march back. We are not hunting anyone.' The sheriff spoke as he too stared into the darkness on either side. 'We must show we are not just visitors from the castle.' He shrugged. 'Who knows? Perhaps we may be fortunate and flush something out of the undergrowth.'

The march continued, the scouts coming back occasionally to grip Branwood's horse and give him messages. Now and again they crossed a welcome glade where the darkness became less oppressive and Corbett recalled the stories people whispered: about the dark wood men, the small people, the eerie nightmare tales about goblins and elves. He was aware that he was in a world totally alien to his own. The King's writ or law had nothing to do with the forest. Corbett started, his stomach curdling with fear as a great stag, his horns high, burst out of the trees before him. The animal glanced arrogantly at the horsemen before quietly slipping away deeper into the forest.

Sir Peter held up his hand, the column stopped and he turned round.

'You see what I mean, Sir Hugh?'

He was about to continue when, from the dark depths of the forest, came the lilting, mournful blast of a hunting horn. The soldiers muttered, horses skittering with fright, and drew swords, the hiss of steel sounding unnaturally loud. Archers unslung their bows. The sound of the horn died away, only to be taken up again, this time closer, more powerful and from the other side of the forest. Arrows whirred round them. Sir Peter drew his sword. Corbett did likewise. Ranulf was almost wild with panic. Naylor shouted orders and the archers returned fire whilst the mounted men tried to protect themselves behind their long, oval shields. Ranulf dismounted and peered amongst the threshing horses.

'Nothing!' he yelled. 'I can't see any of the bastards!'

His shout was echoed by a whirring sound, like the wings of a swooping bird. A soldier stupid enough to lower his shield took a long, feathered arrow full in the chest and the still crisp air became filled with whirring winged death. A horseman fell, eyelids fluttering as the arrow pierced his throat just above his gorget. Corbett turned his horse round.

'Sir Peter!' he yelled. 'Quickly!'

He glimpsed shadows flitting through the trees. Corbett braved the whirring arrows, stood high in the stirrups and pointed. Branwood, his head encased in a great helm, followed Corbett's gaze.

'We'll be surrounded!' Branwood yelled.

He took off his helmet and ordered Naylor to blow three horn blasts, the signal for retreat. The column needed no second bidding. Ranulf remounted and followed Corbett back along the forest track, arrows whirring around him, one even bouncing off the high horn of Ranulf's saddle. Corbett's warning had been prophetic for the outlaws were drawing closer, trying to cut the column off completely. The sheriff's archers were also running or clutching the stirrups of the horsemen. The confusion was indescribable. One horse, maddened with fear, rose up on its hind legs, high in the air, throwing its rider into a clump of bushes. The fellow clambered to his feet to stand, rooted to the spot by panic, until an arrow caught him full in the mouth.

At last the column, in total disarray, managed to distance itself from the ambush. Sir Peter ordered a general halt except for Naylor who galloped back along the track to urge on the few stragglers.

'We cannot stop, Sir Peter!' Corbett gasped.

'We'll retreat in order,' the under-sheriff replied, nursing a small cut on the back of his hand.

Naylor returned. The horsemen threw a screen round the archers and Sir Peter led his bloodied, disorganised troop out of the thinning forest. They did not pause until they were clear of the trees and able to rest in a daisy-filled meadow. A quick count was made whilst soldiers staunched wounds and checked their equipment. Sir Peter sat morosely on the ground, holding the reins of his horse. Eventually he glared sourly at Corbett and Ranulf, still seated on their mounts.

'Master Clerk, you are not going to say I told you so?'

'How many men did we lose?' Corbett snapped.

'All in all,' Naylor replied, 'it could have been worse. One habelor, two archers and three horsemen are missing.'

Sir Peter cursed. 'Tell the men to lead their horses. We'll skirt the town and re-enter the castle by a postern gate.'

Corbett and Ranulf walked with the rest as Sir Peter's soldiers trudged back along the lanes, the horses blown and covered with foam. The men were in no better state. One was grievously wounded, the rest suffering from cuts and slight scratches. The injured soldier, an arrow embedded just below his knee, was forced to sit in the saddle, white-faced and swaying. He would have fallen off if his companion had not removed the arrowhead with his knife, cleansed the wound with some coarse wine and tightly bound the bleeding gash with strips of cloth.

Corbett was thankful to be unscathed. Ranulf seemed relieved just to be out of the forest.

'You look dreadful,' he whispered to Corbett and stared at his master's tousled hair and face scratched by over-hanging branches.

'We could all have died!' Corbett exclaimed. 'That was stupid. What is more, it was no chance meeting. Those outlaws were waiting for us.' He raised his voice. 'Sir Peter!'

The sheriff joined him.

'That ambush,' Corbett said, 'who could have told them?'

Branwood shook his head. 'I don't know, Sir Hugh. But if I do find out, I'll tell you just before I hang the bastard!'

Despite Branwood's route, his return to the castle was observed and his disgrace noted. News of their defeat had somehow gone before and townspeople gathered on either side of the cobbled trackway leading up to the postern gate. Corbett bore it philosophically but he felt for the under-sheriff who couldn't fail to hear the sniggers and muffled laughter. Sir Peter's humiliation was complete. He rode more like a man being taken out to death than the King's representative.

Once back in the castle, Physician Maigret and Friar Thomas came down. The former attended the wounded whilst the friar took personal care of Sir Peter, leading him gently away, murmuring softly as if consoling a beaten schoolboy. Corbett threw his reins at an ostler and stood for a while with Ranulf watching the soldiers unsaddle their horses and stack their weapons. Once the news of their return and their losses had spread, the keening and mourning began. Corbett turned away in disgust.

'Come on, Ranulf. This is a royal castle in the King's shire of Nottingham, not some outpost on the Scottish march.'

They went back to their chamber where they washed and cleaned their own wounds.

'Discretion is the wisest course of action,' Corbett muttered, lying down on the bed. 'I do not think Sir Peter will wish to to see us today.'

Ranulf sat on a stool and chewed his lip.

'Master, who could the traitor be?'

'Anyone,' Corbett replied. 'Anyone in this castle who knew we were leaving. Sir Peter had to display his authority, but was it really worth it?'

'But how is the outlaw to be caught?' Ranulf asked. He moved over to the window but stood warily to one side for he had not forgotten the previous day's attack.

'Our sweet Robin,' Corbett sardonically commented, 'will not be caught by floundering about in the forest. I have no intention of returning there to blunder about waiting for an arrow to take me in the throat. The wolfshead must be enticed out, but what can we use as bait?'

'There is another way,' Ranulf replied. 'If you found his spy here . . .'

Corbett sat up. 'Strange you should say that. Did you notice Naylor went with us into the forest, Maigret and Friar Thomas were waiting for our return, but have you caught sight of Master Roteboeuf?'

'Do you think he could be the traitor?'

'Yes, he might be. He showed little grief over Sir Eustace's death and, as you remarked, is capable of bearing arms. So why didn't he come with us or at least wait for our return?' Corbett chewed the quick of his thumb nail, then grinned at his tousled-headed, white-faced manservant. 'Don't worry, Ranulf, we are hardly likely to go back into the forest but you are right. If we catch the traitor we remove Robin Hood's most powerful supporter and, more importantly, we'll probably hang the murderer of both Sir Eustace and poor Lecroix.' Corbett swung his legs off the bed. 'Let's stay busy, Ranulf.'

'And do what?'

'Well, we can't question Lecroix. He has gone to meet his maker. So let's pretend to be two mummers in a play and re-trace Vechey's steps the night he died. At the same time, we'll send for Roteboeuf.'

Corbett filled his wine cup and went down to the hall. Except for one servant whom Corbett sent to summon Roteboeuf, the place was deserted as the garrison huddled in groups outside in the bailey to hear about the disaster in the forest, tended their injured or, like Sir Peter, sulked morosely in private, licking their wounds.

Corbett went up to the table on the dais. 'Now according to what we know, Vechey left the hall, followed by Lecroix and Maigret.' He walked to the door. 'Our dead sheriff carried a cup of wine which had been tasted for him at table as was everything he put in his mouth. He went up to his chamber. None of the others in the household are affected except Sir Peter, who returned for his wine cup. It tasted rather strange so he threw it away.' Corbett then walked upstairs, Ranulf trailing behind him. They stopped outside Vechey's chamber. 'What happened next?'

'According to our good physician, Vechey made him re-taste the wine. The sheriff then went into the chamber,' Ranulf continued, 'Lecroix with him. The door was locked from the inside and two soldiers stood on guard.'

'Which means,' Corbett replied, 'that Maigret, Friar Thomas, Peter Branwood, Roteboeuf, or indeed anyone else in the castle could have slipped back into the hall and poisoned Branwood's wine.'

'Right.' Corbett pushed the door open and went into the death chamber. It was still squalid and dark: the dirty rushes scuffed into piles, the bed drapes half-pulled, the blankets and sheets all disarranged. The cup holding the stale dregs of wine still stood untouched, as did the scum-covered water in the lavarium bowl and the plate of sweetmeats with the flies hovering over them. Ranulf went and sat on Lecroix's trestle bed whilst Corbett pretended to repeat exactly what Vechey must have done though he was careful not to sip the wine, touch the water or taste any of the decaying sweetmeats. He then pretended to wash and dry his face and hands, careful not to touch the blood-spattered napkin, and went to lie down on top of the stale-smelling blankets.

'Have I missed anything?' he called.

Ranulf shook his head.

'Then in God's name . . .'

Corbett's words were cut off as the door was pushed open and an anxious-faced Roteboeuf came into the chamber.

'Sir Eustace's death is still a mystery, Sir Hugh?'

'Everything's a mystery,' Corbett snapped, getting up. 'Why did Robin go back to the forest? Why does he kill? How were Sir Eustace and Lecroix murdered? And, above all, who was the traitor who would have had us all killed in the forest?' Corbett glared at him. 'Which is why I sent for you.'

Roteboeuf stepped back.

'Why didn't you go with us?' Ranulf challenged. He pointed to the wrist-guard peeping out from underneath one of Roteboeuf's sleeves. 'You are an accomplished archer.'

'I am a clerk.'

'So am I!' Corbett snapped.

Roteboeuf scratched his head and sat on the stool, pulling his hose so tight Ranulf thought they would split.

'Why didn't you come?' Corbett repeated.

'Oh, what's the use?' Roteboeuf sighed. 'In a word, Sir Hugh, I am a coward. No, that's not right. I hate the forest and have no desire to die there.'

'You are Nottingham born?' Corbett asked, ignoring Roteboeuf's excuses.

'Yes, I was born within the walls.'

'So you know the stories and legends of Robin Hood?'

'Everyone does.' Roteboeuf got to his feet and stared anxiously round. Corbett sensed that beneath his cheery exterior, he was suspicious and worried.

'What's the matter?' Ranulf jibed. 'No one likes to die, particularly with an arrow in the throat in some God-forsaken forest. Anyway, what are you frightened of now?'

Roteboeuf forced a smile. 'Nothing! I just feel sorry for

Sir Peter. We all accept there's a traitor in the castle and no man is free from suspicion.' He walked over to Corbett. 'But if you really want to know about Robin Hood,' he whispered, 'why ask me? Go down to the house of the friars which lies at the foot of the castle rock. Ask Father Prior if you can speak to Will Scarlett who serves as a lay brother there.'

'Scarlett? Robin's lieutenant in the old days?'

'The same. You see, Robin was a very young man when he first fled to the forest, Scarlett much older. When the outlaws accepted the King's pardon, Scarlett went home but his wife died of the pestilence. He saw that as God's judgement so now he does reparation behind the friary walls.'

'Why didn't Sir Peter Branwood tell us about this?'

Roteboeuf stared anxiously about. 'What does it matter, Sir Hugh? Scarlett has now accepted the King's peace. If Vechey or Branwood had found out otherwise, they would drag Scarlett from the friary and hang him on the castle walls just for the sake of it. I am telling you because, as the King's Commissioner, you might reassure him.' Roteboeuf stared at them, shrugged and slipped out of the room.

Corbett gazed at the half-open door.

'There goes a very worried man,' he commented. 'Right, Ranulf, let's leave this accursed castle and make hay whilst the sun shines. Let us visit this man Scarlett.'

'What about Achitophel?' Ranulf warned. 'If he is hunting you, surely he'll now be in the town waiting to seize his opportunity?'

Corbett smiled. 'De Craon has been hunting my head for years. So far, thank God, he has never taken it.'

They left the castle by a postern door and followed the winding path down around the crag, past the dark mouths of caves burrowed into the rock. Corbett stopped outside The Trip to Jerusalem.

'No sign of Maltote yet,' he remarked, watching the busy

yard full of horses as travellers, tinkers, pedlars and merchants crowded in to spend the profits of a morning's trade.

They walked down a small side street, the gables of the houses jutting out above them. Children waded knee-deep in the sewer, throwing pieces of offal at the dogs or fending off the pigs with sharp little sticks. They turned a corner, went down a small lane and stopped before the main gate of the friary.

A grumbling lay brother answered the jangling bell and ushered them along paved corridors to Father Prior's room. The latter was hardly welcoming: a tall, severe man, Prior Joachim regarded both Corbett and Ranulf with the utmost suspicion. Only when Corbett produced letters and warrants from the King did the Prior relax and offer refreshment which Corbett courteously refused.

'So.' Prior Joachim steepled his spindly fingers and leaned across his desk. 'You wish to see Brother William?'

Corbett stretched out his legs. 'Father Prior, what is the matter? I am the King's Commissioner. Brother William has nothing to fear from me.'

The Prior rustled some parchment sheets on his desk.

'Brother William has now accepted the King's peace,' Corbett insisted. 'He has nothing to fear.'

'He thinks differently.' The Prior's head snapped back. 'Over the last few months, ever since the outlaw returned to Sherwood, Brother William has refused to meet visitors or accept any gifts. You see, Sir Hugh, Brother William is one of the most famous members of our community. His exploits with Robin Hood are legendary.'

'But now he sees no one?'

'Exactly.'

'Why?'

'I don't know.' The Prior bit his lip. 'We live in turbulent, dangerous times. Perhaps Brother William should answer that himself.'

He led them deeper into the friary, across the cloister garth, past the entrance to the small church and into the gardens. A burly gardener crouched over the herb banks, glowered then turned his back on them as the Prior led his visitors to a stone cell which stood by itself on the borders of a small orchard. He tapped on the door. 'Who is it?' called a reedy voice.

The Prior explained. Corbett heard shuffling steps, a key being turned in the lock and the door was flung open by a tall man dressed in a dark robe. He had a long, scraggy neck and a small, weather-beaten face, but his eyes were surprisingly bright and watchful. Prior Joachim murmured introductions. He said he would wait outside whilst Brother William ushered Corbett and Ranulf into a small, white-washed chamber, stark and severe. The room was dominated by a large crucifix and had only a few sticks of furniture. Corbett noticed how the friar locked the door behind them before gesturing at the bench whilst he sat on a wafer-thin pallet bed.

'I have nothing to offer you.' Brother William's sun-burned fingers flickered an apology.

'We have not come to eat and drink.'

The friar smiled, touched his white hair and winked at Ranulf.

'Do you know this was once as red as yours, hence my name.' His smile died as his eyes became watchful. 'You are here to ask questions?'

'Yes, Brother, and the first is why you are here?'

'To atone for my sins, to pray to God and Christ's mother, to seek reparation for the follies of my youth.'

'What follies, Brother?'

The friar half-grinned and his glance fell away.

'Oh, running as wild as the King's stags,' he murmured wistfully. 'A roaring boy in the forest, taking what I wanted and not caring about tomorrow. Now God has struck me down. My wife is dead and I see the Lord's hand against me. When I die,' he continued as if speaking to himself, 'I'll not be buried here but next to her under the old yew tree in the village graveyard.'

'But why do you hide now?'

'To put it bluntly, Sir Hugh, I am frightened. I lived with Robin, I ran with him, I fought the King's soldiers by his side, I wenched and drank. But now . . .' his voice trailed away.

Corbett sat and watched as Will Scarlett stroked his smooth-shaven chin and stared down at the floor.

'At first,' he began slowly, 'we all fought for Simon de Montfort, the Earl of Leicester, who wanted to make the lords of the soil account for what they did. After his defeat at Evesham, I and the rest, Robin, John Little, Friar Tuck fresh from ordination, Allan-a-Dale and the others, remained free in the forest. I was the oldest, just past my thirtieth summer, yet the blood beat hot in my veins. We fought the tax-collectors and the fat abbots for Robin's soul was stuffed full of de Montfort's ideas: how Adam and Eve were born naked before God, equal in everything.' The friar shrugged his thin shoulders. 'So we robbed the rich and gave to the poor.' He looked up and smiled. 'Well, not everything. We kept some for ourselves but the rest we gave away. It not only made us feel good but safe. We bribed the foresters and verderers and so kept everyone's mouth shut.' He chewed his lip. 'Robin met Lady Mary – Marion as she was popularly called – and one year passed into another. Then the old king died and Edward came north like some golden-haired Alexander, distributing gold and pardons as if they were apples from the tree. Robin accepted. He joined the King's chamber and fought his wars.' The friar's eyes became fierce. 'I accepted the pardon but would not be bought. I stayed in Nottingham whilst the rest drifted away and, when my wife died, I came here.'

'So why are you frightened?'

Brother William got to his feet and went to stand overlooking the window. 'Have you ever been haunted, Corbett? Do you know what it feels like when ghosts gather at your back? Vindictive ghosts spat from hell? Well, that's what's happening now.' He turned round. 'Oh, yes, Robin's back in the forest. Little John appears to have joined him. Perhaps even Lady Mary has left Kirklees Priory.'

'Why did she go there?' Ranulf interrupted before Corbett could stop him.

'God knows,' the old friar replied. 'There was a serious quarrel between her and Robin. She saw his acceptance of the King's pardon as a betrayal of many of us. Perhaps she was right. Now I hide behind these friary walls because I am frightened of a Robin who kills at a whim former members of his coven.'

'Is that true?' Corbett asked.

'Oh, yes. News trickles in here occasionally. Much the Miller's boy found drowned in a river. Hick the Haywain strangled in a field. And who knows?' he added softly. 'Perhaps it's old Will Scarlett's turn next?'

'In which case,' Corbett retorted, 'tell us how we can kill him?'

The old friar turned, eyes brimming with tears. 'I can't do that,' he whispered, 'because I don't know this Robin.'

Chapter 5

A short while later, Corbett and Ranulf left the friary and went down into Nottingham market place. Corbett walked slightly ahead, mystified by what he had learnt. Why had Robin returned, and why the change in his behaviour? He passed Pethick Lane which was usually the haunt of prostitutes, but because of the pestilence in the city the street was barred with heavy beams and iron chains slung across.

A funeral procession of three plague victims was making its way down to St Mary's church. The elmwood coffins bobbed on the shoulders of sweating pall-bearers. The chantry priest walking in front of them, a lighted taper in his hand, could hardly be heard muttering the funeral prayers for the antics of a wild man. He was dressed completely in black from head to toe with a crude skeleton painted on his garb, and danced in front of the procession, furiously ringing a bell.

Corbett entered the market place where people bought and sold, impervious to the death around them. The noise was deafening. Piles of rubbish, heaped up between the stalls or choking the broad gulleys which ran through the cobbled market place, reeked under the hot summer sun. The stench was so offensive anyone who went by had to cover their mouth and nose. Apprentices shouted, 'Lincoln cloth!' Another bawled, 'Good eggs!' A small group circled two fish wives who rolled on the ground, tearing at each other's hair and clothes like any city brawlers. The fight stopped immediately when a cart entered the market place driven by two beadles. At its back was tied a baker, his breeches pulled down about his ankles whilst a sweaty bailiff birched the prisoner's large bottom. A notice, scrawled in red and forcibly carried by the baker's apprentices, proclaimed he had sold rat's meat in his pies. Other punishments were being carried out. Two scolds were next, their faces fastened in iron bridles as they were led down to the river to sit on stools and be ducked in the filthy water.

Corbett and Ranulf stood and watched as the bartering sounds died down and the crowd turned, thronging round the stocks to watch two felons scream unremittingly as their ears were barbarously cropped. Next to them, a tanner who had poured horse piss in his rival's ale was made to sit bare-arsed in the stocks.

'Why are we watching all this?' Ranulf whispered.

'When punishments are carried out,' Corbett murmured, 'the low life always crawl from the gutter.'

Corbett's prophecy was proved correct: the flotsam and jetsam of Nottingham life appeared. The pickpockets or foists, the hookers, the night hawks, the cut-throats and the whores in their strange wigs and heavily painted faces. They stood round relishing the punishments whilst keeping a sharp eye for any unsuspecting victim. A group of retainers from a merchant prince's household, drunken and slobbery-mouthed in their stained livery, forced their way through, singing a raucous song. A pardoner screeched that he had one of the stones used to kill St Stephen whilst a hunch-backed harpist drew scraps of parchment from his jerkin and shouted that he had songs for sale.

'So the villains gather,' Ranulf observed.

'Study them carefully,' Corbett insisted, 'for those

who seem sharp-eyed or wear wrist-guards.'

'You think outlaws from Sherwood would dare venture here?'

'It's possible. Remember the attack on the castle.'

Ranulf, who prided himself on spying out a villain in a crowded street, studied the mob carefully but saw nothing fitting Corbett's description. The punishments over, the crowd broke up, going back to the stalls. Suddenly, behind Corbett and Ranulf, a voice rang out.

'I challenge you, sirs. I, Rahere of Lincoln, Riddle Master and Keeper of Mysteries north and south of the Trent, from whom no puzzle is proof. I challenge you!'

Corbett and Ranulf turned round and stared at a young man wearing a long tawny robe lined with rat's fur over a blood-red shirt and Lincoln green hose. He stood on a barrel shouting out his challenge across the market place. He was sandy-haired and fresh-faced with cheeky eyes, pointed nose, and a voice which carried like a preacher's. He twirled a silver coin between his fingers as he repeated his challenge and Ranulf grinned. He had seen his type before – gentlemen of the road who could answer any riddle and pose another which would leave even the greatest scholar scratching his head for all eternity.

Ranulf stared at the young woman who stood next to the barrel, dressed in a brown smock with white lambswool fringing the neck and cuffs. Her face was hidden in a hood but suddenly she pulled this back and Ranulf's heart missed a beat. All mourning for the Lady Mary Neville abruptly ceased for this woman was breathtakingly beautiful. An oval ivory-skinned face, perfectly formed nose above full red lips, auburn hair under a white linen veil – and those eyes, ice blue with a touch of fire. Ranulf stared at the way the close-fitting smock pulled sharply across thrusting breasts. Her narrow, hand-span waist was circled by a silver cord and red leather boots peeped out from beneath the hem of her dress. She moved her hair from her face, the movement delicate and beautiful as a butterfly.

'You, sir!'

Ranulf tore his eyes away and looked up at the Riddle Master.

'Tell me any riddle and, within twenty beats of your heart, I will give you the answer or this coin is yours.'

'What happens if there are two answers?' Ranulf jested back, quickly nudging Corbett.

'As long as my answer's correct, the coin stays here.'

'What has two legs, then has three and eventually none?' Ranulf shouted, conscious of the crowd pressing round him.

'Why, a man!' the Riddle Master retorted quickly. 'For we are all born with two legs, then in old age we have three with a walking staff, and then in bed, as we die, none whatsoever.'

Ranulf grinned and nodded.

'Give me another!'

'A vessel there is that is round like a pear,

Moist in the middle, coloured and fair.

And often it happens that salt is found there,' Ranulf chanted.

'Very good!' the Riddle Master shouted. 'It's the eye of a man!'

Ranulf agreed then Rahere's face became serious.

'I'll buy you a flagon of ale, sir.' He glanced suspiciously at Corbett. 'But not for your sober-sided companion. Rahere the Riddle Master of Lincoln refuses to drink with a man who never smiles!'

Corbett shuffled in embarrassment and tugged at Ranulf's sleeve.

'Come on!' he whispered as others began to shout riddles. 'Let's go back to the castle.'

They fought their way through the crowd.

'Hey, Master Redhead!'

Ranulf turned.

'Don't forget,' the Riddle Master shouted, 'my sister Amisia and I owe you a flagon of ale. You'll meet us in the taproom of The Cock and Hoop?'

Ranulf was about to shake his head but the young woman was smiling at him. He reluctantly turned away to follow his master through the crowd back into Friary Lane. They were almost at the foot of the crag, the great castle of Nottingham looming above them, when Corbett stopped.

'You'd best go back.'

'What do you mean, Master?'

'To The Cock and Hoop.' Corbett grinned. 'Ranulf, Ranulf,' he whispered, 'you can never resist three things: a goblet of wine, a game of dice and a beautiful face.'

Ranulf needed no second bidding and ran back down the lane. Corbett watched him go.

'It will do you good,' he shouted but Ranulf was out of earshot, already stopping passersby to ask them directions to The Cock and Hoop.

At last he found it opposite St Peter's graveyard. He burst into the musty taproom, bawling at the landlord for service whilst slipping him a penny to hire a table near the tavern's only window. Ranulf ordered a flagon of ale, sat and sipped its cool tanginess as he tried to control the flutter of excitement in his belly. He felt tired, slightly heavy-eyed, still agitated after the ambush in the forest.

'I hate bloody trees!' he muttered to himself.

He leaned back against the wall and watched a skinner, who sat cross-legged just inside the tavern door, neatly sewing together pieces of mole-skin. Ranulf closed his eyes. He could stand in a dark alleyway in Southwark and not turn a hair but that forest, with its green gloom and haunting sounds, would always unnerve him. He thought idly about the deaths in the castle and then that mysterious refrain contained in the cipher: Three kings go to the two fools' tower with the two chevaliers. 'If I could only unlock the secret,' Ranulf muttered under his breath. He thought of the Riddle Master, opened his eyes and grinned at the thought which suddenly occurred to him.

'So you have come for your flagon of ale?'

Ranulf looked up as Rahere sat down on the stool opposite, his sister just as quietly next to him.

'You move like shadows,' Ranulf remarked, extending his hand.

'Sometimes we have to. Your name, stranger?'

'Ranulf-atte-Newgate, servant in the retinue of Sir Hugh Corbett.'

'Never heard of him.'

Beside Rahere Amisia suddenly giggled, her eyes dancing in gentle mockery. Ranulf could barely look at her, she was so beautiful. Rahere snapped his fingers.

'Two flagons of ale, your best, and a glass of white wine – not from your slops and it has to be cool.'

The servile landlord wiped his sweaty face with his hand, bobbing up and down as if Rahere was some great lord.

'He knows you well?' Ranulf remarked.

'He should do. We hire his best chambers and he charges us well.'

'You make such a profit from your riddle-making?'

Rahere spread his hands and Ranulf suddenly noticed how one eye was green, the other brown with a slight cast in it, giving the Riddle Master a rather saturnine look.

'Every man likes a mystery, a puzzle, a riddle.'

The landlord hurried back with the ale and wine.

'Tell me,' Rahere tapped Ranulf's knee, 'where did you learn that riddle about the eye?'

'My mother told me it.'

Rahere leaned back and sipped from the tankard. 'You have never heard of it, have you, Amisia?'

'No, brother.'

The young woman's voice was soft and melodious, and as she sipped daintily from the cup Ranulf gazed hungrily at her. Everything about her was delicate and fine. She reminded him of a beautiful ivory statue he had glimpsed in the King's chamber. And those eyes . . . Never had Ranulf seen such fire in such icy blueness. He looked away and shook himself.

'Do you have any more such riddles?' Rahere asked. 'I tell you, Ranulf, we always buy a tankard of ale for the man who poses a riddle we have never heard and it's three years since I have done that. I'll take yours north,' he continued. 'We hope to spend Michaelmas at the court of My Lord Anthony de Bec, Bishop of Durham.'

'There is one riddle,' Ranulf hesitantly began. 'A secret saying.'

Rahere cradled the tankard in his hands and leaned forward, his strange eyes glistening with excitement.

'Tell me.'

'It's a saying which masks a secret.' Ranulf closed his eyes. 'The three kings go to the two fools' tower with the two chevaliers.'

Rahere pulled a face. 'Hell's teeth! Is that all?'

Ranulf shrugged. 'That's all I know.'

'Who contrived it?'

'I don't know,' Ranulf lied. 'But if you could resolve the mystery, or even point to what it means . . .' He opened his purse and put two silver coins on the table. 'Then these would be yours.'

The Riddle Master extended his hands. 'There, Ranulf, you have my bond.'

Ranulf shook it warmly, pocketed the coins and shouted at the taverner to bring more drink. He felt smug and satisfied, trying hard to hide his excitement. The Riddle Master might help. If he did, Ranulf would profit, and if he didn't, Ranulf would still profit: he was being given an open excuse to slip away from Old Master Long Face and pay court to the beautiful Amisia.

The following morning Corbett rose early. He stared suspiciously at the sleeping Ranulf. His manservant had returned the previous evening, slightly drunk, weaving his way down the corridors of the castle singing the filthiest songs Corbett had ever heard, and he had only with the greatest difficulty extricated Ranulf from a game of dice with some of the surly castle soldiers who were growing increasingly suspicious about his run of luck at every throw. The manservant now sprawled half-dressed, snoring off at least a gallon of ale. Corbett finished dressing, tiptoed out of the room and went down to the hall to break his fast.

Branwood, Naylor, Roteboeuf, Friar Thomas and Physician Maigret were already there. The under-sheriff was morosely chewing snatches of bread and sipping from a tankard. Corbett's salutation was greeted with mumbles and dark looks; the household was obviously still smarting over the previous day's ambush in the forest. Corbett sat on a bench next to Maigret and cut chunks of bread from a newly baked loaf. He felt refreshed and reflected on the recent attack.

'Strange,' he murmured aloud before he could stop himself.

'What is?' Naylor snapped, his pig-like eyes red-rimmed with tiredness.

'Yesterday in the forest those outlaws could have killed us all yet we escaped. It's almost as if . . .'

'They were sending a warning?' Roteboeuf finished the sentence.

'Yes.' Corbett bit off a piece of bread. There's something elusive there, he thought, like staring into murky water and glimpsing something precious lying on the bottom.

'Sir Peter,' he asked, 'do you wish the King to confirm you as sheriff?'

Sir Peter shrugged. 'That's the King's prerogative. He appointed me under-sheriff.' He smiled sourly. 'Perhaps he will insist I step into poor Vechey's shoes?'

Corbett nodded diplomatically and was about to reply when Maigret coughed and cleared his throat.

'I have been thinking over what you asked me, Sir Hugh, about Sir Eustace's death.' The physician's quick eyes darted around as if challenging the others to object. 'The poison,' he continued, 'may have been deadly nightshade or some potion distilled from mushrooms, those poisonous ones which grow under the oak and elm. They are most noxious, especially when picked under a hunter's moon.'

'Would they kill immediately?'

'If the potion was strong enough, yes.'

'Sir Peter! Sir Peter!'

All conversation died as a young soldier, a mere boy no more than sixteen summers old, his hair tousled, eyes staring in terror, burst into the hall.

'What's the matter, man?'

'I've seen them! Two of the men who went missing in the forest yesterday.' The soldier's voice faltered. 'They've been executed!'

Sir Peter sprang from the table, the others followed. Branwood ordered Roteboeuf and Maigret to stay in the castle.

'Sir Hugh! Father Thomas! Naylor!'

They hurried into the bailey where retainers were already saddling horses. The sheriff, shouting curses at the soldier, told him to take a nag from anyone and lead them back to what he had seen.

The sun had not yet risen but the grey-blue sky was lightening with streaks of red as they galloped out of the castle gates, down the winding path and into the still-sleeping town. Branwood rode like a man possessed and

Corbett found it hard to keep up with him. He noticed with wry amusement that Father Thomas was a better horseman than Naylor who kept slipping in the saddle.

I wonder when Maltote will return? Corbett suddenly thought as they thundered past The Trip to Jerusalem into Friary Lane. Any further speculation ended as he tried to keep his horse away from the sewer and a watchful eye on the overhanging tavern signs and the gilded boards of the furriers, cloth-makers and goldsmiths. Thankfully few people were around and those who were flattened themselves against the walls as Sir Peter and his party thundered by. Shop doors abruptly slammed shut as apprentices, preparing the stalls for a day's business, saw or heard the horsemen and fled for safety. Two dung collectors, their carts half-full of stinking ordure, blocked the route until Sir Peter beat them aside with the flat of his sword.

The city gates were hastily opened and Branwood led them across dew-drenched fields, following the same track as they had yesterday which aimed like an arrow towards the dark sombre line of trees. Corbett's stomach lurched in fear. Surely, he thought, not back there?

'Sir Peter!' he shouted. 'What is this nonsense?'

Branwood failed to hear but spurred his horse faster. Corbett hung on grimly, then suddenly Sir Peter reined in, pulling his horse up savagely, shouting at them to stop.

'Well, where, man?' he bawled at the soldier, who looked as if the recent ride had jarred every bone in his body. The young man blinked and stared at the forest. He turned his horse to the side and galloped along the fringe of trees, Branwood and the rest behind. Abruptly the guide stopped and pointed a dirty, stubby finger.

'I saw them,' he gasped. 'I saw them as I came in after visiting my mother in the village.'

Corbett stared hard. At first he could see nothing then Sir Peter leaned over and clutched his wrist.

'Look, Sir Hugh!' he whispered hoarsely. 'Look at that tree, the huge elm!'

Corbett followed his gaze. The blur of white he had glimpsed before now became clear. Two corpses, their dirty white skin gleaming like the underbelly of landed pike, swung by their necks from one of the high branches of the tree. Friar Thomas pushed his horse further forward, Branwood and Corbett followed, whilst the young soldier leaned over his horse's neck to vomit and retch. The bodies were grotesque in death. They were naked except for loin cloths, their faces a mottled hue; half-bitten tongues protruded from swollen mouths, their staring eyes were glazed and empty.

'Two of the soldiers,' Sir Peter murmured, 'who went missing yesterday.'

The horses smelt the corpses and began to whinny and fret. Corbett turned away in disgust whilst Sir Peter began to roar out orders to Naylor to cut the men down and get a cart from the castle to bring the cadavers in.

'Let's return,' the sheriff moodily announced.

'I cannot,' Friar Thomas spoke up. 'I must visit my church. Sir Hugh, you will stay with me?'

Corbett readily agreed; Sir Peter at the best of times, was a graceless companion, but now he looked like a man awaiting condemnation. Friar Thomas murmured a prayer, sketching a blessing in the direction of the corpses, then led Corbett back to his small parish church. This stood about two miles from Nottingham on the road going west to Newark. Around the church were grouped the stone and wooden houses and tiny garden strips of the villeins and peasants.

'Most of them are free,' Friar Thomas proudly announced. 'Or nearly so. They grow their own crops and only spend two boon days working on the manor lord's domain.'

Corbett nodded. The Franciscan seemed well liked. As

they rode into the village he was greeted by a host of thin-ribbed, near-naked children who jumped round like imps from hell, chattering and calling, pointing at Corbett and asking Friar Thomas a stream of questions in high reedy voices. Their parents, faces earth-stained or burnt brown by the sun, also welcomed their priest as they came back from the fields to hear mass and break their fast before returning. Friar Thomas greeted them genially and, by the time they reached the church, a small procession had formed behind him. Outside the cemetery, the friar and Corbett dismounted, two peasant lads taking their horses whilst Thomas led Corbett into the musty darkness of the church. It was a simple building with no pillars or glass windows. The floor was beaten earth, the altar a simple stone slab. Corbett crouched with the rest before a crude wooden altar rail whilst Friar Thomas donned his vestments in an adjoining chamber and came out to celebrate the fastest mass Corbett had ever heard. Friar Thomas did not gabble the words but he spoke swiftly. He moved through the epistle and gospel on to the offertory and consecration before dismissing his parishioners with a swift benediction.

'A quick mass, Father,' Corbett remarked, watching him disrobe in the small vestry.

Friar Thomas grinned. 'It's the belief which counts,' he replied. 'Not the elaborate ritual.' The friar nodded towards the church door. 'My parishioners have fields to tend, crops to harvest, cattle to water, children to feed. If they don't work, they starve. And what then, Master Clerk?'

'Assistance from Robin Hood?'

The friar's fat face creased into a wreath of smiles. 'Well said, Clerk,' he murmured.

'You approve of the outlaw?' Corbett asked.

Father Thomas neatly folded the vestments, placed them in a wooden coffer and padlocked the lid.

'I did not say that,' he replied, straightening up. 'But my people are poor. A girl marries at twelve. By the time she is sixteen she will have had four babies, three of whom will die. She and her husband will wrap the little bodies up in a piece of cheap cloth for me to bury out in the graveyard. I'll say a prayer, wipe the tears from their eyes and quietly curse their misfortune.

'These villagers are the salt of the earth. They rise before dawn, they go to sleep when it's dark, they plough their fields in the depths of winter, leaving their babies under a bush to suck on a wet rag, hoping they will keep warm in the piece of cow hide in which they are wrapped. They make a little profit, and then the tax-collectors come. They fill their barns and the royal purveyors snatch it. The lords of the soil prey on them: if there is a war, their houses burn and they are cut down like grass.'

Father Thomas stuck his podgy thumbs into the dirty white girdle round his waist. 'If the King wants soldiers,' he continued, 'their young go swinging down some country lane, leaving the air full of their chatter and song.' The priest's dark eyes swept up to meet Corbett's and the clerk saw tears brimming there. 'Then the news comes,' he continued, 'of some great victory or some great defeat, and with it a list of the dead. The women come here. They crouch on the dirty floor – the wives, the mothers, the sisters – whilst I,' the friar added bitterly, 'hide like a dog in my vestry and listen to their sobs.' He sighed. 'A year later the wounded return, one without a leg, another maimed. For what?'

'Did you bring us here to tell me this, Father?'

'Yes, I did, King's Commissioner. When you return to Westminster, tell the King what you have seen. Robin Hood is in the hearts of all these people.'

'I know that,' Corbett replied. 'Like you, Father, I come from the soil, and like you I found an escape.' He stepped closer. 'But there's something else, isn't there? You minister here and not at the castle. Your heart's with these peasants. Robin Hood the outlaw, the famous wolfshead, must have made an approach to you.'

Father Thomas turned his back as if busying himself, putting away the cruets in a small iron-bound coffer.

'I asked you a question, Father?'

Father Thomas turned, a defiant look in his eyes. 'If Robin Hood walked into this church,' he retorted, 'I would not send for the sheriff but . . .' his voice trailed off.

'But what, Father?'

'Well.' The friar leaned against the wall and clasped podgy hands round his generous stomach. 'Yes, I brought you here so you can take messages back to the King. But there's something wrong.' He busily washed his fingers in a small bowl of water and wiped them carefully with a napkin. 'In former years when Robin Hood ran wild with his coven, the villagers were never attacked and the outlaw shared his goods.'

'And this time?'

'Oh, the peasants are safe and the outlaw distributes good silver, but it's to buy their silence.' The friar walked to the door. 'We should go.'

Corbett stood still. 'Father, I asked a question and you did not answer.'

Father Thomas turned. 'I know you did, Sir Hugh. Yes,' he continued wearily, 'I have seen the wolfshead. He came here, late one evening, sauntering up the nave like some cock in a barnyard. I was kneeling at the altar rail. When I turned he was there, dressed in Lincoln green, a hood pulled across his head, a black cloth mask hiding his face.'

'What did he want?'

'He asked for my help. If I would give him information about what I saw in the town and the village. Who was moving where? What monies were being transported? Would I tend to the spiritual comfort of his men?'

'And what was your reply?'

'I told him I'd dance with the devil first under a midsummer moon.'

'Yet you said you understood him?'

'No, Sir Hugh, I understand the poverty of my people.' The priest wriggled his fat shoulders. 'This was before the murders in the castle or the killing of the tax-collectors. But I don't know . . . I just did not like the man. His arrogance, his coldness, the way he stood leaning on his long bow. I felt a malevolence, an evil.'

'And what was his reply?'

'He just walked away, slipping out into the night, laughing over his shoulder.'

'Did you tell the sheriff?'

'Sir Eustace or Sir Peter? Never!'

Corbett dipped his fingers in the stoup of holy water just inside the vestry door. He blessed himself. 'I thank you, Father. You'll return to the castle?'

'In a while,' replied the friar. 'You go ahead.'

Corbett walked back into the church, stopping to light a taper before the rough hewn wooden statue of the Virgin Mary. He closed his eyes, praying for Maeve and baby Eleanor, unaware of the figure in the shadows at the back of the church, glaring malevolently towards him.

Chapter 6

Corbett, lost in his own thoughts, let his horse amble back to Nottingham. He was tired, a stranger unused to hunting the evil which hid in the blackness of the forest. He was also distracted by thoughts of pressing business in London where the King would be seething, expecting an immediate solution to the cipher's secret.

Corbett grasped the reins of his horse and half-closed his eyes, listening to the sound of the bees buzzing in the grassy verge on either side of the track, the angry chatter of birds offset by the haunting, bitter-sweet song of the thrush. Concentrate! he thought. Sir Eustace Vechey's death is the key to the matter. He recalled the words of Physician Maigret about the deadly potions used.

'I wonder!' he exclaimed aloud, opening his eyes and watching the white butterflies float on the morning breeze like miniature angels, their wings reflecting the light. Corbett, now intent on the conclusion he had reached, kicked his horse into a gallop and rode into Nottingham.

When he arrived back in the castle bailey, the corpses of the dead soldiers were being laid out on trestle tables to be washed for burial. Beside them women crouched and mourned over their dead. Meanwhile Naylor, assisted by cursing, sweating men-at-arms, brought out two pinewood coffins containing the remains of Sir Eustace and his servant Lecroix. Corbett stared round the bailey. There was no sign of Branwood and he wondered where Ranulf could be. He caught sight of Maigret sitting on a bench at the base of the castle keep, his long face turned to catch the morning sun, a wine cup in his hand, a plate of bread soaked in milk resting in his lap.

'You seem little perturbed,' Corbett remarked, sauntering over.

Maigret opened his eyes and glanced at the corpses being washed and loaded into the coffins.

'In the midst of life we are in death, Sir Hugh. Moreover, what can a physician do about the dead? Will you be on the battlements tonight?' he suddenly asked.

'Why?' Corbett asked, sitting down beside him.

'Well, today's the thirteenth. For the last few months on this date at midnight, the witching hour, three fire arrows are shot over the castle.'

'What?' Corbett exclaimed.

'I thought Branwood would have told you? On the thirteenth of each month, at midnight, three fire arrows light up the night sky.' Maigret shrugged. 'No one knows who does it or why.'

'How long has this been happening?'

'Oh, for six months at least.' Maigret's eyes hardened. He stared at the dark, closed face of the clerk, noting the beads of perspiration on his forehead. 'What do you really want, Corbett? You are a man of few words and yet you sought me out.'

Corbett smiled. I must be careful, he thought. Maigret had first struck him as a typical physician, self-absorbed and overweening, but the man possessed a subtle wit and a sharp intelligence. A possible murderer? he wondered.

'Before you ask, Sir Hugh,' Maigret murmured, 'I have nothing to do with this business. I am a widower who practises physic here in the castle and in the town. I go to church on Sundays and give three pounds of wax a month to my parish church so I will have a chancery priest sing ten thousand masses for my soul when I am dead. I know the properties of medicine but hold no poison. You are free to search my chambers or my house.'

'Sir,' Corbett replied, 'I thank you for your honesty and so I will be equally blunt back. If I was an assassin, where would I buy poison in Nottingham?'

Maigret looked surprised, then his eyes narrowed. 'You are a sharp one, Corbett. Too sharp for your own comfort. I hadn't thought of that. Of course.' The physician leaned forward, putting what was left of the milk sops down for the dogs to eat. 'The answer is simple. If I wanted to procure a noxious substance or some young girl needed to rid herself of a child still in the womb, then I'd go along to that old bitch Hecate. She owns a shop in a three-storied tenement in Mandrick Alley at the back of St Peter's church near Bridesmith Gate. You'll easily see it,' he continued. 'It stands opposite a tavern called The Pig in Glory where, if you have the right amount of silver, you can buy whatever you want.'

Corbett got to his feet.

'I suppose you are going there now?'

'Of course. And if you see my servant Ranulf . . .'

'I doubt it. He left the castle at least an hour ago, his hair prinked and curled, freshly shaven, as smart as Prince Frog going a-wooing.'

Corbett grinned. He would have words with young Ranulf, though that would have to wait. He ordered a surly ostler to saddle his horse again, snatched a quick ladle of water from one of the butts outside the kitchen and rode back into town. In the market place he hired a young urchin, scraggy-haired and dirty-faced, to take him to The Pig in Glory. The young rogue grinned from ear to ear in a black-toothed smile. Corbett, who had offered him a coin to lead him, had to double the fee to stop the urchin telling all and sundry that the sombre-faced clerk he was guiding was off to The Pig in Glory 'to get his whistle blown'. A phrase Corbett half-believed he understood, but decided not to query.

The area behind St Peter's was as dark and noisome as any web of alleyways in Southwark. Large timbered houses which had seen better days crowded in on each other, blocking out the light, turning the rubbish-filled streets into a warren of alleyways packed with every type of rogue under the sun. A few studied Corbett closely but were warned off by his sword and dagger whilst the young urchin proved to be as much a protector as a guide. They entered Mandrick Alley. Above them the higher stories of the houses nestled cheek by jowl. A few tinkers and journeymen sold bric-à-brac, pigeon flesh or the skins of rabbit from shabby stalls. The Pig in Glory stood in the centre of the street, a tawdry blue and gold sign swinging from the broad ale beam jutting out from its eaves. The door of the tavern was thronged with hucksters. A few whores in their shabby gowns and colourful wigs stood laughing with two soldiers from the castle garrison.

Corbett paid the boy his fee, promised him more if he guarded his horse and hammered on the door of the witch's house. He looked up; the windows of the upper stories were all shuttered whilst a small casement above the door was covered in grime and speckled with the corpses of long-dead flies. Corbett pounded again on the door, cursing softly because the knocking was beginning to attract the attention of customers from The Pig in Glory.

'Are you looking for Hecate?' a gap-toothed woman shrieked, her tawdry wig held in one hand whilst she scratched her bald pate.

Corbett turned, throwing back his cloak to show his sword and dagger.

'Yes, I am.'

He flicked a coin at her which she caught in her grimy paw.

Some of the other customers jostled her.

'You won't find her there!' another voice shouted.

Corbett leaned against the door as the crowd began to edge across towards him. Even the boy holding his horse looked frightened. Corbett quickly drew his sword and wished Ranulf was with him.

'I am Sir Hugh Corbett,' he called, 'King's Commissioner!' He glimpsed the soldiers skulking behind the rest. 'And you, sirs, belong to the castle garrison. Come forward!'

The rest of the crowd drew back. The two soldiers sheepishly shouldered their way through and stared dully at Corbett.

'Am I,' the clerk demanded, 'who I claim to be?'

The soldiers nodded.

'Then, sirs, you are under my orders. Take a bench from that tavern and force that door off its hinges. Are you deaf?'

Corbett took a step forward. The two soldiers scampered back into the tavern and returned carrying a rough bench. A greasy-haired landlord came out to protest. Corbett told him to shut up and diverted the rest of the crowd by throwing a handful of coins on to the dirty cobbles. All resentment vanished like mist under the sun. Corbett stood back. The soldiers began ramming the bench against the door until it creaked, buckled and snapped back on its leather hinges.

'Stay outside!' he ordered.

He went down a dank, dimly lit passageway. The first entrance on the right led into the shop and Corbett gagged and swore at what he saw and smelt. The shop was tidy enough, nothing more than a chamber with shelves bearing jars of various sizes, small pouches and wooden boxes clasped and locked. But Hecate was also a skinner, a person skilled at removing the entrails of animals then stuffing them with herbs, turning them into mummified likenesses. A red-coated, glassy-eyed fox stared up at him from the floor. A rabbit, ears back, crouched in frozen stillness. The putrid smell came from the corpse of a small squirrel which lay on the table, its entrails spilling out from its slit stomach. Above these a mass of black flies buzzed.

Corbett left the shop and walked further along the passageway. He opened a small door to a chamber and gasped at the sheer luxury inside. It was like a young noblewoman's parlour. The walls were white-washed and covered in thick woollen cloths of various hues whilst polished gridirons stood under a small carved hearth. There were woollen carpets on the floor, silver candlesticks on the dark polished table, and a half-open cupboard revealed other precious cups and plate. The windows at the back were all glazed with tinted and coloured glass and the room smelt as sweet as a meadow on a summer's day. Two thin-stemmed wine cups stood on the table. Corbett stared around and went into the small buttery in the kitchen at the back of the house. The smell of corruption was stronger here. He pinched his nostrils. Not even his wife Maeve kept her scullery and kitchens so clean and neat yet the stench was terrible.

'In God's name!' he breathed.

He opened a small cupboard door and cursed as the corpse of a grey-haired woman fell out, arms flailing, as if, even in death, she wanted to beat him. Corbett stepped back and stared at the woman's corpse sprawled on the floor, her iron-grey hair spread out around her. Corbett could see no sign of blood or violence. He crouched and turned the body over, pushing the corner of his cloak into his mouth for the woman's face, hatchet-featured in life, was grey and swollen in death, eyes popping, tongue protruding. She had fought for her last breath against the bow string tied tight round her throat. Corbett got to his feet and strode back into Mandrick Alley, gulping the air which now smelt sweet compared to that he had just left.

'Is anything wrong?' one of the soldiers muttered, glimpsing the clerk's white face.

'Yes,' he breathed. 'Hecate's dead.'

The soldier nodded at the tavern where, from the sounds of merriment, they were now spending Corbett's coins.

'They said she'd gone away. She owned a small cottage near Southwell.'

'Well, she's gone!' Corbett snapped. 'And she won't be back! You guard the house.' He nodded to the soldier's companion. 'You go to the castle and tell Sir Peter Branwood: Hecate was a witch and now she's dead so her property belongs to the King.'

Corbett watched the soldier go, paid the urchin, collected his horse and rode back down the alleyways seeking directions to The Cock and Hoop tavern.

He found Ranulf in the small garden, sitting in a flower-covered bower paying court to the beautiful young woman Corbett had glimpsed in the market place. Ranulf rose and sheepishly made introductions. Corbett kissed the woman's cool fingers and studied her closely.

She is lovely, he thought. One look at Ranulf told him that his manservant was smitten. All he could do was stand and stare so adoringly at the girl. Corbett didn't know whether to laugh or cry. If I had a gold coin for every time you were in love, Ranulf, he thought, I'd be the richest man in the kingdom.

'Sir Hugh?'

Corbett smiled at the woman.

'Mistress Amisia, I am sorry, my mind's elsewhere. I am afraid Master Ranulf and I have business to attend to.'

'Yes, yes,' she said. 'A chancery clerk is always busy.'

Ranulf gazed warningly at Corbett.

'Of course,' he answered silkily, 'Master Ranulf is one of the King's most trusted clerks. He will no doubt receive further preferment, if he works hard.'

Ranulf grinned. 'In which case, Master,' he whispered, 'I will finish this wine.'

'As long as you do it in the next mouthful,' Corbett muttered out of the side of his mouth, 'I don't mind. Mistress Amisia, where is your brother Rahere?'

'Spinning his stories in the market place, Sir Hugh. He is most skilled,' she continued proudly. 'Master Ranulf has promised that he will use his good offices with the King to win my brother an invitation to the court at Christmas.'

Corbett stifled a grin. 'Mistress, it's matters such as that which call Ranulf and myself away.'

And, bowing to the young woman, he grasped Ranulf by the sleeve and marched him from the tavern out into the street.

'There was no need for that, Master!'

'Yes, there was,' Corbett retorted. 'Ranulf, I need you.'

He was about to yell that Rahere and Amisia were not just people to while away the time with but one look at Old Master Long Face's sombre expression persuaded him that prudence was the better part of valour. Corbett told him about the corpses of the soldiers, his meeting with Friar Thomas, the fire arrows and the discovery of Hecate's body. Ranulf whistled through his teeth.

'So the good friar has a foot in either camp but has his doubts, whilst the death of Hecate proves that Vechey's killer purchased potions from her. What else, Master?'

'I don't know,' Corbett muttered. 'What perplexes me is the change in Robin Hood's behaviour. He is now more of a killer, an outlaw with only a modicum of care for the common man. And there's this business of the three arrows fired at midnight on the thirteenth of every month.'

'So where are we going now?' Ranulf asked.

'Before I joined you in the tavern I asked the landlord for the name of the most prosperous inn on the roads outside Nottingham. He mentioned The Blue Boar on the Newark road. We passed it on our journey north.'

'What has that to do with Robin Hood?'

'You have met Elias Lamprey?'

'You mean that snotty-nosed clerk in charge of the records in the Court of King's Bench?'

'Well, I am sure he wouldn't agree with your description, Ranulf. However, law and order, the work of Royal Commissioners, Justices of the Peace and the whole question of outlaws are meat and drink to dear Elias.' Corbett grinned. 'I have often nodded off to sleep whilst listening to his stories in some Cheapside tavern. However, one thing Elias always holds as an article of faith is the unholy alliance between outlaws and taverns, the latter being a source of gossip as well as a way of squandering ill-gotten monies.'

They paused at the corner of the street as town pig-killers seized on a sow wandering in defiance of town regulations, pulled it over on its back and cut its throat. Their horses whinnied, startled by the smell of blood. Ranulf yelled at the men to bugger off but the pig-killers replied with obscene gestures and dragged the animal's carcass to a waiting cart. Ranulf spat and looked at Corbett.

'You were saying, Master?'

'Well, two things attract me about The Blue Boar. First, it's the place Willoughby stopped at just after he left Nottingham. Secondly, The Blue Boar seems to prosper during these days of hardship. I think it's worth a visit.'

They made their way out of Nottingham, skirting the city walls till they found the way south to Newark. Ranulf felt more relaxed for the road was packed. Farmers drove their carts; two hedge-priests pushed a wheelbarrow containing all their worldly goods; a group of pilgrims were journeying to Canterbury and a number of peasant families wandering in search of work. After a quarter of an hour's ride, Corbett and Ranulf entered the walled courtyard of The Blue Boar. The place was busy enough, not only with travellers but labourers from the surrounding fields quenching their thirst with stoups of ale. These men sat in the great cobbled yard, backs to the outhouses, sunning themselves whilst their bare-footed children, clothed in rags, played King of the Castle on a great heap of manure. Near the tavern door, peasant women in fustian smocks, their hair piled high on their heads under grimy white rags, stood round a relic-seller, a small squat man with the face of a mastiff and a voice which boomed like a church bell. He had his relics slung on a string round his neck and proudly pointed out the decaying fingers, toes, bits of bone, tissue and clothing of saints Corbett had never even heard of.

Inside the cavernous taproom a more genteel class of customer, the wandering scholars, pilgrims and occasional merchants, broke their fast on small white loaves covered in a fish gravy and pewter jugs of beer. The landlord took one look at Corbett and came bustling up – tall, gross, bald-headed, his face wreathed in a mock smile, eyes a mixture of arrogance and guile. The sort of man, Ranulf thought, who could sniff a profit from across a crowded room. Whilst Corbett ordered the food, Ranulf carefully scrutinised the great taproom, noting the clean rushes on the floor, the walls painted thickly with lime, huge barrels of beer, ale and malmsey in one corner and polished shelves bearing mugs and cups of the finest pewter.

'You keep a fine house, Master . . . ?'

'Robert Fletcher, your honour.' The landlord bowed to Ranulf as if he was the Emperor or the Great Cham. 'But such a room is not for the likes of your excellencies.'

He led them across the taproom, down a small corridor and ushered them into a small parlour, a well-furnished chamber with tables and stools as well as a bed with clean linen sheets and bolsters.

'My special guests are always taken here,' the landlord explained.

Aye, Ranulf thought, noting the bed. Any young gentleman and his doxy.

'And what is your pleasure?'

'Two cups of watered wine,' Corbett replied. 'Perhaps some bread and cheese.'

'Your wish is my command. My own daughter will serve you.'

Bowing and scraping, the landlord backed out. Corbett and Ranulf sat down, grinning at each other. A few minutes later a slim, blonde-haired girl with the face and eyes of a spoilt angel brought in the wine and bread. Ranulf hastened to help her, whispering one compliment after another. The girl's blue eyes rounded in an affectation of innocence though this was betrayed by a lewd smile and the saucy pertness of her manner.

'We have heard of you,' she announced, stepping back and wiping her hands on a very rounded bodice. 'Friar Thomas says you ask a lot of questions.'

'And you are too saucy.'

An old man hobbled into the room. His lined face seemed to crumple round a huge nose; his eyes were small and rheumy and a blood-crusted patch covered the spot where his right ear should have been. He tapped the girl playfully on the rump.

'Come on, Isolda.' He nodded at the guests. 'Don't play the greenwood wanton with these gentlemen.'

'Shut up, Grandfather!' The girl's mouth pulled into a bitter line. 'Shame on you. I am not even allowed to go into Nottingham by myself, never mind the forest.'

She glanced quickly at Corbett but the clerk pretended to be more interested in his drink. Yet the old man had blundered, made a mistake, the first Corbett had detected since arriving in Nottingham. The old man hobbled out as quickly as he could whilst the girl fled back into the taproom.

'That was a mistake,' Ranulf breathed. 'Perhaps you should arrest her, Master?'

Corbett shook his head. 'I suspect, Ranulf, most of the cottagers and tavern-keepers around Sherwood know something about the outlaw. As Elias puts it, no outlaw worth his salt can move or travel without the connivance of innkeepers and, in this case perhaps, their daughters. But when we go fishing it's the trout we catch. We leave the minnows alone.'

Ranulf was about to object when suddenly there were shouts and sounds of commotion from the courtyard. Corbett heard the customers in the adjoining taproom fall quiet then begin an excited babble. He and Ranulf went out, forcing their way through the throng to see a group of mounted men-at-arms wearing the blue and silver livery of the sheriff. The day had grown hot so they had removed their heavy helmets. Corbett recognised Naylor as he bellowed for a cup of water and a stoup of ale, anything to wash the dust from his throat. The real focus of interest, however, was two men, their clothes tattered and weather-stained, faces and hair covered in thick grey dust. They crouched gasping on the ground, whimpering for relief from the cruel ropes tied around their wrists, the other end being attached securely to the saddle horns of Naylor's men. Corbett strode forward.

'Master Naylor, what is this?'

Naylor's face broke into a smile as he recognised Corbett.

'Two outlaws!' he bellowed triumphantly. 'I caught them red-handed with bows and quivers on the edge of the forest.'

'A surprise catch, Master Naylor,' Ranulf teased. 'They just walked up and surrendered?'

The serjeant-at-arms glowered back. 'No!' he rasped. 'They fell into a trap.' He jabbed a thumb over his shoulder. 'One of my men posed as a traveller. These two creatures stopped him on the King's highway with bows drawn. The rest was simple. So concerned were they with plundering, we were upon them before they could recover their wits.' He turned and spat in the direction of the prisoners. 'Robin Hood's men!' he taunted.

One of the prisoners shook his head so Naylor yanked on the rope, pulling the man face down on to the sharp-edged cobbles.

Isolda ran up with a jug of frothing ale in each hand. Naylor drank both in noisy gulps, not caring that the ale ran down his chin and soaked his leather jacket. More flagons were brought for his companions as well as water for the horses. At Corbett's order Ranulf brought tankards of ale for the two prisoners and they lapped greedily, like panting dogs. Naylor watched surlily then put on his helmet, snapped his fingers, and the cavalcade left the inn, the two prisoners stumbling and cursing behind.

'We'd best follow,' Corbett whispered. 'I want to be present when Branwood questions these prisoners.'

They collected their horses and followed Naylor back into Nottingham. The serjeant-at-arms made no attempt to hide his triumph as he moved along the streets, across the crowded market place and up the steep rocky track to the castle gates. Every so often Naylor would stop to proclaim loudly that he had captured two outlaws and that both would swing from the gallows before the day was out.

The castle garrison was awaiting them. Sir Peter Branwood's face was wreathed in smiles. Roteboeuf and Maigret stood beside him, straining to glimpse the two outlaws, now bloody and covered in filth from the city streets.

'God bless you, Master Naylor!' Branwood clapped his hands and helped the serjeant-at-arms down off his horse, shouting for wine to be brought. 'And you, Sir Hugh. You can tell His Grace the King that we do have our successes against these wolvesheads. As well as poisoners,' he continued, lowering his voice. 'Believe me, sir, the city is well rid of Hecate.'

'A pity,' Corbett replied, throwing the reins of his horse to an ostler and peeling off his leather gloves.

'Why so, sir?'

'I believe the killer of Sir Eustace silenced Hecate to stop her chatter.'

'Who cares?' Branwood harshly replied. 'Sir Eustace's death lies at the outlaw's door. The bitch is dead and I will have a little more money to send to the King's Exchequer at Westminster.' He grabbed a cup of wine brought by a servitor, slurped from it and passed it to a grinning Naylor.

Branwood then went across to the two prisoners who seemed little more than bundles of rags as they sprawled amongst the shit and dirt of the castle bailey. He cruelly yanked back each man's head by the hair and spat in their faces. Then he straightened up and glared round at the castle servants, now thronging about: stable boys, ostlers, scullions and wenches from the kitchen.

'This day,' he bellowed, his dark face flushed with emotion, 'we have caught two of the wolvesheads!' Branwood grinned at Corbett. 'According to the law and its usages we will give them a fair trial. And then . . .' He spread his hands and a servant sniggered at the implications of his words.

Branwood spun on his heel and strode up the steps of the keep. The two captives were dragged to their feet, their bonds cut and, flanked by men-at-arms, were pushed roughly up the stairs after him. By the time Corbett and Ranulf entered the castle the trial was ready to begin. Roteboeuf crouched on a stool, his writing-tray in his lap. Sir Peter, eyes glittering, sat on a high-backed chair on the edge of the dais, Naylor and Physician Maigret standing behind. The two prisoners cowered before him like beaten dogs. Corbett kept in the shadows, an unwilling witness to the quick, brutal sham.

Naylor repeated the circumstances of the two men's capture, reporting every gesture and movement. Corbett half-listened, studying the two prisoners carefully. Before their capture the men's clothes must have been poor, little more than a collection of rags sewn together. When Naylor opened a leather sack and dropped their weapons to the floor, these proved to be equally pathetic. Both men had carried long bows yet they were old and split whilst their swords and daggers were of poor quality, dull and blunt-edged. Despite their skin being tanned by sun and wind, the prisoners were emaciated, certainly not outlaws who feasted on the juiciest portions of the King's venison.

'Do you have any information about the wolfshead known as Robin Hood?' Branwood shouted at them.

Both men shook their heads.

'We are landless men,' one of them spoke up. 'We were starving.' He moistened his cracked lips. 'So we came south to live in Sherwood. We know nothing of the outlaw.'

Naylor sighed. Rubbing the side of his face, he walked off the dais towards the two prisoners who cringed as he approached. The serjeant-at-arms stood before them, legs apart.

'My Lord Sheriff,' he said evenly, 'asked you a question. You are to tell him the truth, not lies.'

'We do not lie,' one of the prisoners replied, squinting up at Naylor through bruised, half-open eyes. 'We tell the . . .'

His words were cut off as Naylor smashed him in the mouth and turned back towards the dais.

'My Lord Sheriff,' he commented, 'perhaps a stay in the dungeons might loosen their tongues?'

Branwood nodded. 'Take them away!'

The two men were hustled out, Naylor following. Branwood got up and came towards Corbett.

'A good day's work, Sir Hugh.'

Corbett stared at the sheriff's thin, dark face and noted the cruel malice in his bright shining eyes. You are obsessed, Corbett thought, you hate Robin Hood.

'Torture, My Lord Sheriff, is not permissible.'

'These are outlaws, caught red-handed! They are judged *utlegatum*, beyond the law.'

'Oh, I agree they are outlaws,' Corbett replied. 'But nothing to do with Robin Hood.'

Corbett was surprised at how speedily anger replaced the gleam of triumph in Sir Peter's eyes.

'What do you mean?'he spluttered. 'What proof do you have?'

'No real proof,' Corbett replied slowly, watching one of the castle cats leap on to the great table and push his nose into Branwood's cup. 'No proof, just a feeling.' Corbett shrugged. 'These men are fools, acting by themselves. Naylor was almost allowed to take them.'

'They are Robin Hood's men.' Branwood grinned. 'You will have the proof!'

He stormed out.

Corbett pulled a face and tugged at Ranulf's sleeve.

'Let's just watch this for a while.'

Chapter 7

They followed Branwood down the steps into the dark runnel of dungeons beneath the keep. The stench was offensive and dirt from the passageway slopped over the edge of their boots. On either side were heavy oaken doors with small grilles in the top. Mad eyes stared out from behind these.

Branwood led them, turning and twisting, until they came into a large chamber, black as night despite the torches fixed to the wall and the huge glowing bowls of charcoal. Naylor and others from the castle garrison were stripped to the waist and already their bodies gleamed with sweat. Against the far wall were the two prisoners.

Ropes had been lashed round their wrists and ankles then looped into iron rings fastened to the wall. As Corbett entered, one of the half-naked torturers grunted an order. The soldiers pulled vigorously down on the rope and both prisoners screamed as their arms were stretched to breaking point. The soldiers then went to the blazing bowls of charcoal and picked up glowing piles with their pincers. They shuffled back to the prisoners and pressed the flaming pieces against stomach, chest and armpits. The prisoners screamed, their bodies jerking and dancing against the wall until they became unconscious.

Ranulf swore under his breath. Corbett felt queasy. Branwood spun on his heel and walked away as Naylor ordered buckets of water to be thrown into the prisoners' faces. The men were roused and the torture recommenced. In between the ominous shuffling of the torturers, Naylor would approach both men and press his mouth against their sweat-soaked ears to ask them questions.

'Stop it!' Corbett ordered.

Naylor spun round.

'I am ordering you to stop it!' Corbett snapped, sickened by the gleam of pleasure in the burly serjeant's eyes.

'I take my orders from the sheriff.'

'You'll do what I damned well say!' Corbett roared. 'I act for the King in this matter!'

'You heard him, fellow,' Ranulf added sweetly, drawing his dagger. 'Either you do it or you're guilty of treason.'

Naylor was about to protest but Ranulf took one step forward and the serjeant-at-arms changed his mind. He grunted an order and the two prisoners were cut down. They slumped to the ground like piles of rags.

'I want them taken to a dungeon,' Corbett ordered. 'One of the cleanest in this muck pile. I need a wineskin, two cups and a bucket of cold water.'

Again orders were issued and Naylor hurried off.

'Wait for it,' Corbett whispered.

Sure enough there was a clatter in the corridor outside and Branwood hurried into the torture chamber.

'Sir Hugh, what are you doing? These men are to be tortured and then hanged after Friar Thomas has shriven them!'

'Sir Peter,' Corbett said tactfully, 'you are the King's under-sheriff but I am his commissioner. There are more ways than one of killing a cat. Naylor has had his way. If he continues, these men will soon be dead. Now I am going to have them taken to a dungeon where I'll question them closely. When I have finished, if they are still lying, you can have them hanged, drawn and quartered for all I care. However, if they tell the truth, I'll issue a pardon.'

Branwood's face relaxed. 'Have it your way,' he muttered.

Corbett returned to the castle bailey for some fresh air. He noticed how restless Ranulf had become.

'What's the matter, man?' he snapped. 'Are you missing your lady love?'

Ranulf looked down and shuffled his feet. 'He wants to meet you.'

'Who does?'

'Rahere the Riddle Master.'

'Ranulf, what have you promised?'

'Nothing, Master, it's just that . . .'

'He would like an invitation to the King's Crown Wearing at Yuletide?'

'Yes, Master.'

Corbett turned away. 'For God's sake, Ranulf, we have enough on our minds. Tell him I'll meet him soon. Perhaps we can share a bowl of wine. But at the moment . . .'

Ranulf knew when to cut and run; the words were hardly out of Corbett's mouth before he was hurrying away, back up to his chamber to rub fresh oil into his face as well as search for a small bottle of perfume he had been hoping to sell. He had bought it from a high-class courtesan in London.

'A concoction of ass's milk, balsam and rare ointment,' the woman had lied. 'I bought it from an Egyptian who said it was the same unguent Cleopatra used to rub into her body.'

Ranulf searched amongst his untidy belongings until he found it, his excitement increasing as he thought of the lovely Amisia letting it drip between her ripe, full breasts.

Whilst Ranulf prepared himself, Corbett returned to the dungeons. A surly Naylor showed him to the cell where the two prisoners, their hands and feet shackled, lolled side by side on a bed of filthy straw covered by a threadbare blanket. Corbett asked for a stool and, when it was brought, ordered Naylor to leave them alone. He then pushed the bucket of water nearer the men. They were conscious but in sore pain, groaning every time they moved. Corbett splashed water over their faces, filled the two tin cups full of wine and pushed them into their bruised and eager hands.

'Drink,' he said. 'It will dull the pain.'

Both men gulped. Corbett re-filled the cups.

'You are going to hang,' he began softly. 'If you survive the torture, Branwood will tie a noose round your necks, fasten one end of the rope to a hook and kick you both over the castle walls. Do you want to die like rats on a farmer's line?' He showed them his ring bearing the Royal Arms of England. 'My name is Sir Hugh Corbett. I am Keeper of the King's Secret Seal. I have the power of life and death over you. If you tell the truth, I'll have you pardoned and released. If you lie, you'll both be dead by sunset.' He refilled the cups as the men shuffled and looked at each other. 'Now, you are Robin Hood's men?'

They both nodded.

'Where do you usually hide?'

One man licked blood-caked lips. 'We are the outlaw's men and yet we are not.'

'What do you mean?'

'Go deeper into the forest, Master, and Sherwood is like a city. You have the peasants, the charcoal-burners, the pig tenders, the poachers. Those who live by the law and those who live by the law and those who do not. We began as poachers; usually we lived by ourselves, moving from one cave to another or sleeping in this glade or that.'

'So you did not live in one band?'

His companion spluttered on a half-laugh and gulped from the cup.

'For God's sake, Master, I have heard the ballads myself. Any outlaw band which kept together would soon be hunted down. Its camp fires would be seen from Nottingham. No, Robin Hood can usually be found near the glades and oaks of Edmundstowe. At times we were called in.'

'How?'

'By runners or by hunting horn. Or by messages left pinned to the trunks of certain oaks.'

'And what happened then?'

'We usually gathered in some glade or other. Robin Hood and Little John would appear.'

'What do they look like?'

'They wear brown and green so that through the trees they cannot be seen. They are hooded with half-masks over their faces.'

'Who else is there?'

'Other members of his coven.'

'Is there a woman?'

'Aye, Maid Marion.' The fellow licked his lips. 'Saucy she is, large-bosomed. She, Robin Hood and Little John act almost as one person. Orders are issued.' The fellow shrugged.

Corbett thought of the wench at The Blue Boar inn but decided not to reveal what he knew.

'Were you involved in the attack on the tax-collectors?'

Both men became agitated.

'You were, weren't you?'

'We had no part in the killing, Master, but Robin Hood is a hard taskmaster. The tax-collectors' retinue were hanged because of what they had seen, whilst Willoughby was left alive as a warning.'

'And the plunder?'

'Not much, Master. We got a few coins, each according to what he contributed. Nym and I,' he jerked his head at his companion, 'are relative strangers. A few pence is all we got. The band then broke up to wait for other attacks.'

'So how were you captured this morning?'

'We were starving, Master. The deer have become wise, they are harder to track. Robin Hood has kept to himself and Branwood's soldiers are all over the forest. We dare not go into the villages because of the rewards posted against us.'

'Is that all you know?' Corbett got to his feet.

'We have told the truth,' Nym rasped. 'Robin Hood is mysterious. A will-o'-the-wisp. They say elves and goblins advise him and that he can talk to the trees.' The man held up his hands. 'Master, we are small twigs on a large tree. We have told you all we know.'

Corbett nodded, opened the door and shouted for Naylor.

'Give these men a set of clothes, one loaf and a wineskin.' He dug into his purse and drew out two coins. 'They are to be released unharmed.'

Corbett strode away before Naylor could remonstrate or the prisoners finish their pathetic litany of thanks. He went back into the castle bailey. Branwood was not there. Corbett found him in the hall seated at the great table, a chequer board before him, the black and white squares covered in heaps of coins.

'I am preparing my accounts for the quarter,' he muttered, not bothering to raise his head. 'You found the prisoners interesting?'

Corbett told him what he had learnt. Branwood nodded.

'They'll be released unharmed,' he agreed and leaned back, clinking the coins in his hand and staring at Roteboeuf who sat at the edge of the table carefully inscribing accounts.

'How long do you think they'll live?' Branwood asked ironically.

Roteboeuf lifted his head and shrugged.

'What do you mean?' Corbett snapped.

'I mean, King's Commissioner in Nottingham,' Branwood replied, making no attempt to hide his hostility, 'those two outlaws will not see this week's end. They were captured and then released. What do you think their companions will believe? That they have accepted the King's pardon and talked, of course. They are dead men already.'

'That's none of our business,' Corbett replied. 'And what do you plan now, My Lord Sheriff?'

Branwood looked up, a false smile on his saturnine face.

'We shall wait for Sir Guy of Gisborne and see if he can do better than us. You still await your messenger's return?'

Corbett nodded.

'Until then,' Branwood continued, 'I will count my coins, Roteboeuf will write his accounts, and you will wonder what to do next whilst your servant, so I gather, spends most of his time slipping in and out of the castle.'

'I shall do one thing,' Corbett retorted.

'Which is?'

'Well, Sir Peter, tonight is the thirteenth of June.'

Branwood's eyes narrowed and Roteboeuf's head jerked up.

'Oh, you mean the fire arrows?' Branwood shook his head. 'God knows what they signify. Perhaps some prank. You'll join us for supper?'

Corbett agreed and returned to his own chamber. He felt restless and for a while moved about, either staring out of the window or lying on the bed gazing up at the rafters.

'The thirteenth of June. If I don't break that damned cipher soon,' he exclaimed, 'His Grace the King will want me back in London and others can chase this will-o'-the-wisp of the forest!'

He sat up in bed and plucked at a loose thread on the blanket, wondering when Maltote would return.

'Three kings,' he whispered, 'to the two fools' tower go with their two chevaliers.' He wondered who had composed the riddle. De Craon, Nogaret or Philip himself? What could it mean? Were they names of towns in

Flanders? Would Philip's armies pour across the frontier and strike at certain vital cities as King Edward had in Scotland? Corbett felt his heart sink in despair. Most of the ciphers used by the French chancery could be solved eventually, simply because they conveyed long messages. The longer the cipher, the easier it was to break.

But this short phrase? Corbett's mind moved on. He thought of Vechey's death chamber. How could a man be poisoned in a locked chamber with a servant inside, two guards outside, and no trace of the poison ever be discovered?

'You should apply logic, Corbett,' he declared loudly and thought of the invitation he had recently received from the Chancellor of Oxford, inviting him to give a lecture in the Schools on Aristotle's logic and its effects on the study of the Quadrivium. Corbett smiled. How Maeve had teased him! He wondered how she was faring at Leighton Manor. Would she supervise the bailiffs? The harvest looked as if it would be good but the grain merchants in Cornhill couldn't be trusted as far as he could spit; he really should be present when this year's produce was sold. He thought of someone trying to swindle Maeve and grinned. She would have their head! Corbett's eyes grew heavy. He dozed for a while and was abruptly awoken by Ranulf crashing into the room.

'For God's sake, man, what is it?' Corbett snarled. 'Are we under attack?'

'No, Master,' Ranulf replied, still fresh and eager from his conversation with Rahere. 'But I have an idea about that cipher.'

'Go on!'

'Could it be a poem or a song?'

Corbett narrowed his eyes. 'What made you think of that?'

'Just a thought,' Ranulf lied. 'Perhaps a French song or a Flemish poem?'

Corbett shook his head. 'It might be worth pursuing,' he muttered. 'But for the moment, let's deal with present problems.'

And Corbett told Ranulf what the prisoners had said. Hiding his disappointment at his master's curt reception of his idea, he listened attentively.

'They probably told you the truth,' he remarked. 'The same is true of the outlaw bands in Southwark. The human rats usually scavenge by themselves, but when one of the masters of that Devil's Kitchen plans some great stratagem, such as an attack upon a merchant's house or an ill-guarded convoy, they gather together.'

'The problem is,' Corbett interrupted, 'what Robin and his coven do in between such actions. Where does he hide? Where does he go? Is he well guarded?'

He went back to the table, sifting amongst the papers there. He picked up a quill, sharpened it, dipped it in the ink horn and listed his conclusions.

'First, Robin Hood accepted the King's pardon in 1297, five years ago.' Corbett ran his finger down the report drawn up by the clerk at Westminster. 'Secondly, on the twenty-seventh of November, 1301, the chancery at Westminster issued a letter to Robin Hood, serving in the King's army in Scotland, granting his release from military service there and issuing a safe conduct for him and two companies to come south. On the same day, the royal clerks wrote a letter to Sir Eustace Vechey informing him that Robin Hood was returning to Nottingham, that he was still within the King's peace, was not to be molested and should be allowed to draw on the revenues of his manor at Locksley.

'Now.' Corbett looked up and stared at Ranulf. 'Our outlaw friend must have been back in Nottingham sometime in mid-December. Apparently he did not go back to Locksley but returned to Sherwood where he resumed his old life as an outlaw. At first a little poaching and the occasional assault, but by the spring of this year he was organising ambushes on merchants and convoys, culminating in the murderous attack on Willoughby and his retinue.' Corbett scratched his chin. 'He has the same people with him, a tall man whom Willoughby thought was Little John and a woman, Lady Mary, better known as Maid Marion. He appears to have been dressed in exactly the same way as before, clothed in brown and green, a hood over his head, his face half-masked.

'However, there are two differences. First, according to Brother William Scarlett, he is responsible for the death of some of his old band. Secondly, he robs the rich but there is very little evidence that he distributes his gains to the poor.' He looked up. 'Have I omitted anything, Ranulf?'

'No. The one thing which cannot be explained is the outlaw's change in conduct. He has become more ruthless, vicious even.'

'Umm!' Corbett nibbled the tip of the quill. 'That could be old age, growing cynicism, disillusionment with the King – God knows that would be easy – or determination to reinforce his authority over the outlaw gangs in Sherwood.'

'There are two other matters,' Ranulf added. 'First, he has a confidant here in the castle. Secondly, we suspect a link between the outlaw and The Blue Boar tavern. We could arrest the landlord there and put him to the question.'

Corbett shook his head. 'I doubt if he'd tell us much and we are wasting time on the minnows.' He stared down at the page and studied the dates. 'Let us think of Robin leaving the army in Scotland. Where would he go to first?'

'His home at Locksley.'

'And then where?'

'Brother William said Lady Mary entered the convent at Kirklees Priory.'

Corbett threw down the pen on the table. 'In which case he would have gone there. Whatever happens, Ranulf,' he continued, 'I'll give Maltote one more day, then I'll travel to Kirklees and Locksley to see what I can discover.'

They talked for a while, Corbett being drawn to the window as soldiers of the castle jeered at the two outlaws hobbling out of the gate. The sun began to set like a fiery ball in the west. Ranulf pleaded some excuse and slipped away, his mind full of the comely Amisia, as Corbett summoned up courage to write a letter to the King. He made it short and terse, openly stating that he had discovered nothing.

He'd hardly finished sealing it when a surly servant banged on the door, shouting that the evening meal was ready. Corbett washed and walked down to the main hall. He suddenly stopped half-way down; something he had just done had sparked a memory in his mind. He smiled, solemnly promising himself that he would pursue that line of thought at the proper time.

The evening meal proved to be quite a cheerful affair. Branwood viewed the capture of the outlaws as at least a minor victory against Robin Hood. Maigret was still absorbed in discovering the poison used to kill Vechey and described a long list of possible noxious substances. Corbett listened to them carefully but kept his own counsel. He knew that the traitor and Vechey's assassin was probably seated with them at table. He glanced at Roteboeuf and Friar Thomas who had returned from his parish church, and wondered when the traitor would make a mistake.

Darkness fell, more torches were lit. Ranulf returned much the worse for drink, drawing dark glances from the rest, so Corbett excused himself. He took a sconce torch and, with Physician Maigret still sonorously lecturing him about poisons, helped an unsteady Ranulf to the top of the keep. The cool night breeze whipped their hair. Corbett, who disliked heights, sat on a bench and stared up at the pinprick of stars, Ranulf half-dozing beside him.

'I know why you are here.' Maigret abruptly changed the topic of conversation. 'Everyone in the castle is expecting the three fire arrows.'

'Why?' Corbett mused. 'Why does it happen?'

'God knows!' he answered. 'But I hear you took my advice, Sir Hugh.'

'Aye, and found the woman dead.'

'Too much death,' Ranulf mumbled. 'Master, when will you see Rahere?'

'When I return,' Corbett snapped.

He rose, walked to the battlements and stared down. In the pools of torchlight on the parapet beneath, he glimpsed Branwood, Naylor and other soldiers of the garrison, whilst horsemen milled around the postern gate.

'Every time it happens,' Maigret muttered, coming up behind him, 'Sir Peter sends riders into the city but they discover nothing.'

The bell of some distant church tolled for midnight. The peals had hardly died away when they heard a shout and looked up. A fire arrow streaked against the velvet blackness, followed by a second, then a third. For a while the arrows burnt fiercely against the darkness. Branwood shouted orders, the postern gate was thrown open and the riders clattered out but Corbett could see it was futile: the mysterious archer could have fired the arrows from the roof of any house, from garden or darkened alleyway.

Why three? he wondered as he helped Ranulf back to their chamber. Why three arrows on the thirteenth of every month?

Corbett made Ranulf as comfortable as possible and lay down on his own bed. He tried to recite three Aves but his mind was in turmoil. He now suspected the way in which Vechey had been poisoned but he must move cautiously. He was still distracted by such thoughts when, half-way through the third Ave, he fell asleep.

* * *

The two outlaws released by Corbett had hidden in the fields once they were clear of the city. They ached and found every step painful but were determined to put as much distance between themselves and Nottingham as possible. They ate what little food they had and drank from a brook. They, too, had glimpsed the fire arrows long before they stumbled on to the moonlit trackway which would lead them down to the Newark road. Their relief at being released soon died as they passed the gallows and followed the track through clumps of trees which seemed to crowd in on them from every side. They paused and cowered at the hoot of an owl or the sudden flurry of bracken as a hunting fox chased his quarry.

'We should have stayed in the city,' Nym moaned.

'Nonsense!' his companion muttered. 'The bastard sheriff may have changed his mind and Robin Hood has friends there.'

'Stay clear of The Blue Boar,' Nym replied.

They walked in single file. Nym glimpsed a break in the trees where the track met the Newark road. He breathed a sigh of relief which turned into a gasp of terror as six shadowy figures slipped from the trees, bows at the ready.

'We are poor men!' Nym wailed.

'You are traitors!' a voice called from the trees. 'Master Robin sends his salutations and finds you guilty of divers crimes. Firstly, you should not have robbed without his permission. Secondly, you should not have been caught. And, thirdly, you should not be slinking like rats along a moonlit trackway. What did you tell the sheriff and his friends?'

Nym and his companion gasped in terror.

'We told them nothing!'

'Then, friend, walk on.'

The bowmen stood aside. Nym and his comrade took one step and another, then forgetting their injuries, began to hobble fast towards the end of the trackway. Behind them bow strings twanged and steel-tipped death, eight arrows in all, caught them in the back. Both men groaned, flailing out their arms, and collapsed on to the dry sunburnt grass, choking out their life blood. Behind them the outlaws slipped back into the trees, leaving the corpses sprawled bloodily under the moonlight.

Chapter 8

Corbett woke early, still sweating after his nightmare. He had been standing on a red, dusty plain under black, howling skies, surrounded by thick green forests. At the edge of this stood a huge manor house built entirely of iron. In his nightmare Corbett walked towards it, noticing a shutter banging. As he approached, this was suddenly flung open. A hooded figure peered out, the cowl was pulled back, and Corbett stared into the narrow, red-bearded face of his adversary, Amaury de Craon.

'Welcome to Hell!' de Craon cried. 'What took you so long?'

After he had woken, Corbett lay for a while, wondering what the dream meant. He felt agitated and slightly anxious. He hoped that all was well with Maeve at Leighton Manor then recalled the fire arrows the night before and became aware of the date and how time was passing whilst he floundered about in Nottingham. Across the chamber, Ranulf lay sprawled on his bed sleeping peacefully as a baby. Corbett groaned, got out of bed, washed, shaved and dressed. He remembered de Craon from his dream, wondered if the assassin Achitophel was in Nottingham. He clasped his sword belt round his waist. A distant bell began to sound for morning mass so Corbett went down to the small bleak chapel where Friar Thomas, dressed in a black and gold chasuble for the Mass of the Dead, greeted him.

'I'm offering this for the souls of Sir Eustace and Lecroix.' He smiled at Corbett from the altar. 'May God take them to a place of light.'

A few soldiers from the garrison joined them. Friar Thomas made the sign of the cross and began mass. The service was simple and after the final benediction, as was customary at a Requiem, Friar Thomas recited the *Dona Eis* three times. Corbett listened to the words. 'Eternal rest grant unto them, O Lord, and let perpetual light shine upon them. May they rest in peace. Amen.'

He remembered the friar's remark at the beginning of mass, about God taking the souls of the two dead men to a place of light, and thought of the three fire arrows he had glimpsed against the velvet night sky. Were those arrows a prayer for someone? Some form of tribute? Or a threat?

Corbett left the chapel and went up to Sir Eustace's room which Ranulf had sealed with Corbett's own insignia. He broke these off and went into the musty chamber, took a sheet from the bed, collected a few items and, closing the door after him, went back to his chamber. He was surprised to see Ranulf up and dressed and sitting beside an aggrieved-looking Maltote.

'So the messenger returns!' Corbett exclaimed, pushing the items he had taken from Vechey's room under his bed.

Maltote rose and limped towards him.

'For God's sake, man,' Corbett cried, 'what happened?'

'I went to Southwell as you said, Master.'

'And?'

'Guy of Gisborne kept me there.'

'Why?' Corbett gazed in astonishment at the bandage round Maltote's knee. 'Sit down and tell us what happened.'

'I'll tell you,' Ranulf spoke up. 'Gisborne has gone into Sherwood.'

Corbett closed his eyes and groaned.

'He moved his force in there last night,' Ranulf continued. 'They begin their hunt at daybreak. Maltote rode through the night to tell us the news. He found the castle barred so he stayed at The Trip to Jerusalem.'

'Why didn't Gisborne let you go immediately?'

'He knew you might stop him,' Ranulf answered for Maltote. 'That's why he detained him.'

Corbett went to stare out of the window. He recalled Gisborne's face: red, weather-beaten, with a flattened nose and eyes as hard as pebbles. An excellent soldier and a born fighter, Gisborne had performed many feats on the Scottish march and, if the clerks at Westminster could be believed, had a special loathing for Robin Hood. Gisborne had never accepted the King's granting the outlaw a pardon. However, if chancery gossip could be believed, whilst serving in Scotland, Edward had made Gisborne swear an oath over holy relics that he would never raise a hand against Robin Hood. When the outlaw returned to his depredations, Gisborne, a local landowner with considerable knowledge of Sherwood Forest, had immediately offered his sword to hunt the outlaw down. King Edward had refused but, after the attack on Willoughby, had ordered Corbett north. He'd also sent writs to Gisborne to raise troops but these were only to be deployed when Corbett gave his consent. But Gisborne had been cunning. He had taken Maltote's arrival as Corbett's tacit consent to move and, by detaining the messenger, made sure Corbett was in no position to object.

'Who else knows?' Corbett rasped over his shoulder.

'Sir Peter Branwood,' Maltote spluttered. 'The castle guard called him down immediately.'

Corbett pressed his hot cheek against the cold stone.

'And, of course,' he muttered, 'Sir Peter is furious at Gisborne's actions.'

'Worse,' Ranulf answered. 'He and Naylor have taken a small force out to the fringes of the forest – whether to assist Gisborne or stop him, I don't know.'

Corbett spun round, came back and glared down at the boyish face of his messenger.

'Couldn't you have returned earlier? And how were you wounded?'

Maltote looked at the floor.

'Two reasons,' Ranulf replied cheerily. 'First, he got drawn into a game of dice and lost everything. Secondly,' Ranulf clapped Maltote on the shoulder and grinned at Corbett, 'he tried to redeem his losses by accepting a challenge from an archer.'

Corbett gaped.

'You see,' Ranulf chattered on, 'our good messenger here shot one arrow, picked up a second, tripped over the bow and somehow or other,' Ranulf compressed his mouth to stop himself laughing, 'tripped and gashed his knee.'

Corbett stared disbelievingly at him. He would have given the young messenger his usual lecture about not touching any weapon but Maltote already looked so miserable. His face was pallid, emphasising the pock marks round his eyes, the legacy of an attack some months previously when Corbett had been hunting the insane murderer of London prostitutes. Corbett tapped him gently on the shoulder.

'Let's forget that. Listen, whilst Branwood is gone, I am travelling to Kirklees. Don't ask me why. Just watch what happens here. And, Ranulf, before you ask, I'll see your friend Rahere on my return.'

Corbett left the castle an hour later, Ranulf and Maltote seeing him as far as the Middle Gate. The clerk led his horse through the busy teeming streets of Nottingham, pulling a cowl over his head so as not to attract anyone's attention. In the market place he had to fight his way through the crowd watching a pack of snarling mastiffs

132

snap at a great black bear. This stood roaring its defiance in a flash of ivory teeth and thrusting cruel paws which delighted the crowd and stirred the blood lust of the dogs. Corbett went down an alleyway near St Mary's church, looking for a scribe. A water-seller directed him to the other side of St Mary's and, as he passed the church steps, he stopped and cursed as he saw the naked corpses of the outlaws sprawled there. In accordance with city regulations, both cadavers had been stripped and placed on public view for anyone to recognise. The bodies lolled sideways in makeshift chests and Corbett saw the ugly purple-red arrow wounds in their backs. He breathed a prayer and pressed on.

In the booths and stalls just inside St Mary's graveyard, he found a scribe who etched a crude map of the surrounding countryside, indicating which route he should take to reach the Priory of Kirklees. The fellow took his time, chattering like a magpie about how hobgoblins had been seen sitting on a tomb and feasting on human flesh, and how such evil sprites plagued the roads round Nottingham. Corbett tapped his boot in frustration but at last the man finished. Corbett grabbed the map, paid the fee and left the churchyard.

The visit to the scribe must have cost him an hour. By the time he left the city gate, joining others as they wound their way along the country track, Corbett found his serenity disturbed. By nature he was a solitary man, accustomed to the subtle intrigue of court around him as well as the dangerous street politics of London. This had given him a heightened sense of danger. Now he felt uneasy, certain he was being watched and followed. At first he felt protected by the other travellers but eventually these left the main highway, returning to outlying villages or farms. At last Corbett travelled alone, the silence broken by scuffling in the hedgerows, the occasional burst of bird song or the steady hum of the crickets. Corbett eased the sword in his belt, letting his horse amble gently as he himself breathed in deeply and strained his ears to catch any sound of danger.

As he approached the forest, his anxiety increased. Who was tracking him? he wondered. Was it the traitor in the castle or was it Achitophel? Had the French assassin arrived in Nottingham and was he planning to strike here in the lonely countryside? The line of trees drew nearer.

Corbett stopped and looked round. So far he had travelled through open countryside where an assailant would have to use hedges or a small copse for concealment. He urged his horse on and entered the forest. The sunlight faded and, once again, Corbett became aware that the forest was a living thing; the crackling in the undergrowth, the fluttering of birds, the growing darkness and sense of utter loneliness. Suddenly Corbett heard chatter, the noise of conversation somewhere in front of him, but resisted the urge to whip his horse into a headlong gallop. He peered over his shoulder but could see no signs of pursuit whilst ahead of him he glimpsed other travellers. They stopped, looking back in alarm at the sound of his horse's hooves. Corbett saw one of them unstring a bow so reined in his horse and held up his left hand in a sign of peace.

'Who are you?' the man called.

'An honest traveller,' Corbett replied, 'eager for your company.'

'You are alone?'

'Of course.'

'Then come forward slowly.'

Corbett dug his knees into his mount's sides and the group waited to receive him. They were a mixed band: men, women and children, protected by retainers, a number of families intent on visiting the Blessed Thurstan's tomb at York. Corbett journeyed with them until they arrived at a tavern at some crossroads in time for the mid-day meal.

The place was a hive of activity. Peasants and villeins and travellers of every sort thronged the busy stable yard whilst the taproom was packed to overflowing. Ostlers took their horses and Corbett went inside, sitting by an overturned beer barrel near the window. He felt hungry so asked for a jug of ale, a broth of peas and onions with sippets, and a raston or small loaf made of sweetened flour and enriched with eggs. While eating he watched the other travellers take their ease. A pardoner appeared, pretending to speak Latin but now and again telling the pilgrims anecdotes full of coarse merriment. The taproom was filled with the clatter of jugs and basins, the cries of children, the braying voice of the pardoner, and the low hum of conversation as traders, tinkers and merchants exchanged gossip about the roads and markets.

Corbett stared round. He could see no one who might pose a threat. No one he could recognise from the castle or the town. One of the pilgrims, a young girl, stood up to sing a song in a clear voice. Corbett leaned back, eyes closed, and listened as the girl described the bird song of summer.

'Everywhere summer sings,' she sang.

A tremendous commotion from the yard outside drowned the song as customers sprang to their feet at the alarm: 'Fire! Fire!'

Corbett joined the rest in the yard. Ostlers were dragging horses from the stables and the air was sharp with the acrid smell of burnt straw. Corbett saw a wisp of flame from the end stable but servants carrying buckets of water soon doused the fire. The atmosphere relaxed, the customers laughed and everyone trooped back into the taproom. Corbett took his seat and grasped his tankard, then stopped. He had to stretch out for it, from right to left, but knew he'd never have left his tankard there. Maeve was always nagging him about resting cups and jugs at the edge of tables.

'You are lazy, Hugh,' she would berate him. 'You like to pick up your cup with the minimum of effort. Baby Eleanor loves that too.'

Corbett stared at the tankard. Someone had moved it, but why? A servant rushing by the barrel to get to the door? Or someone with a more sinister intent? He took the tankard and cradled it in his hands. He peered quickly round the tavern. He could recognise no stranger and was sure no one was watching him. He lifted the tankard, sniffed it carefully, and beneath its malty tang caught something more subtle, sharp and acrid. Corbett put the tankard down and breathed deeply, trying to control his panic. Had it been poisoned or was he losing his wits? He remembered the rat-catcher he had seen outside, sprawled on the cobbles, his back to the tavern wall, sunning himself. Corbett went out and stood over him. The seamy yellow-faced man looked up.

'You have business with me, sir?'

Corbett produced a coin and gestured at the man's empty rusting cages. 'Could you catch me a rat?'

The fellow caught the glint of silver and his mouth broke into a toothless smile.

'Can a bird fly?'

He picked up one of his small cages and shuffled across to one of the outhouses where hay and grain were stored.

Corbett sat and waited for a quarter of an hour. At last the fellow returned. Now his cage contained a long-tailed, fat-bellied rat which pushed its snout aggressively against the wire, yellow teeth protruding, blood-red eyes gleaming in fury.

'A prince among rats,' the fellow declared. 'You wanted it alive?' He held out a dirty claw for the coin.

Corbett handed it over.

'There's another for a piece of cheese and your tongue remaining silent about what you see.'

The man shrugged, dug into his greasy wallet and

handed Corbett a piece of spongy cheese so putrid it stank. Corbett placed the small cage on the ground, the piece of cheese next to it. The rat pushed its snout against the bars, tantalised by the smell. Corbett then poured the contents of his tankard over the cheese and, using a stick, pushed it into the cage. The rat attacked it voraciously, peeling off strips like a man would an apple. The cheese disappeared, the rat raised its head, sniffing at the air, then suddenly moved sideways. It rolled on its back, dirty underbelly up, clawing the air. A greenish substance trickled between its jaws as it convulsed in its death throes.

'That's the last time I'm eating that bloody cheese!' The rat-catcher's beady eyes studied Corbett. 'Or better still, Master, perhaps you should be more careful what you drink!'

Corbett went back into the tavern, shouting for the landlord as he tried to control his own fear at the horrible death he had just escaped. He handed over the tankard as well as another coin.

'That is the most expensive meal I have ever bought.'

The taverner looked at him quizzically.

'I want that tankard destroyed,' Corbett insisted. 'And a cup of your best claret. But I will choose the cup and broach the cask myself.'

Guy of Gisborne stopped and peered through the trees on either side. His red face glistened with sweat under his heavy iron helm and mailed coif. He smiled in satisfaction as he surveyed his line of foresters and verderers.

'I'll show the King,' he whispered, 'his sombre clerk and that bastard Branwood how to kill an outlaw!'

Gisborne's heart skipped a beat in pleasure at what he planned for Robin Hood. Gisborne detested the wolfshead with his much vaunted love for the common man, his consummate skill with a bow, his knowledge of the forest and, above all, the way he had on several occasions tricked and ambushed Gisborne himself only to receive the King's grace and favour.

Gisborne ground his teeth and winced in pain at an abscess high in his gum. He had been forced to watch Robin Hood become a member of the King's own chamber, stroll like any lord through the streets of Nottingham or amongst the silken pavilions of Edward's generals in Scotland. Gisborne had seen how the King had favoured the outlaw, granting him special privileges, using the outlaw's skills as the English hunted the Scottish rebel leader Wallace through the wild glens and woods of Scotland. But now Robin had returned to Sherwood. Gisborne forgot his pain for this time the outlaw had put himself beyond the law, stealing the King's taxes and executing his officers as if they were common malefactors. Today would be different. Gisborne would hunt the outlaw down, but not with an armed band of knights, clattering like a peal of bells through the forest. These verderers and foresters would flush out Robin as they would a hart or a wild boar. Gisborne would trap him, mete out punishment, then tie him to the horn of his saddle and ride the wolfshead naked through Nottingham so all could see Gisborne's glory and the outlaw's downfall.

'Sir Guy? My Lord of Gisborne?'

Guy glanced sideways at the dark, elfin face of his chief huntsman, Mordred.

'My Lord, you are pleased?'

'Your lord is pleased.'

Gisborne stared into the green darkness ahead of him. He couldn't position the sun but guessed it was past mid-day and already he was driving bands of outlaws deeper into the forest. A mile on either side of him, lines of well-armed huntsmen prepared to close the next net. Gisborne had deployed his soldiers like the horns of a bull, sweeping the dirt and refuse of the forest before them. Sooner or later he would flush out Robin Hood and trap him against a marsh or rocky escarpment. Or, better still, out in the open countryside where Gisborne's horsemen would seal the trap. Guy rocked himself to and fro as he peered through the surrounding forest. He had spent every penny he had on this venture but the King would repay him and Branwood would have to eat the dust from his cloak.

'My Lord of Gisborne?' Mordred spoke up again.

Sir Guy caught the note of anxiety in the man's voice.

'What is it, man?'

'My Lord, we are moving too fast.'

'Good. It will give the outlaws little time to re-group.'

'Sir Guy, I beg you, the outlaws are fleeing but could be leading us into a trap.'

'Nonsense!' Gisborne snapped. He gripped his sword tighter. 'Give the order to advance!'

'My Lord . . .' Mordred's words were cut off.

Gisborne angrily raised his horn, giving three long haunting blasts, and then ran forward in a half-crouch.

They came to the edge of a glade. Mordred scrabbled at Gisborne's arm but the knight shrugged him off. He felt the blood beat in his temples. He ran across the sun-dappled grass, Mordred and the others loping beside him. In the dark greenness before them, a single horn blast greeted them. Mordred and the foresters stopped. Sir Guy ran on. Another blast of that horn, sombre, sinister, and the air was full of speeding death. The grey, goose-quilled arrows fell like a silent deadly rain. Mordred saw men to his right and left drop, kicking and spluttering, as arrows took them in the throat and chest.

'Sir Guy!' he screamed.

But Gisborne ran on. Another flight of arrows. Now the glade was full of screams. Men sprawled on the ground, jerking in their death throes, dark bloody pools glistening on the green grass. Mordred raised his own horn. One shrill blast and his men fled back into the shelter of the trees. Sir Guy, however, charged on, forcing his way through the bracken on the other side of the glade, his sword held out in front of him. No arrow hit him. He felt protected, a sure sign that God's favour was with him. A hooded figure, face masked, stepped out from behind a tree.

'Welcome to Sherwood, Sir Guy!'

Gisborne turned, his mind seething with fury. He half-lifted his sword and ran, shouting curses at this man who had taunted him for years. Gisborne's foot caught a root and he fell headlong, sword flying out of his grasp. He stared up at the cowled figure bending over him. Gisborne's lips curled in a smile.

'You!'

It was his last word. The dark figure raised his sword then brought it crashing down on the line of exposed flesh between Gisborne's coif and hauberk.

Chapter 9

Corbett reached Locksley later that evening, a small hamlet with barn-shaped buildings on either side of a dusty track, a village green, communal well and rough makeshift church, the simple thatched nave built alongside a rough-hewn tower. Corbett stopped at the ale house, a stone-built cottage with a stake hooked under its eaves. The ale wife, a slattern with shifty eyes and dressed in a greasy smock, served what she termed 'freshly brewed ale'. The other villagers sipped their beer and gawked at this stranger before returning to listen to one of their number recount how he had seen a demon on the edge of the forest, a shadowy form with a face of glowing iron.

Corbett half-listened to the tale as he sat on a bench and watched the door of the ale house. Since leaving the pilgrims just south of Haversage, he believed his mysterious, murderous pursuer had given up the chase but wanted to be sure. He had ridden thirty miles and was saddle-sore, his horse nearly blown, and he was reluctant to spend the night out in the open. The clerk's eyes grew heavy and he dozed, to be woken by a rough hand shaking his shoulder. Corbett jumped, hand going to his dagger, but the man standing over him was old and venerable, his face thin and ascetic though his eyes were smiling and his manner friendly.

'You are a stranger here?' The voice was soft, burred by a strong accent.

Corbett saw the tonsure on the man's pate, the black dusty robes and sandalled feet.

'You are a priest?'

'Aye, Father Edmund. This is my parish, for my sins. I have served the church of St Oswald for many a year. I was told there was a stranger here so I came down. I thought perhaps you were . . .'

Corbett, fully awake, gestured to him to sit on the bench.

'You want something to drink, Father?'

'No, no.' The man patted his stomach. 'Never on an empty belly.'

'Who did you think I was, Father? Someone from Robin Hood's band?'

The priest gripped Corbett's wrist. 'Shush!' Father Edmund threw a warning look at him and glanced quickly round the tavern to see if anyone else had heard his words.

'Who are you?' the priest muttered.

'My name is Sir Hugh Corbett, Keeper of the King's Secret Seal.'

The priest's eyes widened. 'So it has come to this,' he murmured.

'To what, Father?'

'No, come with me.' The priest stood up. 'You haven't eaten and I suspect you haven't a bed for the night. I can give you some broth, bread which is soft, a bed that is hard, and wine which perhaps has seen better days.'

Corbett grinned and got to his feet.

'In the circumstances, Father, your offer is princely and generous.'

They went outside. Corbett unhitched his horse and followed the stoop-backed priest through the gathering darkness towards the church. The priest's house was a red-tiled, yellow-brick building standing behind St Oswald's, separated from it by the cemetery. Father Edmund helped him stable his horse in one of the outhouses, sending his own nag, a broken-down hack, to graze amongst the tombstones whilst he brought water, oats and fresh straw for bedding.

Corbett was then taken to the house, stark, simple but very clean. The floor was of beaten earth covered with rushes fresh from the riverside, green, soft and sweet-smelling. A flitch of bacon hung to cure above the small hearth gave off a tangy, salty smell. The rest of the room was filled with a few sticks of furniture, one large parish chest, a number of coffers, and in the corner, partitioned off from the rest of the room, a small cot bed above which hung a huge wooden cross.

Father Edmund pulled up a stool before the fire and gently stirred the pot until it bubbled over the small fire he had lit. Corbett was then served bowls of tasty soup, thick with vegetables and pieces of meat, brown bread made of coarse rye, and red wine that was strong and tangy. Corbett sipped it whilst waiting for the soup to cool. He grinned at the priest.

'I have drunk much worse in many of London's taverns,' he commented. 'In fact, it would be difficult to find better.'

Father Edmund smiled in appreciation.

'It's my one weakness,' he murmured. 'No, no, I am not a toper but I do love red wine. Do you know, the blessed Thomas of Becket, when he became Archbishop, gave up the joys of the world but the one thing he would never sacrifice was his claret.' Father Edmund's eyes grew serious. 'This comes from a small tun given to me by Robin Hood. Or, as he was baptised in the church next door, Robin of Locksley. Why have you come here, Sir Hugh? To trap and hang him?' The priest moved uneasily on his stool. 'We have heard the stories.'

'What stories, Father?'

'The attack upon the tax-collectors, the brutal deaths.' The priest cradled his wine cup and stared into the fire. 'God knows why,' he breathed, 'but Robin came back from the wars a bitter man.'

'You've met him?' Corbett asked.

'Yes, at the end of November. He visited me here.'

'How did he seem?'

'Weary. Don't forget, Sir Hugh, he is in his fifties and sickened by the sights seen whilst serving with the King's armies in Scotland. He said he'd had enough of King and court and was going to Kirklees where the Lady Mary was sheltering.'

'Was he by himself?'

'Yes. He just walked into the village on foot, that great long bow slung over his shoulder. I asked him where Little John was, or more appropriately John Little. Robin said that John had deserted from the King's armies and they had agreed to meet at Kirklees.'

'Did Robin say what he was going to do in the future?'

'He said he would take Lady Mary away from Kirklees. They would marry in my church and become "Lord and Lady Stay At Home".'

Corbett broke up his bread, crumbled it into the soup and carefully sipped from the horn spoon.

'But he never came back, did he?' Corbett asked between mouthfuls.

'No,' Father Edmund sighed. 'He left here the next morning. Something happened at Kirklees. Something which changed Robin. He didn't return here and the manor at Locksley is now decaying under the care of an old steward.' The priest shook his head. 'I can't understand it. Robin walked up that road and disappeared.' He sipped from his cup. 'I heard no more until the stories began to circulate, so I went to Kirklees. The Lady Prioress, Dame Elizabeth Stainham, is a distant kinswoman of Robin. She had afforded protection to the Lady Mary.' Father

Edmund raised his thin shoulders. 'She could tell me nothing. Robin had arrived. Little John was already waiting for him. The Lady Mary joined them and, instead of going to Locksley, they went back into Sherwood. She, too, was surprised and shocked at the stories she had heard.' Father Edmund stared anxiously at his guest. 'What will happen to him, Sir Hugh?'

Corbett put the earthenware bowl down.

'I won't lie, Father. They'll hunt him down. If Sir Peter Branwood does not catch him, if Sir Guy of Gisborne fails, if I cannot entice him out into the open, the King will send others north. They will double and treble the price on his head and one day they'll find a traitor to betray him.'

The priest looked away but not quickly enough. Corbett saw the tears pricking those sad old eyes.

'Why, Father Edmund? Why did Robin change?'

'Listen,' the priest continued. 'Listen to this, Sir Hugh.'

He shuffled over to the parish chest, unclasped the three padlocks and scrabbled around, muttering. He lifted up the candle, gave a murmur of satisfaction and came back with a small scrap of parchment in his hand. The priest smoothed the parchment out on his lap and, holding the candle over it, began to read.

'Once,' he declared, his finger following the line of words, 'a poor peasant man died but his soul was unclaimed by either angel or devil. However, the peasant was determined to reach Paradise and eventually arrived outside its gates. Here St Peter came before him. "Go away, peasant!" he cried. "Peasants are not allowed into heaven!"

'"Why not?" the peasant shouted back. "You, Peter, denied Christ. I have never done that. You, St Paul, persecuted Christians and I have never done that. You, bishops and priests, have neglected others and I have never done that."

'St Peter,' Father Edmund continued, enjoying the story, 'eventually called for Christ to drive the peasant off and Le Bon Seigneur arrived, clothed in glory, outside the gates of Paradise.

' "Judge me, O Christ!" the peasant cried, "You caused me to be born in misery but I endured my troubles without complaint. I was told to believe in the gospel and I did. I was told to share my bread and water with the poor and I did. In sickness I confessed and received the sacraments. I kept your commandments. I fought to gain Paradise because you told me to. So here I shall stay."

'Christ smiled at the peasant and turned to reprove Peter. "Let this man come in for he is to sit at my right hand and become a lord of heaven." '

Father Edmund finished speaking and stared down at the piece of parchment which he reverently curled up into a thin scroll.

'You may ask, Sir Hugh, who wrote that? I did, but I copied it word for word from a speech Robin of Locksley gave to the villagers on the last Yuletide before he went north to join the King's armies in Scotland. That is why I took you from that ale house. If any man, woman or child in this village thought you meant to harm Robin of Locksley, they would kill you!'

And before Corbett could stop him, the priest threw the piece of parchment into the fire.

'But now it's all over,' the priest murmured. 'The soul of the man who spoke those words is dead.' He smiled and blinked back the tears. 'And I am a babbling old priest who drank strong wine too quickly. I can say no more about Robin Hood.'

They finished their meal. Corbett helped the old priest wash the cups and bowls then Father Edmund insisted that Corbett use his bed.

'You are not taking anything I need,' he declared. 'I am old. From the cemetery outside I have heard the owl hoot my name. Death can't be far off so I spend my nights praying before the altar.' He grinned sheepishly. 'Though I do confess, I spend some of the time sleeping.'

The priest doused the fire, made sure his guest was comfortable and then slipped quietly into the night.

Corbett lay down on the hard bed and thought about what the priest had told him, but within minutes he was fast asleep. He woke refreshed the next morning to find Father Edmund busying himself in the kitchen. Outside the sun had not yet burnt off the thick mist which shrouded the cemetery and church. It was still quite cold. Corbett shivered as he put his cloak round his shoulders and followed the old priest across the graveyard to celebrate the dawn mass.

Afterwards they broke their fast in the kitchen. Father Edmund, in a lighter mood, refused any payment and avidly listened to Corbett's talk of the outside world. At last the clerk got to his feet.

'Father, I must go. Your generosity is much appreciated. Are you sure I cannot pay?'

The old priest shook his head.

'Only one favour or boon I ask,' he replied. 'If the outlaw is captured alive – and I repeat if – I would like to see him before any sentence is carried out. Now, listen.'

Father Edmund busied himself to hide his distress. He dug into his old leather wallet and brought out a small metal badge depicting the head of St James Compostela. He handed this to Corbett and smiled.

'When I was younger and much more nimble, I went to the shrine in Spain and brought scores of these back as proof. Show this to Naismith. He is the old steward of Locksley. He'll know that I sent you. God speed!'

Corbett thanked the priest, assuring him that he would try and grant his favour. He collected his horse and, remembering Father Edmund's directions, rode through the silent village. He followed the cobbled track which wound through the open fields to where Locksley Manor stood on the brow of a small hill. The mist began to lift, the sun strengthening. Nevertheless Corbett found Locksley Manor an eerie, ghostly place. The double wooden gates hung askew on their hinges, the surrounding wall was beginning to crumble, whilst the pathways up to the main door and the yards and gardens were overgrown by brambles and weeds. One part of the roof had already lost its tiles. The windows were firmly shuttered, the paint and wood on the outside beginning to decay.

Corbett left his horse to crop a small patch of grass which surrounded a disused fountain and hammered on the front door, shouting for Naismith. The sound echoed eerily through the empty house. Corbett thought the place deserted then he heard the shuffle of feet and the jangle of keys. Locks were turned and the door swung open. A small, squat, bald-headed man glared up at him.

'Can't a man sleep?' he bawled, scratching his pate, shiny as a pigeon's egg. 'I goes to sleep and wakes to hear a knocking as if Angel Gabriel is here. What's the matter? Is it the last trumpet?'

Corbett hid a smile and politely introduced himself, displaying the ring he wore and, more importantly, Father Edmund's metal badge. Naismith's watery, short-sighted eyes peered up at him.

'Not an angel,' he muttered. 'Perhaps a demon. You'd better come in! You'd better come in!'

Corbett followed him down the dank, dilapidated passageway. He noticed how the plaster on the walls was beginning to flake; the paving-stones underfoot were cracked; some doors were bolted whilst others hung askew. The manor house had been cleared of all its possessions, not even a stick of furniture or a tawdry arras remained. The walls were completely bare. Naismith led Corbett into a small buttery. The clerk gazed round and realised Naismith lived, slept and ate here for it boasted a small cot bed, chest, a table, stools and, rather incongruously, a high-backed chair, cleverly carved with a quilted leather backing and cushion. Naismith sat himself down in this as grandly as a prince.

'What do you want?' he asked guardedly.

Corbett explained and was pleased to see Naismith's hard face soften.

'Father Edmund's correct,' Naismith replied. 'God knows what happened to the master. He comes back from the wars tired and sickened of blood, yet still full of hope. He was only here a few hours then he says he's off to Kirklees. He wants to see the Lady Mary. So off he goes. He said he would return. He swore he would. He said he had gold to refurbish the manor.' Naismith slumped in the chair. 'But he didn't come back,' he continued weakly. 'I hears he goes to Kirklees then back to Sherwood where the killing began.'

'Did he say anything?' Corbett queried.

'He was bitter. Bitter about the King, bitter about life; sad he had left Mary but looking forward to meeting her and John Little at Kirklees. At first I thought that the Robin of Locksley I knew and the murderer in Sherwood were two different people, but they aren't.' Naismith got up and shuffled towards a small coffer. He brought out sheafs of parchment, greasy and finger-marked, and thrust these at Corbett. 'You see, Master, when Robin was in Sherwood he'd often send me messages. Of course, he was wary of any law officer trying to trap him here so we agreed he would always use a purple type of ink and seal each letter with his own secret mark.'

Corbett studied the manuscripts, some faded, others more recent.

'Was he literate?' Corbett asked. 'Could he read and write?'

'A little, but he always got some clerk to write for him. God knows, Master, there's enough wolvesheads, if you'll pardon my saying so, who began their careers in the halls of Cambridge or Oxford.'

Corbett smiled and studied the scraps of parchment.

'And the secret mark?'

Naismith pointed to a small blob of wax on the corner of a manuscript. Corbett took this over to the light and studied it carefully. The wax bore the imprint, rather crude but effective, of a man standing, bow in one hand, arrow in the other. He knew such signets were common for landowners, even yeomen, had to certify documents and protect themselves against forgery.

Corbett quickly read the most recent messages, merely requests for Naismith to sell all the manor's moveables, both furniture and stock, and arrange to have the monies collected late at night.

'What happened?' Corbett asked. 'Did the outlaw return and collect what was his?'

'Sometimes at night. It only happened on two or three occasions. A man would arrive bearing a message from Robin, I would hand the money over and the fellow would disappear like some will-o'-the-wisp.'

'Why?' Corbett asked.

'Why what?'

'Why would the outlaw sell everything he had here?'

Naismith shrugged as if past caring. 'Like Father Edmund, I am an old man,' he said. 'I have done what I can and can do no more. I have served this family since I could walk. If the master orders something, then Naismith does it. But, to answer your question bluntly, I don't think Robin of Locksley wishes to come back here.' Naismith shrugged and looked around. 'After all, the manor is not much: stables, some pastures, a little arable. Perhaps the master may go away.'

'And you can tell me no more?'

'What I know you now know, and that is the end of the matter.'

Corbett thanked Naismith, collected his horse and rode back to the trackway. The morning mist was now burnt off and the sun already felt hot on his back. For a while he listened to the sounds from the fields: the chatter of insects, the cries of the foraging birds, and the haunting, liquid song of the wood dove. Corbett stared round satisfied he was in no danger. His pursuer had either given up the chase or perhaps was waiting for another day and another place. He kicked his horse gently forward then stopped and stared back at the dilapidated manor. Everything pointed to Kirklees. Something had happened there which had tipped Robin of Locksley's mind into a maelstrom of murderous madness. A man devoted to revenge. But why? And how could Corbett trap him?

He sat chewing the quick of his thumb nail. It was already approaching the end of June. The King wanted a reply on the matter of the cipher in the next few days. Corbett felt uneasy. But how could he resolve it, keep himself safe from the assassin Achitophel and track down an outlaw who was as elusive as a shadow in the thickness of Sherwood Forest? He stared down at the ring on his finger. The King had given him one final choice.

'If you can't do it, Corbett,' he had roared, 'if you can't stop this bloody outlaw, then offer him a pardon, an amnesty for all crimes, provided he returns my taxes and pays blood-money for the men he killed!'

Corbett gazed unseeingly across the fields. Should he do so? A bird fluttered in a tree nearby, making him think about the great oaks and elms which surrounded Leighton Manor. A sudden thought made his heart jump. What if Achitophel was not tracking him? Perhaps the murderous assault at the tavern was the work of the outlaw, intent on killing Corbett as he had Sir Eustace Vechey? If that was the case where was the assassin? Was he in Nottingham? London? Or, even worse, out at Leighton Manor, perhaps threatening Maeve and his household? Should he go back there? Corbett kicked his horse forward.

'De Craon would like that,' he spoke aloud. 'That would warm the cockles of his cold heart. Corbett being so distressed he leaves everything to protect his own kith and kin . . .'

In a secret chamber high in the Louvre Palace, Philip Le Bel, King of France, knelt before a statue of his sainted ancestor the Blessed Louis, and prayed for the success of his armies in Flanders. The French King was noted both for his beauty and impassivity, his marble white face, strange green eyes and bloodless lips framed by the lustrous Capetian blond hair.

Yet Philip felt both distracted and excited. He closed his eyes and thought about the troops now camped along his northern borders. Squadrons of heavy cavalry. Rank after rank of Genoese bowmen. The great lords with their foot soldiers, the banners, the golden lilies on a sea-blue background and, furled in the tent of his own commander, the Sacred Oriflamme, the King's own banner, usually kept behind the high altar at St Denis. When Philip gave the word, this banner would be taken out and flown as a sign to the rebellious Flemings that Philip's soldiers would take no prisoners.

He breathed in deeply. His spies in the Flemish towns had sent letters south full of good news. How, in each city those Flemings partial to his cause, the 'Lileantists' or Lily Men, were ready to open the gates to his soldiers. Philip could have hugged himself with glee. Those Flemings who resisted were hopping like fleas on a hot plate, sending plea after plea to Edward of England for help and assistance. But Edward couldn't do that, he was bound by treaty. Oh, he could send gold secretly but what use would that be? The Flemings might hire soldiers and buy arms from the princes across the Rhine, but where would they deploy such men? As one of Philip's spies put it, they were 'like rabbits huddled in their burrow, not knowing through which hole the ferret will come'. Philip knew, his two counsellors seated behind him at the table also, the dark-faced William of Nogaret and pale, red-bearded Amaury de Craon.

Philip crossed himself and got to his feet. He heard a faint cry from the courtyard below and opened the stained-glass window to peer out. For a while he watched the scene below. A huge wheel had been fixed against the wall of the courtyard and a man had been strapped to it, hands and feet lashed to the spokes. One executioner turned the wheel whilst another, using a slim iron bar, broke the man's arms and legs and pounded his naked body. Now and again the prisoner would regain consciousness and scream for mercy as his bruised body quivered in pain, but the torture went on. Philip watched the scene: the soldiers on guard, the great mastiffs near the execution platform barking excitedly at the scent of blood, the careful precise movements of the executioner.

'How long?' he said softly over his shoulder.

'A week, Your Grace.'

Philip nodded and closed the window. The man had suffered enough.

'If he's still alive by tomorrow morning, hang him in the small orchard near the chancery. That will encourage my clerks to be more careful with the secrets entrusted to them.'

'It's good for the man to suffer,' de Craon began slowly. 'But Corbett now has that cipher, Your Grace. If he unlocks the secret . . .'

'I agree,' Nogaret added harshly. 'Your Grace, I beg you to change your plans.'

'Nonsense!' Philip replied. 'I devised that cipher myself. To change it now would cause confusion, perhaps even delay. Edward of England's envoys are already busy at the papal court, trying to urge that fat lump who calls himself Pope Boniface VIII to issue letters condemning our design on Flanders.'

'And we are paying the Holy Father to delay,' Nogaret replied.

'In which case,' the French King breathed, 'Edward of England may have to wait until hell freezes over!' He sat down in the high-backed chair. 'We still have Achitophel. Has he written back?'

De Craon pulled a face. 'He could find no news in London so forged messages to Corbett's manor at Leighton to discover his whereabouts.' De Craon smiled. 'Achitophel was in Nottingham before Edward's beloved clerk arrived there.'

'Nottingham?' Philip looked puzzled.

'Good news, Your Grace. Edward of England is having difficulties in controlling the roads north to Scotland. There's talk of murder and outlaws.' De Craon grinned. 'Another fly in the English ointment.' His face became hard. 'But is it wise to kill Corbett?'

Philip stared at his enigmatic Master of Secrets then burst out laughing. His two counsellors watched, stony-faced.

'Your Grace?'

Philip wagged a finger at de Craon.

'You are concerned, Amaury! I can follow your mind. If we kill Edward of England's beloved clerk then Edward will retaliate by killing one of mine.' He leaned over and pinched de Craon's wrist. 'In this case, perhaps you?'

De Craon blinked and schooled his features. He had no illusions about his royal master. Men said Philip of France had a stone instead of a heart, dedicated to one pursuit and one pursuit only: the glory of the Capetian name. His dream was to build an empire as great as Charlemagne's. De Craon stared obliquely across the table. He or even Nogaret were mere stepping stones in such a grand design.

Philip shook his head and stared at the alabaster carved statue of St Louis.

'Don't worry about Master Corbett. Achitophel has his orders. The clerk is to die in a way which will provoke very little suspicion, and Edward of England will soon have more to worry about than the death of a mere commoner. Now.' He moved the chess pieces aside and quickly sifted amongst the parchments on the table. 'Everything is ready?'

'Everything,' Nogaret agreed. 'Except the date.'

Philip leaned back in his chair and rocked himself gently. He was sure God would give him a sign. He heard another cry from the courtyard and stared at the number of candles flickering in front of St Louis' statue.

'By the end of June,' he murmured, 'the harvest should be ready and ripe for plucking.' He counted the number of candles again, ten in all. Philip leaned forward. 'Send the cipher to the Marshal. Tell him he is to cross into Flanders at first light on the tenth of July. Oh, by the way,' he jerked his silvery head towards the window, 'the fellow's cries are disturbing me. I have changed my mind. If he's still alive by dusk, hang him!'

Chapter 10

Corbett found his reception at Kirklees Priory far from cordial. For a while he was forced to kick his heels in the great gatehouse before a grumbling lay sister led him across the dry grass to the Prioress's private parlour. Dame Elizabeth Stainham was just as frosty in her welcome. Tall and thin, with sharp features, she coldly acknowledged Corbett's greetings. Dame Elizabeth only mellowed, inviting him to sit and partake of some wine and sweetmeats, when the clerk brusquely informed her of his status at court and the King's confidence in him.

'Well, well, well!' she murmured and sat back in her chair, pulling at the sleeves of her dark brown gown. Corbett noticed with amusement how these were edged with white fur and the smock beneath fashioned out of glistening satin. He gazed round the opulent room: the woollen rugs on the floor, the heavy polished furniture, the slender wax candles in their holders, the bowls of rose water, the Venetian glasses on a silver tray and cloths of gold, silver and damask hanging on the walls. Dame Elizabeth, he concluded, lived as grandly as any countess and the white wine she served him was cool and fragrant to the taste, proof that the Prioress bought her wines from the best merchants in York or London.

'Sir Hugh?'

Corbett blinked. The Prioress had asked a question.

'My Lady, I am sorry, the journey was fatiguing.'

Again the false smile.

'Sir Hugh, I asked you what has the King's Commissioner to do with our humble house?'

'Nothing really, My Lady. We are more interested in a visitor you had quite recently, as well as a woman who stayed here. You know them both well: Robin of Locksley, a distant kinsman of yours, and the Lady Mary?'

Dame Elizabeth may have been able to mask her emotions with a cold demeanour but Corbett could have sworn she nearly dropped her wine glass. The Prioress put this back on the table and Corbett caught the nervous shaking of her hands and the flicker of anxiety in her eyes.

'Dame Elizabeth, you seem upset?'

The Prioress licked her thin lips.

'Not upset, Sir Hugh, more angry. We have heard of the outlaw's depredations. I am ashamed that we share the same blood! Even more distressed that we gave shelter to a woman who now runs wild with wolvesheads in the darkness of a forest!'

'My Lady.' Corbett leaned forward, placing his hands on the desk which separated them. 'The King is determined that this outlaw be brought to book and yet, according to what I have discovered, Robin of Locksley left the King's army in Scotland determined to marry the Lady Mary and live out his days in peace at Locksley. The priest there, Father Edmund, has said this. The outlaw's old steward repeats it. So, what happened to change Robin's mind?'

The Prioress rose to her feet and began pacing up and down, pretending to adjust the wimple on her head or smoothe the voluminous sleeves of her gown. Corbett could see she was still trying to hide her agitation.

'My Lady,' he added softly, 'I am the King's Commissioner in this matter and have asked you a question.'

The Prioress stood still and glared at him. Corbett flinched at the hatred in her eyes.

'I detest Robin of Locksley!' she spat out. 'I always have! His love of the common man. The way the vulgus recount his exploits. His swaggering arrogance and his violation of the King's laws, only to be rewarded by that same King himself.' Dame Elizabeth paused, clenching her hands.

'So why?' Corbett interrupted, studying the woman's hate-filled face. 'Why did you give sanctuary to his love?'

'Because he asked me to!' she spat back. 'Because I felt sorry for the Lady Mary. Because I thought I could rescue her and lead her back to the path of righteousness.'

Oh, I am sure you did, Corbett thought. You would have been only too happy to see the relationship end. To hide a woman Robin loved away from his eyes and those of the world.

'Did the Lady Mary become a nun?'

'No, she professed no vows but stayed here like other ladies, widows and women who seek refuge from the world of men. And she was happy until . . .'

'Until Robin returned?'

'Exactly!'

'Why did the Lady Mary come here in the first place?' Corbett asked.

'When Robin accepted the King's pardon, one of the conditions was that he serve for a while with the royal army in Scotland. Lady Mary was disappointed, deeply hurt that Robin could forget her so quickly and put the King's wishes before her.' Dame Elizabeth smiled thinly. 'Like many men, Robin made promises he never kept.'

'But he did come back?'

'Oh, yes, swaggering through the gatehouse. He and that great hulk, John Little, sitting on their war horses like lords come to judgement.'

'And the Lady Mary?'

'For a while she and Robin were closeted in the guest house.'

'And then?'

The Prioress shrugged and sat back in her chair.

'Like any silly girl, Lady Mary's head was turned. She packed a few belongings and rode off with the love of her life.'

'Yet they did not return to Locksley but to their outlaw ways in Sherwood?'

'I cannot answer for that,' Dame Elizabeth snapped. 'But when you catch him, *if* you catch him, Sir Hugh, you can ask him that question just before he's turned off the ladder on the gallows.' She leaned back, steepling her fingers. 'If you do not believe me, ask any of the sisters in this nunnery.'

Corbett was glad to escape that oppressive room. He was uneasy at what Dame Elizabeth had told him but there was nothing he could do. Whatever had turned Robin from a peace-loving soldier into an outlaw, ever ready to violate the King's peace, was still not resolved.

The problem was nagging at Corbett when he arrived back in Nottingham the following day. He found the castle in an uproar. Sir Peter Branwood met him in the outer bailey and, before Corbett could even ask for Ranulf or Maltote, led him across, through the Middle Gate, to a coffin which lay before the altar in the small chapel. Corbett, tired and bruised after his journey, watched wordlessly as Sir Peter swept away the purple pall, prised open the coffin lid with his dagger and pulled back the gauze covering.

Corbett took one look and turned away, gagging. Gisborne lay there. The embalmer, or whoever had dressed the body for burial, had done his or her best and the blood had been washed from the jagged neck, but the decapitated, bruised head still lay askew. Corbett recognised Gisborne's features despite the face being covered with purple-red bruises, as if the head had been bounced like a ball. He sat down on the altar steps and watched as Branwood re-sealed the coffin.

'So Gisborne met with failure?'

'You could say that,' Branwood sarcastically replied. 'He lost over a dozen of his own men. My Lord of Gisborne,' he tapped the side of the coffin, 'would not be advised and tried to take on the outlaw horde. We went to assist but returned within the hour. Gisborne was already too deep in the forest.' Branwood sheathed his dagger. 'Yesterday evening his body was pitched on the Brewhouse stairs with his head alongside in a barrel of pickled pork. If I may advise, Sir Hugh, in your next letter to the King, perhaps you could tell His Grace that with regard to Nottinghamshire outlaws, their capture and execution should be entrusted to those officers the King has appointed here.'

'I shall tell him that,' Corbett muttered as Branwood strode out of the chapel.

The clerk got wearily to his feet, picked up his saddlebag and cloak, genuflected to the altar and wandered across the inner bailey to his own chamber in King John's tower. He found this deserted but checked that everything was as he had left it, including those items he'd filched from Vechey's room. He washed, changed and lay for a while on the bed, half-dozing until woken by Ranulf and Maltote.

'Was your journey successful?' his manservant asked.

Corbett pulled a face.

'You have heard of Gisborne's defeat and death?'

'The whole town is buzzing with the news,' Ranulf replied.

Corbett rubbed his eyes.

'And you, Ranulf, any success with that cipher?'

He mournfully shook his head.

Corbett rose and stretched. 'Maltote, be so kind as to fetch some wine and perhaps some bread from the buttery. Tell that surly cook the King's Commissioner demands it.'

He waited until the messenger had slipped out of the room.

'Ranulf, this mystery of the outlaw.' Corbett threw up his hands in exasperation. 'If a man like Gisborne cannot trap him then what chance do you and I have? The cipher is still a mystery and time is passing. Once those French troops cross into Flanders, the King will need us in London. Oh, by the way.' He walked over to Ranulf. 'On my journey to Kirklees, someone tried to poison me. Did you tell anyone here where I was going?'

Ranulf's face looked the picture of innocence as he raised his hands. 'As God is my witness, Master, I did not even discuss the matter with Maltote.'

'Well, someone tried to kill me. Either the traitor in the castle or . . .'

'Achitophel?'

Corbett nodded.

Maltote returned with a jug of wine, three cups and a platter containing some small white loaves and strips of dried bacon. They sat round the table, Corbett sharing out the food as he listened to Ranulf chatter about what had happened in the castle since his departure.

'And the fair Amisia?' he interrupted. 'Have you seen her today?'

'No.' Ranulf grinned. 'Maltote and I were separating some of Sir Peter's soldiers from their coins.'

Corbett chewed his bread and half-listened as Ranulf gleefully described how some of Gisborne's foresters, after their return to the castle following their master's death, had boasted how easy it was to beat Maltote at hazard. Ranulf had been only too eager to put the matter straight with what he called his 'miraculous dice'.

Corbett had finished eating and taken out his writing implements when there was a loud knocking on the door.

'Come in!' he shouted.

A castle servant entered, a man Corbett did not recognise behind him.

'It's Halfan!' Ranulf exclaimed. 'The landlord of The Cock and Hoop.' His smile faded at the landlord's sombre look.

'He wants to see you,' the servant explained. 'Sir Peter Branwood told me to bring him here.'

'Very well,' Ranulf replied. 'You may go. Halfan, what's wrong?'

The taverner waited until the servant closed the door behind him.

'Master,' the landlord's eyes flickered, 'I have bad news!'

'What is it? The Lady Amisia?'

'No, no, the wench is well. It's her brother, Rahere the Riddle Master. He was found murdered this morning in an alleyway just off from the tavern. Someone had garrotted him.'

'What?' Ranulf sat down on a stool.

'Probably thieves,' the landlord continued. 'He always carried a heavy purse and this has now gone. They took his belt and boots. The rogues must have been stalking him from the market place.'

Corbett looked at Ranulf's white face and hastily refilled his cup.

'And the girl?' Corbett asked.

'As I said, she's safe. Hysterical, so I called the local physician who gave her some wine and valerian drops.'

Corbett remembered the bow string round Hecate the poisoner's throat.

'Come on, Ranulf, Maltote!' he urged.

He fairly hustled the taverner and his two companions out of the chamber and down the steps. Taking great care to stay away from the castle garrison, they slipped through the postern gate of the inner bailey and down into the town.

The Cock and Hoop tavern was quiet as they entered. The landlord explained that he had done the 'Christian thing' by having the corpse laid out in one of his outhouses for the coroner's visit.

'God knows what will happen,' the fellow muttered. 'The wench is almost witless and all the coroner could declare was murder by person or persons unknown.'

He led them across the cobbled yard, lifted the latch and took Corbett and his companions into a sweet-smelling stable. The man nervously lit oil lamps placed on the wall and pulled back the sacking covering the corpse stretched out on freshly laid straw.

'Two corpses in one morning,' Corbett muttered.

He knelt beside the Riddle Master, trying not to look at the blue-black face, protuberant eyes and tongue. He looked at the cord wrapped round the man's neck. Maltote had already backed out, his face turning a tinge of green, whilst Ranulf was caught between grief for his new-found friend and distress for the loss his sweet Amisia must now be suffering.

'It's the same,' Corbett muttered, getting to his feet. He carefully pulled the sheet back over the man's face.

The taverner extinguished the oil lights and they went back into the yard.

'Apart from Ranulf,' Corbett asked, 'did this Rahere speak to anyone else?'

'He was well known.' The landlord scratched his balding pate. 'But he kept to himself. Sometimes he would set us a riddle. He was always either here or in the market place. He did say he wanted to visit the castle, and on one occasion I think he left Nottingham.'

'When?'

'According to one of my customers, about three days ago. He left in a hurry but then returned.'

Corbett stepped back. Three days ago he had begun his journey to Locksley and Kirklees. He looked angrily at Ranulf.

'I told no one in the castle.' Ranulf was quick-witted

enough to catch the drift of Corbett's thoughts. His eyes fell. 'Or here. Except Amisia.'

Corbett dug into his purse and brought out a coin which he flashed before the inn-keeper's shrewd eyes.

'This is for the corpse. A swift burial in a town cemetery. And this,' he plucked out a second coin, 'is permission to go through the dead man's baggage.'

The taverner needed no second bidding but took Corbett, Ranulf and a now gaping Maltote up to the dead man's chamber.

'It will be empty,' he explained. 'The wench, I mean the Lady Amisia, is in another chamber.'

Corbett thanked him. Once the taverner had disappeared, Corbett ordered Ranulf and Maltote to search the chamber and pile the dead man's belongings in the middle of the bed.

At first there was nothing: clothing, belts, baldricks, hose, change of boots, some spoons, a chased silver cup. But then Ranulf, eager now to make up for his mistake, pushed aside the bed and, using his old skills as a burglar, began to test the floor boards. He cried out in delight as he prised one loose and brought out a small coffer. It was no more than a foot long and the same wide, secured by three locks. Ranulf handed this to Corbett who, without a second thought, broke all three locks with his dagger. He then sat on the edge of the bed, sifting through the parchments.

'Ah!' Corbett put the manuscripts aside, grabbed his dagger and jabbed at the bottom of the casket, lifting the wooden slats to reveal a secret compartment. He plucked out a small medal and a roll of parchment which he quickly studied.

'Our friend Rahere was in truth a Riddle Master,' he commented wryly.

Corbett tossed the unfurled parchment at Ranulf, who scanned the Norman French: signed by William of Nogaret and sealed with the Privy Seal of France, the letter instructed all seneschals, bailiffs and officers in the kingdom of France to give every support to the King's most trusted servant, Rahere.

'It was dangerous to carry this,' he remarked.

'Not really,' Corbett answered. 'Many French merchants carry such warrants.'

He handed the medal over and Ranulf scrutinised the portrait of a king sitting on a throne.

'Who is it?' Ranulf asked.

'Philip's grandfather, the sainted Louis. To an ordinary English harbour official, such a medal would appear innocuous. However, they are only given to very trusted servants of the French King. If Rahere showed such a medal, together with that strip of parchment, he'd be allowed access to any castle or town, be able to draw monies or demand military support. Ranulf, your good friend Rahere, God rest him, was Philip's most trusted agent as well as that skilful assassin, Achitophel!'

Corbett perused more pieces of the parchment. 'And who would suspect a Riddle Master? I tell you this, Rahere or Achitophel, God damn him, was responsible for the deaths of at least a score of my agents. And if I carried out an investigation into the circumstances surrounding their deaths, I am sure some witness would remember that, coincidence upon coincidence, Rahere the Riddle Master was somewhere in the vicinity when they died. We always did wonder how Achitophel could not only kill people in France but also in England. Of course a travelling minstrel, especially a man of his skill, would be welcome anywhere.' Corbett laughed sourly. 'I wager there are at least six members of the King's own Privy Council who would be prepared to sing his praises, afford him protection, provide hospitality, write out safe conducts and references.'

'Well, how did he know you were in Nottingham?'

'Oh, I expect the Lady Maeve, perhaps Lord Morgan

Llewellyn, the Earl of Surrey, even the King himself, has been skilfully approached by this trickster and handed the information over to him without a second thought.'

Ranulf, staring moodily at the floor, nodded and glared at Maltote who was softly tut-tutting under his breath.

'You can shut up!' he hissed. 'You liked him as much as I did! Master, do you think Amisia is also guilty?'

Corbett pursed his lips and shook his head. 'I doubt it. It's a fairly common trick. I mean, apart from the Lady Maeve, how many other people know of the human filth we wade through, Ranulf? It's a well-known device,' Corbett continued bitterly, 'and one used time and again. A group of monks go through Dover; seven are genuine, the eighth is a spy. A collection of merchants go to Canterbury; all seem honest burgesses but one's a spy. Or the troupe of jugglers, the gaggle of students. In this case, Ranulf, it's the beautiful sister who'll attract attention, not the merry rhymester.' Corbett added. 'Yet she will still have to be questioned.'

'But,' Maltote interrupted briskly, 'if Rahere came to Nottingham, Master, he had no guarantee of meeting you.'

'Achitophel was no back-street thug or roaring boy, Maltote,' Corbett replied. 'He was a skilled assassin. He would search out the terrain, plan his move and carry out murder as swiftly and silently as a plunging hawk. Three days ago I left for Locksley. Ranulf chatters to Amisia, Amisia chatters to her brother who hastens after me. And what better way of killing one of the King's clerks? All the coroner would declare was that I ate something which did not agree with me. I would be dressed for burial, coffined and laid beneath the sod before anyone really knew who I was.'

'I am sorry, Master,' Ranulf apologised. 'I was tricked like some coney in the hay.'

Corbett shrugged. 'Don't apologise, Ranulf. Your friendship with Rahere might still bear fruit. You see

Rahere, or Achitophel, would have two orders. One was to kill me but the second would be to discover if I had broken the cipher.' Corbett stared directly at his manservant. 'You did discuss the cipher with the Riddle Master?'

Ranulf closed his eyes. 'Yes,' he mumbled. 'But, as God is my witness, I never gave him the reason why.'

'You wouldn't have to,' Maltote tactlessly retorted, and got a swift kick in the shins for his pains.

'Of course,' Corbett continued, ignoring the pantomime, 'Achitophel soon realised we hadn't broken the cipher, and planned my death. That's why he wanted to meet me. Like an executioner who studies a man's weight and stance before putting the noose round his neck and turning him off the ladder. Perhaps I might reveal some weakness or details of a journey I was planning.' He looked over at Ranulf. 'I don't suppose he was any help with the cipher?'

'No, Master, but what's in those pieces of parchment?'

'Nothing remarkable. Letters from friends and acquaintances which may be ciphers carrying instructions and other messages. My colleagues at Westminster will enjoy studying them.' Corbett sifted amongst the pieces of paper on the bed. 'Nevertheless . . .'

'Who killed him?' Ranulf suddenly asked.

Corbett began to laugh softly, much to the surprise of Ranulf and Maltote who could count on the fingers of one hand the number of times Master Long Face laughed in a week.

'Master, what is so funny?' Ranulf snapped.

'Can't you see, Ranulf? Rahere or Achitophel made the greatest mistake which can beset any assassin or hunter. Indeed, he has much in common with Gisborne. In both cases the hunter became the hunted. We know there is a traitor in the castle. He would watch us and become intrigued by your constant visits and deep conversations with a mere Riddle Master in a Nottinghamshire tavern.'

Realisation dawned on Ranulf.

'Of course!' he breathed. 'And the traitor would think Rahere some agent of the King, a spy providing valuable assistance to us here in Nottingham?'

'Correct! Did you see anyone from the garrison keeping a close watch on you, Rahere or this tavern?'

Ranulf shook his head. 'Never once.'

'Of course our traitor would have to be very careful. And what do you do with a problem you can't resolve, Ranulf, eh?' Corbett pulled a face. 'The simplest solution is to remove the mystery and murder Rahere. For his part, Achitophel was so intent on watching us, so confident in his own disguise, he would never suspect danger from another quarter. I suppose he left the tavern this morning on some personal errand, was attacked, quickly garrotted, and his purse and boots removed to make it look as if he was the victim of some alleyway assault.'

'Amisia will blame us,' Ranulf mournfully replied.

'No,' Corbett assured him. 'For the moment, Ranulf, do not tell her why we are here, or indeed anything about her brother's secret profession. She will take time to recover from this grievous wound alone. Further revelations might drive her out of her wits.'

Corbett resumed his sifting amongst the pieces of paper on the bed.

'What are you searching for, Master?'

'Achitophel or Rahere was an intelligent man, a well-paid agent, a trusted spy of King Philip, but he would not know the cipher until you gave it to him. Tell me, Ranulf, if you were in his position, bored, waiting for events to develop as you lounged about some tawdry provincial town, what would you do? You are, by nature,' Corbett continued, 'a solver of riddles.'

'I would try to solve this one,' Ranulf reflected. 'I would see it as a challenge.'

'Exactly! Of course, Rahere would never tell you but he

would have to satisfy himself. Remember, Ranulf, he was a well-placed agent who knew the minds of his masters in Paris. What I am looking for is some indication of the path he followed.'

'He always told me it could be some poem or song,' Ranulf crossly added.

'So we will ignore all those,' Corbett muttered, much to Maltote's delight.

Corbett checked the papers again. Most of them bore riddles or rhyming poems. One piece, however, caught his eye and he plucked it out. Corbett studied this carefully: a crude portrayal of a chess board.

'I wonder?' he scratched his head and sat on the edge of the bed.

The landlord came back and asked if there was anything they wanted. Corbett absentmindedly asked for some wine, a quill, and an ink horn. Then, with Ranulf and Maltote craning over his shoulder, he began to add to the manuscript, writing down each piece: king, queen, bishop, knight, castle, pawn.

An hour passed, the wine jug emptied and Corbett's exasperation grew.

'You see,' he commented loudly as if talking to himself, 'every cipher is based on something: the titles of books, verses from the scriptures, the names of angels or the first letter of certain towns. But this is different.'

Ranulf jabbed a dirty finger.

'Why is the piece of parchment so neatly divided down the middle?' he asked. 'It's as if Rahere specially creased it, to cut the chess board neatly in half, four rows of squares on either side.'

Corbett held the piece of parchment up to the sunlight pouring through the unshuttered window.

'I wonder?' He got to his feet. 'Look, Ranulf, Maltote, put everything back as you found it. Amisia will soon awaken. Ranulf, stay here and comfort her. Swear the landlord to silence about what we have done. Assure Amisia that I will give her every protection but see if you can learn anything fresh about her brother's activities. Maltote, you come back to the castle.' Corbett became lost in his own thoughts again, the piece of parchment wrapped tightly in his fist.

With Maltote trailing behind, he went back to the castle, taking care to go up the Brewhouse stairs through the postern gate, slipping along the walls, making sure no-one stopped or bothered them. For the first time since his arrival in Nottingham, Corbett felt a thrill of pleasure. Somehow he might break the cipher. He laughed softly at how Philip's own agent had provided the key.

Once back in his chamber Corbett laid his writing implements out on the table, ordering Maltote to help in drawing up crude chess boards.

'Remember, Maltote,' Corbett insisted, 'a perfect square, eight by eight.'

Corbett then began to fill in the squares with the names of the chess pieces. At first Maltote watched but soon grew bored and lay for a while on his bed staring up at the ceiling, wondering where Ranulf was and how long they would stay in this benighted castle. Across the room Master Long Face scratched his head, muttered and swore to himself as pieces of parchment were tossed aside. The sun began to dip. Servants came up, declaring the evening meal was ready, but Corbett told them to go away.

Ranulf returned much the worse for drink, declaring loudly that Lady Amisia was more rested and comforted by their assurances.

'Especially,' Ranulf shouted, 'by the promises Sir Hugh Corbett, Keeper of the Secret Seal, has given her.'

Corbett ignored him and continued with his studies.

'Aren't we going to have something to eat?' Ranulf moaned.

'Not in this castle,' Corbett replied. 'Tighten your belt and think of the banquets awaiting us in London.'

Ranulf shrugged, pulled the dice from his wallet and began to show Maltote the finer points of cheating.

At last, just when they were beginning to despair, Corbett grunted, 'I've got the bastard!'

Ranulf and Maltote wandered over. Corbett looked up, his eyes red-rimmed with tiredness.

'This chess board,' he said, 'has the solution.'

He was about to continue when there was a loud knocking on the door.

'Come in!' Corbett shouted.

Sir Peter Branwood, followed by Roteboeuf, strode into the chamber.

'Sir Hugh,' Branwood queried, 'is all well?'

Corbett stared down at the scrap of parchment.

'Oh, yes, Sir Peter, I think all is well.' He smiled apologetically. 'I am sorry, we are involved in business which does not concern the wolfshead.'

Sir Peter looked nonplussed.

'I will explain later,' Corbett gently added.

'Do you want any victuals?'

'No, no, we have drunk enough.'

Branwood pulled a face and made to leave.

'Sir Peter!'

The under-sheriff turned, one hand on the latch.

'Yes?'

'Why should Lecroix hang himself in the cellar?' Corbett abruptly asked.

'God knows. Remember, Sir Hugh, the castle was under attack. Perhaps he felt safer there.'

Corbett nodded absentmindedly. 'Yes, yes, perhaps he did.'

Once the under-sheriff had left, Corbett went back to the crude chess board he had sketched on a piece of parchment.

'Forget the outlaw,' he whispered. 'You, Maltote and Ranulf, I thank you. Apart from Philip of France, his generals on the Flemish border, perhaps Messieurs Nogaret and de Craon, we are the only people who know where his armies will attack. Look, I'll explain.'

Chapter 11

'Let's pretend we are playing chess. We are the white pieces.' Corbett smiled at Ranulf. 'Philip's favourite colour: he sees himself as the Lord of Light. We would arrange our chess pieces as follows, going from left to right: Castle, Knight, Bishop, Queen, King, Bishop, Knight, Castle. In front of each of these pieces we'd have a Pawn. However, let's forget these and the left-hand side of the board from Castle to Queen. Instead we'll concentrate on the four pieces to the right. We now have King, Bishop, Knight, Castle.' Corbett took up his pen. 'Let us insert the letters of the alphabet above these four as follows:'

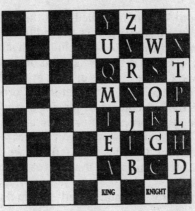

He finished the rough sketch. 'And now the cipher: "The three kings go to the tower of the two fools with the two chevaliers".'

'Master,' Ranulf interrupted, 'the cipher talks of chevaliers, a tower and fools, not knights, a castle and bishops.'

'In French chess, Ranulf, chevalier is knight, the tower is the castle and, perhaps perceptively, the piece we term "bishop", the French call "fool"!' Corbett pointed with his quill. 'The three kings could be any of the letters in that column above the king. The same applies to the two knights or chevaliers, the bishops or fools and their castle or tower.' Corbett tapped the greasy piece of parchment. 'Some of my conclusions are based on guesswork but I have a rough map of the Flemish border towns and, using this cipher, have tried to discover which border town would fit the riddle.'

'Why have you only used one half of the chess board?' Maltote crossly interrupted.

'Don't you remember?' Ranulf snarled. 'The Riddle Master had neatly creased his chess board into two. Continue, Master,' Ranulf added with an air of superiority.

'One word,' Corbett replied, 'fits the cipher based on this chess board and answers the riddle. COURTRAI!' Corbett wrote the name out carefully. 'The three kings are the letters A, I and U. The two knights or chevaliers are the letters C and O. The bishops or fools are the letter R twice whilst the castle or tower is the letter T.' Corbett unrolled a greasy piece of parchment displaying a crude map of the Franco-Flemish border. 'Courtrai is a good choice,' he mused. 'The Flemings would never expect the blow to fall there. What Philip intends to do is over-awe this city, force it to capitulate, then spread the news as his forces advance on the next.'

'In other words,' Ranulf added, 'Philip does not intend

to flood Flanders with soldiers but hop from one principal city to another?'

Corbett threw his quill down. 'I think so,' he muttered. 'I hope so, because that's the best I can do. No other Flemish city agrees with this cipher.'

'What now?' Ranulf asked.

'Maltote, I want you and Ranulf to go into Nottingham and buy whatever victuals we need; a jug of wine, bread, fruit and marchpanes will suffice.'

'And you, Master?'

Corbett piled together the pieces of manuscript on his table.

'I am going to write down all I have learnt or seen since arriving here. Everything I know about Sir Eustace's death as well as anything and everything I have discovered about this outlaw.' Corbett rubbed his eyes. 'I have suspicions, vague unsubstantiated ones, particularly after my journey to Kirklees. Now I want to fit the pieces of the puzzle together. If I can make no sense of it by this time tomorrow, we shall return to London. If I can . . .' Corbett shrugged. 'Well, we'll cross that bridge when we come to it.'

Ranulf and Maltote needed no second bidding, though on the stairs Ranulf told Maltote to wait and went back to see Corbett.

'Master!' he called, closing the door softly behind him.

'Yes, Ranulf?' Corbett asked. 'I thought you had gone.'

'Your promise, Master.' Ranulf fairly danced from foot to foot. 'I mean, it was you who unlocked the secret of the cipher.'

Corbett smiled. 'We don't know if it's correct, Ranulf. We won't know until Philip moves. In any case, you will be responsible. I shall tell His Grace the King that your involvement in this matter was invaluable.'

'But what if it's wrong?' Ranulf cried, ever wary of what the future might hold.

'In which case, Ranulf-atte-Newgate, it will be too late to do anything. By then the King will have given you a solemn promise to elevate you to the post of clerk in the Royal Chancery.'

Ranulf fairly skipped down the steps. Once they were out of the castle, he solemnly assured Maltote that when he reached high office he, Ranulf-atte-Newgate, would not forget his friends.

They visited Amisia at the tavern. Ranulf once again offered his condolences and gave more money to the landlord for Rahere's body to be treated, coffined and transported to St Mary's for burial.

'What will happen to me?' Amisia asked, seated on the edge of the bed, her beautiful face now white and swollen with tears. The soft-hearted Maltote just stared at her pityingly whilst admiring Ranulf's delicate care of her.

'Everything will be all right,' he assured her. 'Master Long Face, Sir Hugh Corbett,' he explained, 'has a great deal of influence at court. Tell me,' he added, 'did your brother own any property or tenements in England?'

Ranulf could have bitten out his tongue for where else would Rahere have property, but Amisia didn't seem to notice. She closed her eyes and rocked herself gently.

'We had money,' she answered, 'from the sale of our father's property and Rahere was always well supplied with gold and silver.'

'And where did this come from?'

'One of the Lombard bankers . . . Luigi Baldi. That's right!' Amisia's eyes opened. 'Luigi Baldi. He owns shops in London, in Lothbury.'

'Then this is what we will do,' Ranulf confidently assured

her. 'You will go to London and lodge with the Minoresses, a small order outside Aldgate. Meanwhile, I will visit this Luigi Baldi to ensure your inheritance is kept safe.'

Ranulf was fairly swaggering when he left the tavern.

'Can you do that?' Maltote asked. 'Rahere was a traitor. His body should be gibbeted and all his property confiscated by the Crown. I know that,' he added defiantly, 'because Sir Hugh told me.'

'There's the law,' Ranulf explained loftily, 'and there's Sir Hugh. Now, Old Master Long Face may appear to be dour, with a heart like flint.' Ranulf pursed his lips and shook his head. 'But, mark my words, once a man's dead, he won't push matters. Moreover, if his solution is correct, the King will grant him anything he wishes. Whatever,' Ranulf caught Maltote by the sleeve, 'we clerks of the chancery have considerable influence in these matters.'

By the time they had bought the victuals and returned to the castle, Corbett was again immersed in his 'scribbling', as Ranulf termed it. He stopped to eat some bread and cheese and drink a little wine then returned to his task. Ranulf asked if they could walk round the castle. Corbett lifted his tousled head and crossly told him to stay where he was. Maltote and Ranulf diced for a while. Darkness fell and the castle grew silent, apart from the calls of sentries on the parapet walks or the occasional ringing of the bell. Ranulf and Maltote wrapped themselves in their cloaks and both slept fitfully. Every time they woke, Corbett was still seated at the table, bathed in a circle of candlelight, writing furiously or staring, face in hands, down at a piece of parchment.

They both rose, heavy-eyed, just after dawn. Although Corbett was grey with exhaustion, he began to interrogate them on different details, going back to the table to continue his scribbling. Ranulf and Maltote gained permission to go into the town. Obeying Corbett's order they kept to themselves. When they returned, the table was cleared and Corbett lay fast asleep upon his bed. He awoke just after noon, still lost in his own thoughts. He shaved, washed and changed, ate some of the provisions Ranulf had brought, then curtly ordered both of them to pack.

'Are we returning to London, Master?' Maltote asked hopefully.

'No, no. Your saddlebags are packed?'

Both Ranulf and Maltote nodded. Corbett handed Maltote a sealed package.

'You are to leave the castle with Ranulf. Ride as hard as you can to Lincoln. You, Ranulf, are to seek an audience with Henry, Earl of Lincoln. You will find him in the castle there. Now,' he handed a small scroll to Ranulf, 'give him this. Tell him to read it alone.' Corbett rubbed his eyes. 'He will then give Maltote an armed escort to London.

'You are to ride like the devil, Maltote, and deliver your package to the King in his own chamber at Westminster Hall. Meanwhile, Ranulf, ask the Earl of Lincoln for soldiers and go to Kirklees Priory. On her allegiance to the King, the Prioress is commanded to accompany you and the Earl of Lincoln, with whatever troops Lincoln can raise, back to Nottingham.'

'Why the Prioress?' Ranulf asked.

Corbett opened his mouth, then shook his head.

'No, the less you know the better.'

'Won't Lincoln object?' Ranulf asked, wary of the hard-bitten Earl whose fierce temper and colourful oaths were known even to the humblest page boy at court.

'The Earl will do as I say,' Corbett maintained. 'The letter is marked with the King's secret seal and the same applies to the writ for My Lady Prioress. They will come. They may object, they may plead, but they will come. Now go! And, Ranulf, I should be grateful if you would ask Sir Peter Branwood and Roteboeuf to join me here.'

'What's going to happen?' Ranulf persisted.

'Do as I say,' Corbett reiterated. 'You must be back here within three days.'

Ranulf and Maltote left and a few minutes later Sir Peter Branwood, Naylor, Friar Thomas and Roteboeuf walked into the chamber.

'Sir Hugh, you wished to see me? I thought I would bring the rest of my household.'

'Yes,' Corbett murmured. 'It's best if I see you all. I think,' he continued, 'I know how to trap and kill Robin Hood.' He saw the look of surprise in Branwood's eyes.

'What has happened?' the under-sheriff asked. 'Have you discovered the traitor?'

'No, no,' Corbett replied. 'I think the solution to this outlaw's depredations must be a military one. My belief is that the Prioress of Kirklees has given comfort and sustenance to the wolfshead. She may be able to provide us with information of his whereabouts. You see,' Corbett leaned forward, 'Robin Hood definitely has an accomplice in this castle but it could be anyone: a cook, a scullion, a chamber maid or a soldier. However, we are not here to catch minnows. I have reached the conclusion, Sir Peter, that the solution must be a military one. I have asked the Earl of Lincoln to bring the Prioress here for questioning. If we obtain the information I need, I am going to ask you and the Earl to join forces in laying siege to this outlaw in the forest.'

'How can that be done?' Friar Thomas asked. 'It would be like trying to encircle the sea.'

Corbett grinned and scratched his head.

'It may take weeks, Father, but it can be done. Sir Peter, you have seen the way the King's army advanced through Scotland?'

Sir Peter, his face flushed with excitement, nodded.

'Sir Hugh, I can guess what you intend. To move forces from glade to glade, turning each into a small fortress.'

'Exactly,' Corbett replied. 'So far any military expedition into the forest has been a visit. This time the forces will camp there. We will use Lincoln's soldiers, what's left of Gisborne's party and the castle forces. Sir Peter, you will begin preparations now. Put the entire garrison on a war footing. I am sure Master Roteboeuf will be kept busy drawing up supplies, and Master Naylor marshalling the men. Friar Thomas, I know you are a man of the people. I rely on you to seek out those who know the forest ways, the secret paths and trackways.' Corbett got to his feet. 'We will try once more and if that fails, Sir Peter, I shall return to London to inform His Grace that you and I have done all we can and the matter is now in his hands.'

Sir Peter got up. 'Sir Hugh, on this occasion I agree with everything you have said. But what about Sir Eustace's death?'

Corbett chewed his lip. 'I think I know how Sir Eustace died. Somehow or other, his cup was poisoned.' He stared around. 'Where's Physician Maigret?'

'In the city on some errand or other.'

Corbett nodded. 'Sir Peter, enough is enough. We all have our tasks to do. Ranulf and Maltote are taking messages to Lincoln. I expect the Earl three days from now.'

Corbett watched Sir Peter and his household leave. He locked the door behind them, breathed a sigh of relief and lay down on the bed eager to catch up on the sleep he had lost.

He woke later in the afternoon and a short walk round the castle proved that Sir Peter already had preparations in hand. The stables, forges and smithies were busy. Horses were being groomed, saddles repaired and foodstocks being moved up from the cellar into the small outhouses of the inner bailey. Corbett ambled around smiling then slipped through the postern gate, down the Brewhouse stairs and into the hot, stinking streets of Nottingham. For a while he moved amongst the market stalls until, confident no one was watching him, he hastened up an alleyway, crossed the street and rang the bell of the Franciscan friary.

Father Prior was hardly welcoming.

'The affairs of this world should be left outside the friary gate!' he snapped.

'Oh, no, Father, this friary is very much at the heart of my world,' Corbett retorted. 'I need to see Brother William. I am asking courteously but, if you object, shall use my authority.'

Father Prior pulled a face but quickly agreed. He led Corbett across the grounds to the old outlaw's cell. Brother William also received Corbett coolly.

'You are leaving for London, Sir Hugh? You have come to say goodbye?' The friar's eyes were guarded. Corbett could see he was only making conversation until Father Prior was well away from the door of the cell.

'I shall return to London after I have trapped the wolfshead Robin Hood,' Corbett replied. 'And you, Brother, are going to help me.'

The friar sat down on a stool.

'I am a man of God. The affairs of this world do not concern me.'

'That's the second time I have heard that remark,' Corbett replied. 'God knows you can help *me*, Brother.' Corbett drew his sword from its sheath.

Brother William's eyes rounded in fear. 'What is this?' he gasped.

'Our past never leaves us alone,' Corbett continued evenly, tip-toeing backwards towards the door. 'Just when we think it's all shadows something springs out to trip us up. I mean you no harm, Brother, just as . . .' Corbett pulled the door open and swung the tip of his sword under the chin of the huge gardener standing there. Corbett grinned. 'Why eavesdrop, John Little? Or is it Little John?'

The huge giant of a man, his iron-grey hair hanging down

to his shoulders, stood with his hands hanging by his sides, his massive fists curled in frustration. Corbett's sword had not wavered but now lay against the man's exposed neck. Behind him Corbett heard Brother William move.

'Don't do anything stupid, Brother!' Corbett called over his shoulder. 'After all, you are a man of God. And I swear, by the same God, I intend you no harm. You, John Little, are a declared outlaw. Your head can be taken by any man. But we have matters to discuss, haven't we?'

The giant's clear blue eyes never left Corbett's face and the clerk could see he was wondering whether to attack or concede.

'I mean you no harm, John Little,' Corbett repeated softly. 'Come.' He waved the man in. The giant bowed his head and shoulders and entered Brother William's cell.

Corbett left two hours later. Neither John Little nor Brother William had been forthcoming. They had refused to answer his questions but sat staring at him, listening to all he said. At last Corbett had borrowed pen and parchment: he wrote out a letter of safe conduct summoning both to appear before him as the King's Commissioner in Nottingham Castle.

Corbett spent the next few hours watching Branwood prepare for the military expedition into the forest. The rest of the time he kept to himself, reviewing his theories like any good clerk preparing a memorandum to place before the King. Corbett tried to hide his nervousness. He just hoped Ranulf would carry out his task and that Maltote was able to reach the King.

On the day after Ranulf and Maltote left Nottingham, Corbett visited the Lady Amisia at the tavern and gently questioned her. He found her intelligent, witty, and clearly innocent of any involvement in her brother's crimes. He listened with amusement to the promises Ranulf had made to her on his behalf.

'It's true, My Lady,' Corbett confirmed, getting to his

feet. 'When I return south, I will be honoured if you will join us. We shall ensure your safe lodging with the Minoresses.'

With the girl's thanks ringing in his ears, Corbett went back to the castle.

He attended Rahere's funeral mass later that day, listening with half an ear to how the priest deplored the 'dreadful murder' of this stranger in their midst. Corbett watched the body being taken out to the graveyard and escorted the tearful Amisia, resting on the arm of the landlord's wife, back to the tavern.

Corbett slept fitfully that night, his dreams plagued by nightmares of being lost in a dense, sombre forest where the very trees came to life, hunting him down, until he woke bathed in sweat. For the rest of the day he kept to his own chamber; he carefully examined the items he had taken from Sir Eustace's room and almost shouted with relief when he heard the cries of the sentries and the noise of many horsemen entering Middle Gate.

Corbett made himself presentable and went down to the hall where a dust-stained Ranulf was busy making the aged but still fiery old war horse the Earl of Lincoln as comfortable as possible.

'Corbett, you bloody scribbler!' the old earl bawled, his fierce face glistening with sweat, bulging blue eyes glaring at Corbett as if he held him responsible for every bump and bruise of his journey. 'Come on, man,' the earl shouted at Ranulf. 'I want some bloody wine. Hello, Branwood!' he bellowed as the sheriff entered the hall. 'Can't catch a bloody outlaw, can you? For God's sake, someone, remove my boots. Lord, my arse is as sore as a maid on her wedding night!'

Corbett bit back a smile and quietly applauded the earl's cheerful bullying of anyone who came within earshot. Henry de Lacey, Earl of Lincoln, was no fool, however and Corbett caught his sly wink.

'You've brought your men, My Lord?'

'Scores of the idle buggers! Men-at-arms, some household knights, and more archers than there are hairs on my arse. And, believe me,' the earl roared with laughter, 'my arse is hairy! Go outside, Corbett, and see for yourself.'

He took the hint and wandered into the inner bailey where men wearing the red and green livery of the earl thronged the courtyard.

'Maltote's gone to London,' Ranulf murmured, coming up beside him. 'But that old earl, Master! He curses everyone, and he's drunk at least a pint of wine since entering Nottingham.'

'That old earl,' Corbett softly replied, 'is a cunning old fox and I think he's guessed why he's here.' Corbett smiled at Ranulf's puzzlement. 'Wait a while, Ranulf, and all will be clear. Oh, by the way, the Lady Amisia sends her regards.'

They went back into the hall where Lincoln had tossed his boots into a corner. Whilst one of his squires tried to put soft buskins on his feet, another was being drenched in water as the earl washed his hands and face and bellowed for a cup of sack, a goblet of wine, anything to wash the filth from his throat.

'Oh, by the way,' Lincoln shouted, 'that soft-arsed Prioress! God knows, she's a snooty bitch. She's here too, Corbett. She was in a bloody half-faint when I left her, silly mare! Hadn't she ever heard a man curse before?'

Ranulf was fighting so hard to stifle his laughter, Corbett thought he would have an apoplexy. He took his leave, hearing the old earl roaring at Branwood that he hadn't travelled to Nottingham for a bowl of stew and he hoped they would dine well that night.

As Corbett hurried out of the hall, he smelt the savoury fragrances from the kitchen and realised Branwood was preparing a banquet to celebrate the hunting down of Robin Hood.

'You wait till you see the Prioress,' Ranulf muttered, still stifling his laughter.

'What do you mean?'

'Well, have you ever heard the story of the lecherous clerk, the miller's daughter and the miller's wife?'

'No, why?'

'Well,' Ranulf laughed, 'the Prioress has. Lincoln insisted on roaring the story out at the top of his voice with a few choice embellishments of his own.'

Lady Elizabeth Stainham had recovered at least some of her poise by the time Corbett met her in her comfortable quarters above Middlegate. Nevertheless she stood quivering with fury, her face white, eyes wide dark pools of malice.

'Master Corbett,' she snarled.

'My Lady, my title is Sir Hugh.'

'You can call yourself whatever you wish! I shall complain to the King about being dragged from my convent and forced to travel here in the company of that!' She flicked a finger at Ranulf.

'Ranulf-atte-Newgate, My Lady.'

'Yes. And the earl, a foul-mouthed . . .'

'You mean the King's cousin, Henry de Lacey, Earl of Lincoln, Guardian of the Prince of Wales and the King's most successful general in Gascony?'

The Prioress bit her lip as she realised she had gone too far.

'What do you want?' she snapped, flouncing down into a chair.

Corbett nodded to Ranulf. 'Please wait outside.' He looked at the young nun who had accompanied the Prioress. 'And you too.' He smiled. 'My manservant has a number of droll stories that may interest you.'

Lady Elizabeth made to rise again.

'You, My Lady, will sit down!' Corbett ordered. 'I must take some of your time. If you had told me, the King's

Commissioner, the truth the first time we met, then your journey and this meeting would not have been necessary. If you have objections to speaking now, then take them to the King. I assure you, you will spend your remaining years on bread and water in some forlorn nunnery at the other end of the kingdom.'

Ranulf heard these last few words as he closed the door behind him. He was tempted to eavesdrop for he knew Master Long Face was closing in on his quarry. However, the door was thick and the young nun rather pretty. Ranulf soon had her giggling at his own tale about the miller's wife, the miller's daughter and the lecherous clerk.

An hour later Corbett left the room, a smile on his face.

'I think your Prioress needs you,' he murmured. 'She has to unpack and prepare herself for this evening's banquet. And you, Ranulf . . .'

He took his manservant by the elbow and led him down the stairs, whispering quiet instructions about what he was to do that evening. Corbett then returned to his chamber, prepared himself, and wrapping certain items in his cloak, went down to the great hall for what Sir Peter Branwood grandly termed his 'victory banquet'.

The under-sheriff had done his best to transform the hall. The floor had been cleaned, tapestries hung against the walls and the great table had been moved from the dais to accommodate all of Sir Peter's household as well as de Lacey, Corbett, Ranulf, and a very grim-faced Lady Prioress. Sconce torches spluttered against the darkness whilst the tables, covered in white cloths, were bathed in pools of candlelight. Sir Peter's cooks had prepared a veritable feast: mutton cooked with olives, royal venison, chicken boiled and stuffed with grapes, a dressed peacock, bowls of salad, pike in galantine sauce, buttered vegetables, and the best wines from the castle cellars. Everyone except Corbett ate well and drank deeply, though Lincoln kept a wary eye on the clerk, sensing a mystery. Once the main dishes had been served and cleared away, Sir Peter stood up and gave a charming speech welcoming the Earl of Lincoln, toasting his martial prowess.

'Well, Corbett,' Branwood concluded with a grin, 'this grand design is all yours. What do you propose?'

'A story,' he began, rising to his feet and looking around. He pushed back his chair and stood behind it, leaning on the back. 'Many years ago this kingdom was riven by civil war. He glanced at de Lacey who shifted uneasily. 'Simon de Montfort, Earl of Leicester, fought His Grace the King. De Montfort had a dream which turned into a nightmare of treason and treachery – the idea that every man is equal before the law. Now de Montfort met with defeat but one of his followers, Robin of Locksley, kept the dream alive, albeit tinged with self-profit. Robin objected to the harsh forest laws and became an outlaw in Sherwood where he robbed the rich and helped the poor. He fought mailed men, knights, sheriffs, verderers, but to my knowledge never raised a hand against an innocent man, woman or child.'

Corbett stared round the now silent group at the table. Branwood looked puzzled, Naylor sombre, Roteboeuf had his head in his hands, Maigret the physician seemed half-asleep but Friar Thomas was listening intently, as was the Earl of Lincoln and the Lady Prioress who, by her flushed cheeks, had apparently drunk deeply to hide her discomfort. Corbett glanced down the hall where Lincoln's henchmen and knights of the household were gathered. Ranulf, standing by the door, nodded imperceptibly, his face illuminated by the sconce torch spluttering above him. Corbett could tell from the look on his servant's face that Ranulf had others with him waiting in the shadows. Corbett took a deep breath.

'Now this outlaw's fame became widely known and when our King came north he offered Robin Hood a pardon. The outlaw accepted and his band broke up. Will Scarlett entered a monastery, Little John, his lieutenant, went back to his small village of Haversage, whilst Robin's love, the Lady Mary, took refuge in a nunnery at Kirklees. Robin went to fight in the King's wars in Scotland but grew sickened of the slaughter and wrote to the King asking to be released from military service. His Grace the King, who always liked a merry rogue, gave Robin licence to return home and sent a copy of the same to Sir Eustace Vechey and Sir Peter Branwood, sheriffs of Nottingham. Robin came south with two companions, William Goldberg and a man called Thomas.'

'Two companions?' Friar Thomas asked.

'Yes, they're mentioned in the King's letter of safe conduct.'

'We know all this,' Naylor interrupted. 'Then for some strange reason the wolfshead broke his word and went back to Sherwood Forest.'

'Ah!' Corbett smiled. 'You are wrong. Robin came south only to be murdered! I will not go hunting the outlaw tomorrow, Sir Peter, that was a ploy to protect myself until the Earl of Lincoln arrived.'

Chapter 12

An immediate clamour broke out but the clerk stood silent. Eventually Lincoln raised his hand as a sign for him to continue.

'Oh, Robin of Locksley returned,' Corbett continued, walking round to stand behind the Prioress. 'He visited his manor at Locksley, paid his respects to old Father Edmund, then recommenced his journey, eager to see the Lady Mary at Kirklees Priory. He also hoped his henchman, Little John or John Little, would be waiting for him for they had agreed to meet there. However, on that lonely forest track he and his two companions were maliciously attacked. William Goldberg and the man called Thomas were killed immediately. Robin escaped but had received his death wound. Perhaps he crawled away. In any event his assailants left him for dead.' Corbett tapped the Prioress on the shoulder. 'Nevertheless, the wolfshead was made of sterner stuff. He managed to reach Kirklees Priory for the ambush, I suspect, occurred near the Priory gates where John Little was waiting for him. It's fortunate he was, isn't it, my Lady?'

The Prioress flinched.

'Now,' Corbett continued, 'our Prioress told me how Robin had ridden into Kirklees. She lied. Robin was a poor horseman, and would have walked. She also said Little

John was with him. Another lie. The outlaw's lieutenant had agreed to meet him there.'

'So?' Lincoln bellowed. 'What happened then?'

'The dying Robin was taken up to the lonely, isolated gatehouse at Kirklees. True, My Lady?'

'It's true,' the Prioress replied, entwining her fingers tightly and staring down at the table top. 'The wolfshead had a jagged, bubbling wound in his neck. I did what I could.'

Corbett glanced round the table. Branwood looked as if he was carved out of marble, his mouth sagging open.

'Ranulf!' Corbett called. 'Bring in John Little!'

Ranulf walked into the hall, the huge giant lumbering like a bear behind him whilst Brother William brought up the rear. Naylor stood up, thrusting back his chair.

'That man's an outlaw and a wolfshead!' he cried, his hand going to his dagger. 'He can be killed on sight!'

'If you interrupt these proceedings again,' Corbett snapped, 'I'll have my Earl of Lincoln hang you from the beams of this hall! Master Little, you heard what I said. Do I speak the truth?'

The ragged, bearded giant nodded. Even Corbett flinched at the hatred in the huge man's eyes.

'Robin was dying,' Little John began, his voice surprisingly soft but tinged with a rustic burr. 'The nun's correct. She did what she could but, there again, God knows what potion she gave Robin. After he had drunk it, he grew a little stronger and asked for my long bow.' The giant's eyes filled with tears. 'He was dying and told me to open the casement window. I fitted an arrow to the string and helped him pull it back. He shot it good and true over the park.' Little John paused. 'Robin laughed. He knew his kinswoman the Prioress hated him but she couldn't refuse him Christian burial. Robin told me to find where the arrow had fallen and bury him there. After that, Maid Marion,' the giant coughed, 'the Lady Mary, came rushing up. Robin was failing.' He shrugged and wrung his great hands. 'That was it. As the light failed, so did Robin. For a while he slept, muttering about days in the forest. Sometimes he would laugh, sometimes shout out Marion's name. Once or twice mine. At last he fell silent. The Lady Mary was prostrate with grief. I bent over the bed. Robin's eyes were closed and his face cold.'

The man scratched his beard. Despite his great size and girth, he looked like a little boy remembering a terrible accident. 'Next morning I went out. It took me many an hour to find where the arrow had fallen then I dug the grave. She,' he flung out a hand at the Prioress, 'that high-faced bitch, objected!' He smiled mirthlessly. 'But, I threatened to break her neck if she refused. I finished the grave. Before he died, Robin had whispered about poor William and Thomas so I went back along the trackway and found their corpses. They were both dead, arrows in their necks and chests. I laid them alongside Robin. The grave was deep and broad. I covered it with earth. I went back to the nunnery to comfort the Lady Mary but she was witless, beside herself with grief. I told the Prioress I would return every so often to check that grave. I never did. I didn't want to be seen in public. As for the Lady Mary . . .' Little John shrugged.

'She's dead!' the Prioress interrupted. 'She had set such hopes on Robin's return. After his death, she pined away. Wouldn't eat or drink, became lost in her own dreams.' Her eyes snapped. 'I told my community she had left with Robin. No one knew the truth. However, in death I bear no man ill will. Robin is gone and so is the love of his life. I placed her alongside him.'

Corbett stared at the hard, taut face of the Prioress. He wondered if she had secretly loved Robin and her later hatred had stemmed from his indifference.

'What did Little John mean about the potion?' he asked.
The Prioress shook her head.

'Why didn't you report Robin's death to the King?'
Lincoln shouted. 'After all, he was under royal protection,
carrying letters of safe conduct.'

'How could I?' the Prioress protested. 'Robin had been
killed near Kirklees! You've heard the rogue Little John –
my dislike of Robin was well known. After all,' she
glared at Corbett, 'I was one of the few who knew he was
coming!'

'I thought of that,' Little John added. 'Robin didn't
know who his assailants were, describing them as masked
and hooded. I came to Nottingham to seek out Brother
William. And then,' the fellow scratched his head, 'I began
to wonder. Robin was attacked on the thirteenth of
December. His assailants must have been waiting for him.
Now I reasoned that many knew about Robin's leaving
Scotland but few could actually plot his footsteps. Only the
King and his clerks at Westminster or someone here who'd
received letters saying that Robin was coming back. The
only people who knew that were the sheriffs, Sir Eustace
Vechey and Sir Peter Branwood. And, of course, their
clerk.'

'Little John shared his anxieties with me,' Brother
William interrupted. 'I, too, became frightened. I begged
Father Prior to give Little John a position as gardener at
our house and he agreed. I listened to what John had told
me and drew two conclusions. Either His Grace the King
or someone in Nottingham was the murderer.' Brother
William stared at Sir Peter Branwood. The King loved
Robin. He would not lift his hand against him in such a
treacherous way. This left me with one conclusion:
someone in Nottingham, who knew Robin was journeying
south, planned that ambush. God knows, there were
enough lords in this shire who hated Robin. At first I
thought his murder was an act of revenge then we heard

these mysterious stories of how Robin was once again hunting in Sherwood Forest, but this time he was different. Oh, he bought the peasants' silence but this Robin was harsh, his hand against every man, ruthless in quelling any opposition, even killing those who had once been close to him.' Brother William wiped his mouth on the back of his hand. 'Of course, I knew it was not Robin of Locksley but someone using his name.' He spread his hands. 'Yet what could we do? If I tried to object, who would believe me? What proof did I have? And as for Little John here, his size alone prevented him from walking the streets of Nottingham. So we both hid in the friary where no one could harm us, for whom could we trust? Not even you, the King's Commissioner.'

Corbett tapped the giant on the chest.

'But you fired the arrows?'

The giant's face broke into a gap-toothed grin.

'Three fire arrows,' Corbett declared. 'Your requiem every month on the thirteenth, the date Robin died.'

'He fired them,' Brother William intervened. 'He would slip out of a postern gate and loose them into the night sky. A reminder to Robin's assassin in Nottingham as well as a prayer, three times repeated, that God would comfort our dead friend's soul.'

'But you never knew who the assassin was?' Corbett continued. 'And that was the evil beauty of his plan. The Lady Prioress here could not reveal Robin's death. Who would believe her? Some might even accuse her of having a hand in it. After all, her intense dislike for her kinsman was well known. Little John might have his suspicions but he was an outlaw and could be killed on sight. Brother William had no proof. And, as he has said, any of Robin's old companions who did suspect went the same way as their master. Now.' Corbett walked briskly up the table. 'My Lord of Lincoln, I would like a man-at-arms on either

side of Sir Peter, his clerk Roteboeuf and Master Naylor.'
Corbett drew his own dagger and stood behind the burly
serjeant-at-arms. Branwood sat slumped on his chair.
Roteboeuf blinked like a frightened rabbit but Corbett saw
Naylor's hands go beneath the table.

'Please sir,' he ordered, 'your hands where I can see
them.'

The serjeant-at-arms peered over his shoulder. Lincoln's
soldiers thronged around. Reluctantly Naylor did as
Corbett asked. Lincoln barked out orders. Branwood,
Naylor and Roteboeuf offered no resistance as their swords
were taken from them.

'In the castle,' Corbett continued, 'Sir Eustace Vechey
must have thought a nightmare had returned. He had
fought Robin in the old days. Now the outlaw was back,
causing even more mischief. Now I don't think the old
sheriff knew what had happened but, as the outlaw's
depredations grew worse, he did suspect a high-placed
traitor in the castle. A lonely, suspicious man, Vechey
would trust no one but, as his mind began to ramble, so did
his tongue. Perhaps he began to hint at things; even his face
or eyes may have betrayed something. So he had to die and
you, Sir Peter, killed him, as you murdered Robin Hood
and took his place in Sherwood Forest!'

'This is nonsense!' Branwood shouted, trying to assert
himself. 'My Lord of Lincoln, the clerk raves. He is as mad
as a hare on a moonlit night!'

Branwood's protests were belied by the expression on
his face and the beads of sweat coursing down his cheeks.
One of Lincoln's knights grasped him by the shoulder and
pushed him down on to his chair.

'No, Sir Peter, you are a murderer,' Corbett continued
evenly, staring at him from the other side of the table. 'You
hated Robin of Locksley for past humiliations. You
resented his acceptance into the King's grace and, I
suspect, despised the King himself for showing such

mercy to a man you would have killed. You, together with Sir Eustace, received the letter from the royal chancery at Westminster, saying that Robin was returning to Nottingham under royal protection. You noticed the dates and the times and planned that ambush. Your two creatures here, Naylor and Roteboeuf, were responsible. I am sure, when my story's finished, one of them will be wise enough to turn King's Evidence and confirm this. You killed William Goldberg and the man called Thomas. You left Robin of Locksley for dead.

'Perhaps at first you thought you might leave it at that but then you saw what opportunities presented themselves. What a way to revenge yourself on the dead man's name and reputation! On the King himself, as well as line your own pockets! And it would be so easy. Who could prove what you had done? Everyone else, from the King in London down to the lowliest serf in Nottingham, believed Robin of Locksley had returned to his old ways. As I have demonstrated, only three other people knew of his death. One, a former outlaw, would not be believed and could be killed on sight; then there was a friar, old and weary, immured in his own monastery and a Prioress who hated Robin.'

'But it's impossible.' Lincoln spoke out. 'How could Branwood here move from the castle to the forest?'

'My Lord, beneath this castle lies a warren of secret tunnels and passageways known only to a few. Everyone is concerned that someone could steal into the castle by these secret routes, it is equally true that such tunnels can be used for people to leave the castle – as Sir Peter discovered to his own profit.' Corbett sipped from his wine cup before continuing. 'I have studied the attacks of the outlaw over the last three months. They did not occur daily but once or twice a month, the most profitable being the attack on the King's tax-collectors. In their role as outlaws, Sir Peter, Naylor and Roteboeuf left the castle by their secret routes. Perhaps the clerk occasionally stayed behind to

197

cover for his master's absences. Some of the tunnels, I understand, come out into the town, a few well beyond the city walls.

'In one of these passageways Branwood and Naylor would change into Lincoln green, as well as their hoods and masks, and go to their pre-arranged meeting place in the forest. Those two outlaws Master Naylor is supposed to have captured provided some insight on how the outlaws would assemble at a certain place when the signals were given. Let us take, for example, the attack on the tax-collectors.' Corbett drummed his fingers against his belt. 'It would have taken Sir Peter no more than a few hours. Naylor acted the role of Little John and the wench from The Blue Boar that of Maid Marion. The outlaws would assemble, orders would be issued and the attack made.'

'You claim we could do all that?' Naylor sneered.

'Oh, yes,' Corbett retorted. 'The wench from the tavern would not know your true identities but just act a part. The rest of the outlaws would be summoned before the tax-collectors even left Nottingham, closely followed by one of your coven. The tax-collector's cavalcade would be slower than men moving on foot through a forest.' Corbett narrowed his eyes at the candle flame. 'Willoughby said he was captured late in the afternoon and fell asleep after dark. No more than five or six hours. Once he was asleep, his retinue was massacred, the spoils shared out and Branwood returned to the castle.' Corbett pointed at Roteboeuf. 'Perhaps you stayed to explain away Sir Peter's absence, claiming he was in his chamber or the town? Anyway, who would notice? Father Thomas busy in his parish? Poor old Vechey, troubled and confused? Or Lecroix, slow-witted and anxious about his master?'

'But surely,' Friar Thomas interrupted, 'Branwood would be recognised.'

'Oh, come, Father. A mask and a hood, the voice deliberately changed. Words kept to a minimum. After all, didn't you tell me yourself that the outlaw approached you in your own church? Did you suspect?'

Friar Thomas smiled and shook his head.

'No, of course not, Father,' Corbett continued. 'In your mind Robin was still alive. And who would suspect the upright, law-abiding under-sheriff was really the outlaw in disguise? The wench from the tavern? Well, as I've said, she played her part. Tomorrow morning she and her father will wake up to find my Lord of Lincoln's men searching every nook and cranny of their house.'

'Did Vechey suspect?' Father Thomas asked.

'Oh, no! He was too busy hunting the traitor in the castle who was providing the outlaws with vital information. Branwood skilfully planned his death.' Corbett pulled the bundle from underneath his chair and took out a soiled napkin. 'Do you remember, Physician Maigret, where you saw this last?'

'Why, yes,' the physician cried, peering across the table. 'That's the one from Vechey's chamber. He used it to wipe his mouth.'

'No, he didn't!' Corbett replied. 'When Sir Eustace went up to his chamber he was carrying a goblet of wine. He sipped that then he and Lecroix ate some of the sweetmeats. Afterwards, Sir Eustace washed his hands and face. He picked up a napkin, dried himself and retired to bed.' Corbett chewed his lip and stared at Branwood. 'But we both know, Sir Peter, that the napkin Vechey used was coated in the most potent poison you could buy from that witch Hecate – deadly nightshade. Oh, yes, I have heard of a case in Italy where a woman dipped one of her husband's shirts in such a potion and killed him. Now, naturally, Lecroix would not use the same napkin as his master, I wonder if that's what Lecroix meant by the last words he said to us before he died? Do you remember, Maigret? "My master was tidy."'

'Yes, I do,' he replied. 'And you are right, Sir Hugh. Vechey would have gone to bed, his lips and hands coated with that noxious substance.'

'Ah, but what would have made it easier,' Corbett continued, 'was that Sir Eustace had sores on his mouth. These would give the poison direct entry into his blood and other humours. Yet that napkin, Sir Peter, was your greatest mistake. The next morning you, with the rest, came up to see Sir Eustace's chamber and, during the confusion, exchanged one stained napkin for another. And you were very cunning. The replacement napkin carried wine stains and sweetmeats, even blood, as if Sir Eustace had opened the sores on his lips. Now, Physician Maigret.' Corbett passed the soiled napkin over. 'Pull across a candle. Examine the napkin left in Sir Eustace's chamber and, bearing in mind what I have told you, what is wrong with it?'

Maigret did as he was told. At first he shook his head but then he glanced up, smiling. 'Of course,' he said. 'There are the stains from the sweetmeats and there are the blood marks, but the two are quite separate. The blood stains are quite distant from the other marks. They should be together, even mingling.'

'Exactly!' Corbett retorted, taking the napkin back and tossing it down the table at Lincoln. 'That's what I concluded when I re-examined it.'

'But,' Maigret exclaimed, 'Sir Peter too was ill.'

'Oh, I think that's due to one of two reasons. Remember, Sir Peter did not go to you until after Sir Eustace's body had been discovered. This could have been due to Sir Peter's trying to pose as a possible victim himself, or perhaps he had tinged himself, or thought he had, with some of the potion from the poisoned napkin.' Corbett pulled a face. 'Who would suspect? Branwood probably left the napkin there before the banquet began. It was the one thing in that room Vechey would not share with Lecroix, a mere servant.'

'You speak true, Sir Hugh.' Friar Thomas spoke up. 'I remember that morning. Sir Peter came to Vechey's chamber wearing gloves. I am sure,' he concluded flatly, 'that those gloves, together with the poisoned napkin, disappeared into a fire.'

'And Lecroix?' Maigret asked.

'Oh, well, he had to die. There was always the risk he may have noticed something or Vechey may even have shared his suspicions with him. Now, do you remember, Sir Peter, I asked you why Lecroix should hang himself in the cellars? You said because the castle was under attack or because Lecroix may have been looking for more wine; after all, we did find a small wine cask smashed. Of course, I know different now. There was plenty of wine in the castle and the cellar with its secret trap doors and passageways would be the last place a man would go if he wanted to hide. Lecroix was not as stupid as he looked. He may have been searching for the secret passageway out of the castle. He may even have suspected the truth, following his master's death, and reached the conclusion that he might discover what the outlaws had taken. In other words, My Lord of Lincoln, if His Grace the King wishes to regain his taxes, I am sure they will be found somewhere in the cellars or secret passageways of this castle.' Corbett paused and stared at Branwood who had now regained his composure and glanced coolly back. 'The rest,' Corbett raised his eyes to the roof, 'was easy. We went into the forest but you had already sent orders ahead and led us into that ambush. The same is true of poor Gisborne.' Corbett smiled ruefully. 'All was confusion that day. I was leaving for Kirklees. You, Sir Peter, were ostensibly furious with Gisborne, hurrying about so no one could really know what you were doing. Naylor and Roteboeuf stayed to sustain the sham whilst you slipped down the tunnels, gathered the outlaws, and Gisborne blundered into your trap.' Corbett looked up at the Earl of Lincoln who sat fascinated by what he was hearing.

'My Lord, you doubted whether anyone in the castle could enter the forest and return. Nottingham is a small city. You are beyond its walls, even after riding through busy streets, in twenty minutes. Can you imagine how quickly it can be left by going down a secret passageway? Who knows? Perhaps we can find one of the tunnels. My reckoning is that after leaving the castle cellars Sir Peter could be in the heart of Sherwood, plan an ambush, carry it out and be back in the castle with an absence of only four or five hours. And who would notice? Sir Eustace, when he was alive, was a broken man, whilst there was always the ubiquitous Roteboeuf ready to say that Sir Peter had gone thither or hither. And, to complicate the mystery, sometimes Branwood would not go but send Naylor instead, just to muddy the waters a little further.'

Corbett sat down and looked around. He had never seen people so motionless, such a captive audience.

'My story is nearly done,' he remarked quietly. 'A clever scheme though flawed from the start. When I wrote down what had happened to me I began to detect a pattern.' Corbett ticked off the points on his fingers. 'First, the attack on the castle on my first day here. How did the outlaws know which room I was in? Secondly, that ambush in Sherwood Forest. At the time I dismissed it but hindsight makes wise men of us all. Wasn't it strange that none of us was hit by those arrows? Branwood and Naylor had to keep me safe because slaying the King's Commissioner would have been pushing matters a little too far.' Corbett stopped and stared down the table. He was sure Branwood was almost smiling. 'You'll hang!' he remarked. 'You are a traitor and a murderer, as are Naylor and Roteboeuf and anyone else who assisted.'

Corbett's sombre words had the desired effect. Roteboeuf, his face white and haggard, sprang to his feet, knocking the chair over. Lincoln's soldiers closed in.

'It's true!' he yelled.

'Shut up!' bellowed Branwood.

'Oh, for God's sake!' Roteboeuf struggled in the arms of the soldiers. 'Sir Hugh, I am a cleric. I claim benefit of clergy and will confess all, giving names and dates.' He stopped and stared beseechingly at Corbett.

'The King's mercy will be recommended,' he replied quietly.

'Shut up, you lying bastard!' Branwood yelled. 'You snivelling coward!'

Roteboeuf, however, heartened by Corbett's words, fell to his knees.

'It's true!' he sobbed. 'Branwood hated Robin Hood. He was obsessed with the outlaw. He found the tunnels leading from the castle. He, Naylor and myself used often to go down there. Sir Eustace never suspected anything. Then, late last autumn, just after the feast of All Saints, the letters came about Robin of Locksley leaving the King's armies in Scotland and Branwood drew up this scheme. We left the castle by a secret route, masked and hooded. Locksley's two companions were killed outright, we left Locksley himself for dead.' Roteboeuf licked his lips. 'We were hasty, frightened of being so close to Kirklees. We took his possessions, including his signet ring. At first Branwood contented himself with thinking the outlaw was dead. He forged letters to his steward under the stolen seal to obtain and sell Robin's few possessions at Locksley.'

Roteboeuf was about to continue when Naylor darted across the table, picked up a knife and, roaring with rage, tried to lunge at him. The knife was knocked from his hand. At Lincoln's command, Naylor's arms were pulled roughly behind his chair and tied together. Roteboeuf talked on. How Branwood had devised the scheme to pose as Robin Hood. How easy it had been to enter the forest and recruit the many outlaws there. How he and Naylor acted as spokesmen. How they had planned the attack on the tax-collectors and other such ambushes. How Sir Eustace at first did not notice anything but then became suspicious about a high-ranking traitor in the castle, whereupon Branwood decided to kill him.

'They killed others,' Roteboeuf sobbed. 'The only fly in the ointment was those fire arrows loosed on the thirteenth of every month. Branwood suspected that one of Robin's old companions knew the truth, so he dispensed ruthless justice to any amongst the outlaws who opposed him. He killed Vechey. Naylor killed Lecroix, Hecate, and the young man in the tavern, the Riddle Master; Sir Peter believed he was another spy. I swear this is the truth!' he cried, eyes wild. 'I will swear the same before the King's Justices!'

Lincoln got to his feet. 'Sir Peter Branwood, King's Under-Sheriff in Nottingham, I ask you solemnly, do you have any defence against these allegations?'

Branwood lifted his face from his hands. 'Defence?' he whispered. 'Defence, you silly, wine-sodden, old man! Against what? Killing an outlaw and doing what he did? After all, if the King can pardon Robin of Locksley and take him into his own chamber, why can't he pardon me?' He turned and glared at Corbett. 'It was worth it!' he snarled. 'I brought the outlaw down with his swagger, his Lincoln green and his love of the common man. I made two mistakes. No, three! I should have taken his head like I took that silly fool Gisborne's. I should have killed Roteboeuf. And above all, Corbett, I should have killed you!'

Lincoln strode down the table and beckoned to his soldiers.

'Make him stand up!'

The soldiers hustled Branwood to his feet. He spat defiantly at Lincoln who struck him across the face then dragged the chain of office from round his neck.

'Sir Peter Branwood, you are a thief, a murderer and a traitor! I arrest you for high treason, as I do you, John Naylor! As for you,' he glanced disdainfully at the kneeling, sobbing Roteboeuf, 'you will be detained until the King's pleasure is known. Sir Hugh.' He looked at Corbett. 'Sir Hugh . . .'

Corbett came round the table and stared at Branwood who looked defiant despite his dishevelled appearance and the burgeoning bruise where Lincoln had hit him.

'You are wrong, Branwood,' Corbett murmured. 'Robin of Locksley was an outlaw but he was also a dreamer, an idealist. He had a genuine love for the common man whereas you are a silent assassin, a conniving thief and a bungling traitor. You used your high office for cold-blooded murder as well as for the theft of the King's money. God forgive me! You are the only man I ever wanted to see die!'

'Take them away!' Lincoln ordered.

The soldiers pushed the three prisoners out as Lincoln went to the top of the table and filled wine cups. He brought one back to Corbett and thrust this into the clerk's hand, telling his soldiers to seal the hall doors. Then he stared round the assembled company.

'Robin of Locksley is dead. He deserved a better end, as did those others whom Branwood so coldly murdered. The traitor will stand before King's Bench at Westminster and his trial will be very brief. For the rest, you are bound to silence on what you have seen and heard tonight.' He sipped from the wine cup. 'Though I gather the truth will soon be out.'

Lincoln gazed round the sombre, shadow-filled hall.

'The King must come here,' he murmured. 'This place has to be purged and cleansed!' He summoned one of his household knights, whispered to him then glanced at the Prioress. 'My Lady, I will give you suitable escort back to your convent tomorrow morning. John Little, I suggest you stay in the friary with Brother William till fresh letters of pardon are issued. For the rest,' he shrugged, 'these proceedings are now finished. You are all free to leave.'

Corbett and Lincoln watched as everyone filed out of the hall, still subdued and shocked.

'You are probably right, Corbett,' Lincoln murmured. 'We'll find a great deal in the cellars. Perhaps tomorrow I will visit Sherwood myself and give the outlaws there something to remember, now they are bereft of their leaders.'

'The Blue Boar tavern?' Corbett asked.

Lincoln grinned. 'My mounted serjeants will meet you there before dawn. But, Hugh, listen. Why did Roteboeuf tell you about Scarlett?'

'They couldn't touch the old outlaw,' Corbett replied. 'He was wary and kept hidden by Holy Mother Church. So Branwood gambled. I was given Scarlett's name to see if the old friar knew anything as well as to depict Branwood as the righteously angry royal official!' He shrugged. 'Scarlett knew little but I glimpsed that huge gardener and began to wonder. Was he John Little, and if so why was he hiding? Had Branwood known of his presence, he would never have sent me there.'

'A ruthless man,' Lincoln murmured.

'Yes,' Corbett replied. 'Determined to play both roles. He even sacrificed his squire Hobwell to sustain the sham. It was all a sham,' he murmured. 'The Prioress was unwittingly dragged into it: she couldn't explain Robin's death or that of Marion so pretended they'd both fled back to Sherwood. Branwood's depredations there only corroborated her story.'

'Well, it's finished,' Lincoln remarked. 'Branwood will

go in chains to Westminster. Do you want an escort to London, Hugh?'

Corbett shook his head. 'Ranulf and I will now be safe. And besides, I must return to Locksley. There's one man, an old priest, who must be told the truth.'

Conclusion

Smithfield Market in London was already hot and packed with people even before the bells of nearby St Bartholomew's Priory tolled for morning mass. The throng pressed in but not to attend the stalls and booths which had all been packed away. The crowds were drawn by the huge black scaffold set up in the middle of the market place, fascinated by the flames leaping from the massive copper cauldron and the grim, red-masked executioner. In one corner of the scaffold a huge post had been placed, a gibbet with a long rope dangling down; the executioner's apprentice was already setting up a thin narrow ladder in preparation for the grim ceremony about to commence.

Corbett was present, Ranulf beside him. Maltote had volunteered to look after their horses in nearby St Bartholomew's. All of London, even the great barons and ladies in their silks and costly raiment, had fought for a place. Corbett was there only at the King's express command.

'You will see the bastard die!' Edward had roared. 'You will be my witness! And die he will!'

The clerk lifted his face to catch the cool morning breeze. Corbett hated executions. He only wished he could collect his horse and ride past the Barbican north to Leighton Manor. However, the King had been most insistent. Naylor had already been hanged, drawn and quartered: his limbs, oiled and pickled, now hung over Nottingham's city walls as a warning to all would-be wrong-doers. Roteboeuf had been more fortunate: he had pleaded benefit of clergy, turned King's Evidence and been issued a pardon on one condition. He was to be denied food and water or any possessions and ordered to walk barefoot to the nearest port. There he would be exiled, forbidden to re-enter England on pain of death. His master Branwood had been tried before a special Commission of Justices. The former under-sheriff had arrogantly con-fessed to all his crimes, openly deriding the King. He'd passively accepted the sentence of the Chief Justice of King's Bench that he 'be taken to a lawful place of execution and there, at a time appointed by the court, hanged by the neck, cut down whilst still living, his body sliced open and disembowelled, his head to be struck off and his limbs quartered. The head to be set upon London Bridge and the quarters of his body sent to four principal cities of the kingdom'.

Corbett opened his eyes. 'I don't care what the King said!' he muttered out of the side of his mouth. 'Once Branwood is here, I'm leaving!'

Ranulf nodded absentmindedly. He was thinking of the voluptuous Amisia, now a moderately wealthy resident of the convent of the Minoresses, and above all of the King's fulsome praise of his work in breaking the French cipher. Ranulf closed his eyes and muttered a rare prayer. He only hoped Corbett had been right. All he could do was wait and see. The King, at Corbett's insistence, had closed all ports and limited sea passage to and from France. Accordingly, Philip would never know whether Achitophel had been successful or not. Nevertheless, the news from Paris was that something was about to happen. Jacques de Chatillon, Philip's uncle and commander of the French armies in Flanders, had according to one of Corbett's spies paid a quick visit to the Louvre Palace. He was now back on the

French border. Edward's allies in Flanders, the mayors and principal burgesses of some Flemish cities, were beginning to report movement by French troops. Little news came, however, of Courtrai. Edward had held on to the secret as long as he could, his spies in Flanders reporting little or no activity in that vicinity.

Ranulf looked up as the crowd suddenly roared. A black-garbed, macabre procession preceded by a blast of trumpets entered the market place. Ranulf glimpsed the nodding black plumes fixed between the horses' ears. Two dark-garbed executioners, a host of city officials following, clustered round the ox-hide hurdle on which Branwood had been fastened. Royal archers went before, beating a way through. The procession stopped at the foot of the scaffold. Branwood was untied and, preceded by six tormentors dressed like devils, hustled up the steps.

Corbett took one brief look but Branwood was unrecognisable, hair and beard now straggly, his body one open wound from neck to crotch. Two of the tormentors pushed him to the railing of the scaffold for the crowd to glimpse, then back towards the ladder and the waiting noose.

'I have seen enough,' Corbett whispered.

Followed by Ranulf, he fought his way back through the crowd, into the cool darkness of the archway of St Bartholomew's Priory where a white-faced Maltote stood holding their horses' reins.

'Come on!' Corbett urged.

They mounted and made their way out. Corbett shielded his eyes from the sight of a figure jerking on the end of a rope as the drums began to rattle out their death beat. In a few minutes they were clear of the market place, pushing their way through the narrow alleyways into Aldersgate. At last Corbett reined in.

'It's all over, Ranulf,' he whispered, leaning over to pat his horse's neck. 'We will ride to Leighton. The Lady Maeve is waiting for us.'

'And Uncle Morgan?' Ranulf interrupted.

Corbett rubbed the side of his face. 'Oh, yes, we must not forget dear Uncle Morgan!'

'And after that, Master?'

Corbett half-smiled. 'You are free to go back to London. I think I'll stay at Leighton to see what news arrives from across the channel.' He grasped Ranulf's wrist. 'But whatever happens, by Yuletide, Ranulf, you will be a man of substance, a royal clerk, ready to climb the greasy steps of royal preferment.'

On the same day Corbett rode to Leighton the French army marched on the city of Courtrai. Philip believed no force could withstand the cream of French chivalry: phalanx after phalanx of heavily armoured knights, columns of men-at-arms and serried ranks of Genoese bowmen. The French were confident of success. They, the chivalry of Europe, the finest army in Western Christendom, would ride down the simple artisans, weavers and burgesses of Flanders.

By nightfall of that same day, Philip and all the great lords of Europe were shocked to hear that this army was no more. The French had attacked but the Flemings were waiting: Philip's knights charged courageously, time and again, only to break against the massed cohorts of Fleming foot soldiers with their long pikes and short stabbing swords. Courtrai was a disaster for Philip and what was left of his army fled in haste back across the border. All the French King could do was kneel before the statue of his sainted ancestor and bitterly wonder what had gone wrong.

Around Nottingham the forest stood silent, a sea of green under the darkening sky. Hoblyn the outlaw crouched beneath the spreading branches of a great oak tree, his eyes never leaving the trackway.

Times had changed but Hoblyn, now past his fifty-sixth summer, was philosophical. As a youth he'd run wild with Robin Hood. When the great outlaw leader had accepted the King's pardon, Hoblyn had tried the path of righteousness but found it difficult to follow. He had returned to the forest, killing the King's deer, keeping a wary eye out for royal verderers and looking for the occasional unprotected traveller.

Then Robin had come back and Hoblyn had rejoined the band. Like the rest, he wondered the reason for some of Robin's actions but saw no need to question him. Robin was always a will-o'-the-wisp. He was the son of Herne the Huntsman and wove magic to blend with the trees and talk to the birds and animals as well as the goblins and elves who lurked in the forest. Now Robin had gone again. Something terrible had happened in Nottingham. The taprooms of different taverns were full of tittle-tattle: how Robin had killed the sheriff; how he had wrought vengeance on the sheriff's evil serjeant-at-arms, John Naylor; how Robin had gone away but one day would return. Hoblyn could not make sense of it. All he knew was that the outlaw and his chieftains had gone. No more would the horn sound, summoning him to a meeting or to receive whispered instructions.

Hoblyn shrugged and spat. He did not care. He was sure Robin would come again. He tensed as he heard the jingle of harness, the soft clip-clop of hooves. Round the corner of the forest track came a solitary rider. Hoblyn peered through the gathering darkness and grinned. By the looks of him the traveller was a well-fed priest. Hoblyn slipped his mask over his face, pulled his cowl forward and hurried at a half-crouch to the edge of the track. He fixed an arrow to his bowstring, waited till the rider was almost upon him and stepped out on to the path. Hoblyn pulled the bow string back, the sharp-edged arrow pointed directly at the priest's chest.

'What do you want?' the cleric shouted, all a fluster, gathering his reins.

'Well, for a start, the wineskin you have hung on your saddle horn.'

The priest released it and the wineskin dropped with a thud to the ground. Hoblyn moved slightly to the right.

'And the purse swinging from your belt. Be careful!' he lied. 'There are a score of others on either side of you!'

The priest licked his thick lips and stared into the darkness. He heard a crackle and rustling in the undergrowth and, gabbling with fright, unhitched the purse and let it fall.

'I am a priest,' he spluttered. 'I do God's work!'

'As do I!' Hoblyn retorted. 'Spreading God's wealth amongst the poor. You may ride on, priest!'

The priest gathered the reins of his horse in his hands. Hoblyn stepped aside to let him pass.

'Who are you?' the priest spat, glaring down at the masked, cowled figure.

Hoblyn smiled. 'Why, don't you know? This is Sherwood. Tell your friends that Robin Hood has come again!'

Author's note

The battle of Courtrai was, as described in this novel, a major disaster for Philip IV, a precursor of those great defeats of the fourteenth century when massed knights suffered against groups of disciplined, well-armed and determined peasant foot soldiers.

The secret diplomatic war preceding Courtrai is also as outlined. A survey of the documents in the Public Records Office, particularly in Categories C.47 and C.49, will illustrate the heightened suspicion of the French felt by Edward I and his commanders at this time. Edward was bound by treaty to Philip and could not openly aid the Flemings. His relief at Philip's defeat is clearly evident in his correspondence following news of Courtrai.

The use of ciphers is also interesting. Some are still unbroken; others, such as that used by Edward III in 1330 in his correspondence with the Papacy, could only be solved when the historians gained access to the Vatican archives.

Nottingham too is as described, a Danish burgh built around a castle where secret passageways and galleries abound. Indeed, in 1330, when the young Edward III wished to depose his own mother and her lover Roger Mortimer, he and a number of household knights managed the coup by using one of these secret passageways to enter the castle and arrest Mortimer.

The story of Robin Hood is one of the most famous in western folklore, but did the man himself exist? My theory that he did and fought with Simon de Montfort is based on a very curious Latin poem on Folio 103 of the *Registe Premonstratense* (Additional Manuscript M.55 4934–5 in the British Library) which indicates that Robin Hood was known by 1304.

Andrew Wyntoun, a Scottish chronicler, in his work 'Original Chronicle of Scotland' written in 1420 also records (under a verse bearing the date 1283) that 'Little John and Robin Hood were alive then and waging their war against the Sheriff in Sherwood'.

Earlier still, in 1341, John Forduen, a canon of Aberdeen, included in his 'Scottish Chronicles' for the year 1266 the following assertion: 'About this time there arose from the dispossessed (i.e. those who fought for de Montfort) and banished that famous Robin Hood and Little John with their companions. They lived as outlaws amongst the woodlands and the thickets.'

The Assassin in the Greenwood is based on the theory that Robin Hood lived in the reign of Edward I and, according to the evidence mentioned above, was pardoned by that King. I have also woven in other references, such as Little John's being a servant of the sheriff, Robin Hood's bitter feud with Guy of Gisborne and his doomed romance with Maid Marion. The outlaw's death at Kirklees may have been as described – eighteenth-century antiquarians described his tomb there which bore an inscription not only to Robin Hood but to 'William Goldberg and a man called Thomas'.

The position of sheriff in Medieval England was also as described in this novel. Many sheriffs entered secret alliances with outlaw bands (e.g. the Coterels in Leicestershire in the mid-fourteenth century, who even had the effrontery to capture the King's Chief Justice). Branwood would not have been out of place among these men. In the end, however, the Robin Hood story is an amalgam of many legends and this novel must be viewed as just one interpretation of them.

A selection of bestsellers from Headline

All Headline books are available at your local bookshop or newsagent, or can be ordered direct from the publisher. Just tick the titles you want and fill in the form below. Prices and availability subject to change without notice.

Headline Book Publishing, Cash Sales Department, Bookpoint, 39 Milton Park, Abingdon, OXON, OX14 4TD, UK. If you have a credit card you may order by telephone – 0235 400400.

Please enclose a cheque or postal order made payable to Bookpoint Ltd to the value of the cover price and allow the following for postage and packing:
UK & BFPO: £1.00 for the first book, 50p for the second book and 30p for each additional book ordered up to a maximum charge of £3.00.
OVERSEAS & EIRE: £2.00 for the first book, £1.00 for the second book and 50p for each additional book.

Name ....

Address ....

....

....

If you would prefer to pay by credit card, please complete:
Please debit my Visa/Access/Diner's Card/American Express (delete as applicable) card no:

Signature .... Expiry Date ....